On the bed she lay. Her nightdress had been starched broderie anglaise. The sheet and blanket had been pulled back from her, carefully and neatly, so that an exact triangle of white sheet had lain against the quilt. Now the nightdress and the sheet and quilt were crimson. Blood still oozed through the cotton weave of the nightdress and because the cloth was wet, the outline of her breast showed through it. She looked at them with blank-eyed horror.

Also by Ann Cleeves
Published by Fawcett Gold Medal Books:

A BIRD IN THE HAND

COME
DEATH AND
HIGH
WATER

Ann Cleeves

FAWCETT GOLD MEDAL • NEW YORK

A Fawcett Gold Medal Book
Published by Ballantine Books
Copyright © 1987 by Ann Cleeves

First published in Great Britain in 1987 by Century Hutchinson Ltd.

ISBN 0-449-13348-6

Manufactured in the United States of America

First Ballantine Books Edition: May 1988

For my parents, who live in North Devon,
with thanks for their encouragement

*C*harlie Todd, hidden behind black leather and helmet, began the steep descent to the shore. He felt like Mr. Toad at the start of his wild, outrageous adventure, and bent low over the handlebars of his motorcycle. It was easier to imagine, when he was going downhill, that he was riding a more powerful machine, and Charlie Todd was a great believer in the imagination. Imagination, after all, had made him a fortune. He looked down over the river. The mud was turned into golden sand by the September afternoon sun, and the island, tear-drop shaped at the mouth of the estuary, was deceptively clear. It looked very close. He could see the Land Rover moving slowly over the rocks at the south end. John would be on his way to collect the weekend guests. Charlie was not looking forward to the committee meeting, but as he did not like to cause disappointment, he quickly put all thought of it from his mind. The lane was narrow, the typical Devon hedges a tangle of bramble and hawthorn, and for a while he was forced to concentrate on the road. There was no need to hurry because John would wait for him, but he did not want to cause the others too much inconvenience.

1

Not today. He drove round a sharp bend, through a small, overgrown wood, and once more the estuary was spread before him. He had bought the island nearly five years before, and since then he had spent every summer there. He supposed that he should feel sad at the prospect of leaving it behind, but Charlie Todd never felt regret. He looked forward with commitment and passion and enjoyment to his new venture, was totally immersed in his new enthusiasm. But because he was a great believer in imagination, it did occur to him that the others might be a little sad that the island was to be sold.

"Mummy, do you have to go out now?" The girl dribbled grimy tears. "You promised last night that you'd help, then you went to that meeting. Daddy wouldn't let me wait up for you."

Pamela Marshall looked at her watch. She would already be five minutes late for Jerry. She would not usually have worried about that, but today she had to talk to him before they met the others.

"I *am* sorry darling. Perhaps Daddy can help. He'll be home soon. Or Edward. It's his chess night isn't it? He'll be in at five."

"None of them can do French as well as you."

Sian hated French and worried about it. Pamela looked at her watch again, and then at the immaculate kitchen, cluttered already with school bag, dirty sandwich box, gym kit, and then at her unbelievably untidy, bedraggled daughter. She stifled her irritation.

"I can't stop now, darling. You know it's my Gillibry weekend, but I'll be back on Sunday afternoon. Forget about French tonight. Do your other homework, and I promise that I'll help you on Sunday night."

Sian smiled and Pamela's irritation disappeared. Her daughter might be untidy and not very academic, but she was no disgrace to her. She was at least pretty.

"I must go now," she said, "or the others will have to wait for me. There's plenty in the freezer. If Daddy does happen to be late, just help yourselves. Or perhaps it

2

would be nice if you and Edward could have a meal ready for him when he gets in.''

She kissed her pretty daughter on the forehead, tied her expensive, hand-knitted Guernsey casually around her neck, and hurried away before her son or her husband could distract her further.

With relief Jasmine Carson locked the front door of her flat behind her. Despite its comfort and convenience she hated it. For thirty years she had taught biology at a private girls' school and her rooms there had been her home. They had been high ceilinged, impressively proportioned. When she retired it had seemed sensible to buy somewhere appropriate to her needs, and she had chosen a ground-floor flat in a new well-appointed block on the sea front. She had always been congratulated on her common sense and while she had been tempted to move somewhere older, to a cottage perhaps with a garden, she had resisted in favour of central heating and a built-in kitchen. Now she was too proud, too afraid perhaps of making a worse mistake, to move again, and knew that the flat would be her home until she died. She supposed that she would get used to it. Already she could bear what had seemed the unbearable heat of the communal areas, and she presumed that the older residents, most of them elderly, would come to realize that she had no interest in the lives of their children who lived in Milton Keynes or Johannesburg, would stop showing her photographs of apparently identical grandchildren.

She drove inland from Gillicombe, the seaside town which she had made her home. The road followed the bank of the estuary and as the tide ebbed, the island became an island no longer, different from its surroundings not in substance but in kind, a lump of sandstone surrounded by muddy sand. That is my real home, she thought. She felt as tensely excited as a young girl off to a dance, hoping that her lover would be there, expectant of adventure, new experience: Then:

Romantic old fool, she thought. What's so special about

3

the place anyway? Fifty acres of sandstone at the mouth of the estuary, and it only becomes an island at high tide. Not a proper island. Not remote at all. Only three miles from the biggest tourist town in North Devon.

But whatever she made herself think, she knew that the pain of rheumatism in her hips and her spine disappeared as she drove along the river to meet the Land Rover, and that the real reason for tolerating the dreadful flat on the sea front was that at night, from her bedroom window, she could see the light of the Gillibry buoy.

It was a pleasant walk down the hill from the main road to the quay. A breeze blew from the sea. The two young men had hitch-hiked from Gillicombe, but were content to walk the last mile.

"I don't understand," said the tallest, lazily, "why you keep coming to the island. You were never that keen on ringing, even when we were kids. Now you hardly ever bother to come out with the North Devon Ringing Group. I don't even know if you've still got a valid ringing permit. But you're still a member, still pay the subs, and now you're on the committee."

"I'm on the committee," said the other, Mark, "because you co-opted me."

"I mean, I understand why it's so important to me. I've got that boring job in the shop, most of my friends—like you and Jon—have gone away to college, and there's not much else to do round here. But you're different. You're into all sorts of things—music, politics. You've loads of friends at university."

"I suppose so. But it is special, Gillibry, isn't it?" He seemed ashamed then of being so serious, and when a motorbike—apparently without a silencer—drove so fast down the lane behind them that they had to climb into the hedge, he was pleased to be distracted.

"Wasn't that Charlie?" he asked.

Nick, the tall one, shrugged.

"Probably. He's an appalling driver. He'll get himself killed one day."

4

"What happens to the island if he dies?"

"Didn't you know? He's left it to the observatory in his will. It's the sort of grand gesture he's good at."

"Do you think he's mad?"

"Of course he's mad. Mad as a hatter."

"No, I mean medically mad. Certifiable."

Nick shrugged again.

Mark continued: "I don't suppose that he can be. If he were properly mad he wouldn't be able to make that much money."

"It's an odd way to make a living, writing daft children's stories. Have you ever seen them?"

"Yeah. I think they're really good. But I suppose if he had been medically mad his family would have locked him up years ago. He always was the black sheep, wasn't he? Until he got rich. Then they decided that he was just eccentric."

Nick shifted the rucksack on his back. He had his own view of the Todds.

"It's your first committee meeting isn't it?" he said. "I hope that you don't find it too boring. They're all the same. Nothing ever happens."

Jerry Packham lingered over his work, pleased at last with the result. His bags were ready and subconsciously he listened for Pam's car, for the change of gears on the steep lane. He knew that she would be late. She always was. It was one of her ways of stressing the nature of the relationship between them. She would be expecting him to be waiting at the gate for her as usual. But today he was reluctant to leave. He wondered for one mad moment if he should tell her that he did not want to come, that he was too busy, that he wanted to finish the series of paintings, but he knew that he did not have the courage. He would finish the affair, but not yet. She had dominated the partnership so completely that he hesitated to take the lead even in separating. Besides, he wanted to see Charlie.

He had first illustrated Charlie's stories for a joke, before they were published. Charlie had lived in his village

5

then, and they had shared the same local. Charlie had been convinced even then that the stories would make his fortune. Jerry had never been at art college. He had left school at fifteen and become apprenticed to a sign writer. When the man retired he had taken over the business and expanded it. He had begun to design menus, posters, had even tried a set of postcards and found that they had been easy to sell. The sign writing became less important. In his spare time he enjoyed sketching and had been persuaded to sell the results through the numerous gift shops in Gillicombe. The illustrations had been fun to do; he had let himself go. There had never been any formal arrangement between himself and Charlie. He had never really believed that the books would be accepted for publication, and when they were, it seemed right that they should come under Charlie's name, that Charlie should get all the publicity and most of the money. The television serial had made the stories famous, and Jerry had taken no part in that.

It had been one of Jerry's birdwatching friends, George, who had suggested that Jerry should get an agent to negotiate a better contract with the publisher.

"Those books are made by the illustrations," George had said. "They're superb. Without them, I doubt if Charlie would have been published at all."

So he had received a more generous proportion of the royalties in the most recent series of books. He had become used to seeing his drawings reproduced in comics, on children's sketch pads, on sweet packets. He was comfortably off, but he was bored by the characters in Charlie's books. Each story seemed the same as the last. It was time to try something new. He had been offered other commissions and had decided that he should tell Charlie that he would not be available to work for him, at least for a while.

Now he was working on a children's encyclopedia of the countryside. It was very different from the illustration of Charlie's fantasies, but he was enjoying the precision and the subtlety of it. He was looking at a recently completed colour plate of leaves and trees when he realized

6

that the doorbell was ringing, and he hurried, rather pleased with himself, to meet Pamela.

As he looked down over the island, Doctor Derbyshire experienced, as he always did, a sense of achievement and of pride. Charlie might have financed the observatory, but the idea had been his. Without his organization, his persistence, Charlie would have grown bored with the negotiations to purchase, would have given up the project. Charlie was like a child and the doctor knew how to handle him.

Mrs. Derbyshire drove her husband to the quay. He disliked driving. He fussed over his luggage and made her check again that his favourite jersey was packed. She sighed with maternal irritation. He had not been happy since his retirement from general practice. She was grateful for the island. It stopped him mooning around the house, sulky and petulant as a schoolboy. That had been a dangerous time and she had been worried. The planning and the intriguing had given him life again, given him a future.

Paul Derbyshire looked at his watch and then over the shore. The Land Rover was on its way. John was a reliable boy. He looked forward to the committee meeting, planned his chairing of it. The committee were all well-meaning, enthusiastic people, but needed a strong chairman to give them proper direction. His wife watched his enjoyment with satisfaction, and planned a private, pleasant weekend. They were a happy couple but she understood nothing of the complexities of his affection for the island. She saw it as a toy, a distraction. It kept him busy.

But, It's the only contact I have with real beauty, he thought as he waited for the Land Rover. It's the daughter I never had, my creation.

She would never have imagined him capable of such lyrical folly. She waved at the other birdwatchers and drove off to her knitting and a nice glass of sweet sherry.

When John Lansdown first moved to the island, every trip to the mainland was a challenge. There was no track.

7

The Land Rover was driven south from Gillibry over steep green rocks, through seaweed-filled pools on to the shore. There, the sand could be soft and the gullies deceptively deep. If the tide had not ebbed sufficiently there was a danger of being stuck halfway across the channel. It had made him nervous. The Land Rover was his responsibility. Now he knew the way and was used to the Land Rover. Only in thick fog was he still wary. Automatically he counted the seals on the sandbank and estimated the number of waders on the shore. He hoped to persuade the others to try the new cannon net and would need to know what they could expect to catch. His reaction to the September committee weekend was ambiguous. The committee members were competent ringers and knew the observatory system. Some of them were friends. It was easier, perhaps, than having a group of strangers to stay, certainly easier than the schoolchildren who were the observatory's usual visitors, but he always felt that he was on trial throughout the weekend and that the committee was assessing his competence to run the place. He knew that Elizabeth felt the same. She supervised all the domestic arrangements in the observatory, and though it was organized like a youth hostel, she cooked three meals a day for the visitors. The thought of Elizabeth brought back the pleasure of anxious excitement which he had been feeling since she had told him that she was pregnant. She had insisted that no one else should know. He wanted to tell everyone he met—it meant after all that now she really belonged to him—but she had a kind of superstition about it. It was natural, he supposed, because of the miscarriage she had suffered when she was married to Frank. He was certain that nothing would go wrong. How could it, when things were going so well for them? They both loved the island. In the precarious world of natural history he had a secure job. Charlie Todd might be an eccentric neighbour, but he subsidized the Gillibry Trust's funds so that although John and Elizabeth were not well paid, they received more than they would have done from any other

conservation charity, and their home was reasonably warm and well maintained.

He turned the Land Rover sharply, and then he could see the people waiting for him at the quay. What can they be talking about? he thought. They're all so different. What can they have to say to each other?

Carefully, aware that they were watching, he drove the Land Rover from the sand on to the stone slipway. It had been a jetty once. Ships had sailed from there to the Armada. Now the estuary had silted up. There was sand and saltmarsh, and the people waiting there with their bags and suitcases looked slightly ridiculous. He jumped down and opened the back of the Land Rover.

"We've been discussing the paddock heligoland," Miss Carson said immediately. "When I was on the island last I was appalled. It should be repaired at once. Charlie says that he can give us some wire mesh. Perhaps we could organize a working party."

Of course, they would have that in common. They were passionate ringers. He thought that Jasmine was the school-mistress of stand-up comics and cartoonists. She was big-busted and formidable in thick woollen stockings and lace-up boots. She climbed without fuss, without a hint of rheuma-tism, into the back of the Land Rover.

"If you want us to do the work, it'll have to be soon. Mark goes to college again at the end of the month, and I'm very busy."

Nick spoke aggressively, more loudly than was necessary.

How ungracious he is, John thought. He does do more than his fair share, but he enjoys it. I hope that he's not going to be rude all weekend. Elizabeth does hate it.

But Miss Carson was disposed to be conciliatory.

"Of course," she said. "You know that we depend on you and Mark. We must talk again about attracting new, younger members."

That, too was a perennial item on the agenda. We must attract new members, but we will not accept their new ideas or give them any responsibility. The observatory had recruited a number of schoolboys over the years, but only

9

Mark and Nick were left. The others had drifted away, disillusioned by the slow pace of change on the island, the refusal to accept new ways of doing things, tempted by girlfriends, rare birds, beer. John wondered sometimes why Mark and Nick stayed. He suspected that Nick might enjoy the alliances and plotting as much as the older members did, but Mark was different. He had a wild and wicked sense of fun, a wide circle of friends, other interests.

As he always did, Charlie Todd climbed into the front seat, the only comfortable seat of the Land Rover, without giving anyone else the opportunity of doing so. John was never sure whether this lack of courtesy was caused by Charlie's usual absentmindedness or by cunning. It was probably absentmindedness. He was a small, round man with curly white hair, like a doll's wig, and a perpetually dazed but happy expression. People spoke to him slowly as if he were deaf, or very old, or a child. He could have been any age from fifty to seventy.

"George phoned up," Jasmine Carson barked suddenly. "He couldn't get through to you. He won't be able to get here until tomorrow, but he said not to pick him up. He'll walk out straight after the tide."

The others climbed in then, Pam Marshall and Jerry Packham taking care to sit on opposite sides of the Land Rover, Paul Derbyshire peevish about leg room and the splash of oil on the seat. It was all the same as every other committee weekend.

The south of the island had been leased to the council and was managed by its Recreation Services Department. This meant little more than that the little bins were emptied occasionally and that the area was open to the public. In the summer families walked over to experience a tide on a real island, to picnic on the beach or the grass. There was nothing else to do there and no one was there now. John noticed briefly that Pam was looking as glamorously well-kept as always, that Jerry was not staring at her with his usual rapt attention, then with an irrational progression of thought, wondered if Liz would marry him now. He knew her so well, yet could not predict how she would react if

10

he asked her again. He was frightened of upsetting things between them. It was her secrecy, her power to surprise which attracted him so deeply.

Through use a track had been worn from south to north over Gillibry and the island rose steeply away from the shore. The observatory was at the far north end, at the point of the tear-drop, like the figurehead of an old carved boat. It looked down over the rest of the island. In contrast Charlie's house was hidden in a fold in the ground, surrounded by the only trees which would grow on Gillibry. It was just more than halfway along the track, in a natural bowl, so that the cliffs to the east and the west of it were high and rocky, but the house was sheltered. In the summer flowers grew in the garden. The house itself was a prefabricated wooden chalet which Charlie had imported specially from Sweden. It was incongruous with bright paint and shutters and could have been taken from one of the illustrations of his books. The house was known on the island as the Wendy House. No one could remember who had named it. John stopped in the dip in the road and waited patiently as Charlie collected together the plastic carrier bags and brown-paper parcels which made up his luggage.

"You'll be up to eat with us as usual?" John asked.

"Certainly. Oh, certainly. It will be a very important meeting, you know. There's something that I've been thinking about for a long time. I know that you'll be most interested to hear all about it."

He was still talking as he disappeared through the stunted, wind-shaped sycamores to his home.

At that point the island was separated by a drystone wall, part of which formed the southern boundary of Charlie's garden. The public was not allowed beyond it, and this northern half of Gillibry formed the trapping area of the observatory. The traps stood over any cover which might attract birds, over small clumps of bushes, over a stream, in Charlie's garden. On the windswept moor to the north of the Wendy House they were the only break to the skyline, but for the white walls of the observatory. The

11

observatory was formed from a complex of lightkeepers' cottages. The lighthouse had long since fallen into disrepair and been demolished, but the cottages were still strong. They were as smart as if still owned by Trinity House, freshly whitewashed and painted. They and the outhouses had been built around a cobbled courtyard, and inside had been transformed into dormitories, single rooms, a laboratory and common room. There were a well-equipped kitchen and dining room, and on the first floor a staff flat. From the outside they looked unchanged. As he drove through the white wooden gates into the yard John heard the rhythmic pounding of the generator. There was no mains electricity on Gillibry. He wished that Elizabeth had waited for him to start it. It was an awkward and cumbersome machine and sometimes had to be cranked with a handle. He knew that she was frightened of the machine, had been even before she was pregnant, but she would never ask him to help her.

As soon as they arrived John went to the kitchen to find Elizabeth. The guests could take care of themselves. They always had the same rooms. Committee weekends followed the same pattern every year. Soon Doctor Derbyshire would open a bottle of Scotch in the common room, someone would put a light to the fire and they would wait for Elizabeth to ring the bell for supper.

Elizabeth was stirring a pan of soup over the Calor-Gas stove. She was three years older than him, but did not look it. Her hair was thick and black and long. She was slim still, in jeans and a sweater.

"How do you feel?" he asked.

She turned to him and pulled a face. "Lousy. I've been sick four times and I always seem to be tired."

"I'm sorry."

"I'm not. It's supposed to be a sign that the hormones are working properly. You might have to give me a hand with breakfast tomorrow morning, though. I'm not sure that I'm up to frying bacon. Are they all settled in?"

"I suppose so. George won't be here until tomorrow morning, but he's going to walk. It's a shame. I wanted to

have a go at cannon netting waders over the tide and he's had a lot of experience. Charlie seemed very excited about something.''

''Charlie's always excited about something. Has Nick been behaving himself?''

''Mm. So far. I think that Mark is a good influence on him. He's not usually quite so obnoxious when Mark is around.''

''What about Pam and Jerry?''

''I'm not sure, but I think that Jerry might be coming to his senses. He doesn't seem quite so zombie-like and admiring as usual.''

''I do hope so. I like Jerry so very much.''

They did not need to discuss Miss Carson. Jasmine was always the same.

In the common room they had left the curtains open, but had lit tilly lamps. The generator would have provided them with electric light, but the tillies were a committee weekend tradition, an affectation, a nostalgia for the time when the observatory was being developed, before the generator had been installed. It was not cold but the driftwood fire added light and atmosphere. It was a comfortable room, with rugs, big armchairs and a lot of books. It should have been a relaxed, enjoyable time. Paul Derbyshire had opened a bottle of whisky. They all held a drink. Usually it was a period of quiet conversation—restrained, academic, about birds and ringing. But as the tide swept in on either side of the long room, so that it could have been a ship moving forward through water, the occupants seemed unable to pretend even to friendship, and there was a mounting sense of tension and irritation.

Pam Marshall wandered to a writing table, where the daily log of birdwatching activity was kept, and there was a card index of ringing totals and recoveries. She had changed, and was wearing a plum-coloured velvet skirt and a simple cream blouse, quite appropriate to the occasion. She would never have worn anything unsuitable, but no one else had changed and the different clothes added to

13

the impression that she was ill at ease, trying for some reason to impress.

She flicked through the pages of the book, then said loudly: "This is really too bad. The log is nearly a week out of date. John should make more effort over things like this."

Her petulance surprised the others. Usually she tried very hard to be charming.

"Nothing to make a fuss about, surely," commented Jasmine Carson without looking up from the scientific journal she was reading with the aid of thick-glassed, heavy spectacles. "I'm sure that the day sheets in the ringing room will be made up. You could always transfer the figures to the log now if you wanted to."

"Oh, it's not that important. I just like to see things properly done."

Her voice was brittle. She looked at her watch. "I want to see Charlie. I don't suppose I've time to go down to the Wendy House now."

Jerry Packham answered with authority: "I shouldn't bother Charlie if I were you. There'll be time for that later."

He looked embarrassed, as if surprised at his own ability to be forceful. Nick shot a significant, gossip-laden look towards Mark, but Mark did not respond. Nick seemed offended by this lack of response, and with a desire to give offence turned to Paul Derbyshire. With bad-tempered sarcasm he said: "You'll be available to join the working party to mend the paddock heligoland trap, will you, Doctor?"

He achieved his objective. The doctor began to mutter excuses about being very busy, and not being as young as he was. He was notoriously idle.

Nick interrupted brutally: "Don't worry. I expect Jerry, Mark and I will manage. We usually do."

Mark usually managed to disperse his friend's aggression with a joke, a piece of clowning, but he seemed hardly to have heard. He seemed unaware that the others were looking at him, expecting him to work his magic, to

14

form the committee into a friendly, cohesive group. He was small and squat with long arms and a squashed, undefined face, as if the features were moulded from plasticine. He stood abruptly, walked to a window and looked out to the lights on the shore. There was a general sense of disappointment and resentment, as if he had let them down. The silence was broken only by the sound of the tide and the hiss of tillies, then Jasmine Carson said:

"John tells me that he would like to try cannon netting the waders over the tide. I haven't heard a weather forecast. We'd have to be sure that the conditions are right. John has borrowed the equipment from the North Devon Ringing Group. He says that they have had considerable success, but I don't know if it's the right technique for us."

"For goodness' sake," snapped Pamela. "We've got to try something new occasionally. If you had your way we'd still be shooting the bloody birds to identify them."

Just then the bell rang for the meal. The noise was simultaneously a further jar to strained nerves and a release of tension. Deliberately slowly, they walked together into the dining room.

They sat together around one long table. John and Elizabeth ate with them. Usually at the observatory, meals were cheerful, functional affairs, but for committee weekends some effort was made to add a little style. There was a tablecloth on the big, Formica-topped table, with wine provided by Paul Derbyshire, and Elizabeth served the meal. (Schoolchildren were sent to the kitchen to collect their own plates.) Charlie had not arrived, but he was always unpunctual, and they started without him. John seemed not to notice the group's uneasiness, and began to talk about cannon netting, trying to persuade everyone to join his enthusiasm.

"We'd be crazy not to try it. We could double, treble, our wader catches in one day. The conditions here are ideal."

"Isn't it dangerous?" Jasmine Carson was still cautious. She seemed unmoved by Pamela Marshall's outburst.

15

"Not if it's properly set up. I've had quite a lot of experience. We used cannon nets on the Wash when I was at college. I've got the right endorsement to my licence."

Elizabeth was sitting next to Mark. She ate little, was less exuberantly involved in the conversation than usual. She seemed to be saving her strength, moving with economy. Usually she communicated with her hands and her eyes and a tremendous theatrical range of voice.

Mark smiled at her. "You're very quiet," he said. "Are you all right?"

She was fond of Mark. She had known him since he was a schoolboy and was tempted for a moment to tell him her secret, but she nodded.

"I'm fine. Just a bit tired."

Charlie came in then. Nobody took very much notice of him. The conversation did not stop. He was wearing baggy trousers, a jersey with knitted patches on the elbows, and carpet slippers. Elizabeth got up quietly to fetch his soup. When she returned they had started to discuss the working party to mend the trap.

Doctor Derbyshire called across the table to Charlie: "It was generous of you to offer to buy the wire mesh. Most generous."

The thanks were automatic. Charlie always did provide the extras which the modest membership fees could not cover.

But now he looked up, peered over his soup, and said earnestly: "I've been meaning to talk to you about that. I should have thought about it before. It hardly seems worth bothering to mend the traps. You see, I'm going to sell the island."

He continued, noisily, to eat his soup.

2

There was no spontaneous reaction. At first they were too shocked. Charlie seemed calm, unexcited. Perhaps he was playing one of his practical jokes. Then the silence became awkward, challenging. Charlie stopped eating and looked around, inviting response. Pamela Marshall gave a well-bred, high-pitched little laugh, but Jasmine spoke for them all.

"I think, Charles, that you had better explain."

The stern schoolmistress voice came at just the right moment. She looked across the table at him with a controlled ferocity which had been one of her favourite methods for maintaining discipline. He surrendered immediately to her authority, lowered his eyes, and when he spoke it was with a naughty child's defensiveness.

"It's a very worthwhile cause," he said. "I saw it on the television when I was at my friend's. A canal boat, which is a theatre too. It goes along the canal giving performances and the cast live on the barge. But the boat needs restoration, and the Arts Council have stopped giving them any money."

He looked around the table. They were all staring at

him: no one would help him out, no one would make the explanation easier. It was nearly high tide. The island was separated from the mainland. In the silence they could hear the waves breaking over the rocks and the slipway at the north end. He caught Jasmine's eye and started again.

"They seemed such nice people. I phoned them up and offered to help. They were so excited and grateful. They are very young. Then I realized that I didn't have much money left. The film made most of the money and that was a long time ago. The books don't seem to be selling so well lately . . . They said that I could live with them on the boat."

"Do I understand," said Jasmine Carson, "that you intend to sell the island to finance their hare-brained scheme? You are a foolish man, Charlie Todd."

She could not have given a worse insult.

"But what about the observatory?" Nick demanded. He had lost the pose of petulant aggression. There seemed nothing to him without it. They had become so used to the act that now he was unrecognizable, without personality.

"I thought," Charlie said hopefully, "that the trust might like to buy the observatory. At a realistic price, of course. I wouldn't want to be greedy, but it costs rather a lot of money to restore a canal boat."

"My dear man." Paul Derbyshire's voice was shrill with impatience and unhappiness. He was a small man, thin and nervous, and now his face was red, the colour of raw meat. "How could the trust purchase the observatory? It hasn't the money to buy a roll of wire netting without your help."

"I could make it a condition of sale that you stay in the observatory," Charlie said. He felt that he was being extremely reasonable and looked with distaste and surprise at the angry, irritated faces. What a boring, unimaginative lot they were. His words seemed only to fuel the professor's impatience.

"We'd never be able to survive here if we had to pay rent for the buildings. Even if the landowner allowed us to retain the use of the observatory the rent would be astro-

18

nomical and we could not expect to have the same unrestricted access to the trapping area. Anything might happen here. Imagine a café at the north end, caravans in the paddock, an ice-cream van on the beach. And everywhere people."

He hesitated, imagining the horrors of the invasion of Gillibry's privacy. He tried to calm himself and said, as reasonably as he could: "My dear Charles, you must reconsider."

But Charlie was stubborn. He was dreaming of life as a travelling player, moving from village to village along the canal. The observatory no longer had any relevance to him. It was as if it had never existed. With some attempt at dignity, but sounding like a child fighting over a long-discarded toy, he said: "It's my island. I can do what I like with it."

Elizabeth gathered the soup plates together. As she moved she become the focus of their attention. They ignored Charlie and watched her as if she was performing a dance or a mime. When she went into the kitchen they waited in silence for her return. There was too much to be said to Charlie and no one felt up to the task. Elizabeth returned, carrying a huge casserole containing the main meal. She always made an effort for committee weekends and they turned their attention gratefully to the food. She acknowledged their compliments with a smile as stylized as the ritual clearing of the plates, but Mark at least noticed that she had been crying. John abruptly left the table and did not return. They watched him go in astonishment. Still nothing was said.

John's leaving, the empty place at the table, was a statement that things were not right with them, but the statement having been made, those remaining began to speak of other things. They were snapped out of shock as if by a slap on the face.

Nick worked as assistant manager in a shop, one of a chain owned by Charlie's family. Threatened by the silence, he began to talk compulsively about the holiday

trade, the foibles of the tourists, the problems of their imported staff.

"But it's been a good season," he said. "We've done very well." Then with a studied lightness: "Perhaps you should ask your family to fund the boat project, Charlie. They should be able to afford it this year."

"I thought of that," said Charlie simply, "but it didn't work. They don't like me, you see."

Jerry Packham was sitting next to Pam Marshall at the table and they had been talking quietly together. Pam was involved in the politics of conservation, was ambitious. She was efficient and enjoyed the power over the use of land. She was a Devon Conservation Trust Committee member and was discussing with him the purchase of a reedbed on the outskirts of Gillicombe, for a reserve. She was fighting to get the purchase approved. He was sure that eventually it would be.

"Perhaps you could persuade the Trust to buy the island," he said.

She shrugged. She had not appeared particularly distressed about the sale of the island. There were other places to go. It would be inconvenient. Perhaps it would be in her interest to form a protest group to save it, but she was not emotionally involved. Perhaps it would be in her interest for the sale to go through.

"They couldn't afford it," she said. "Besides, they're very ambiguous about ringing."

Jerry called across the table to Charlie. He still spoke quietly but they all heard him: "I need to see you some time this weekend about work. When would be best for you?"

"Meet me early," Charlie said. "I like to see the tide coming in. I'll be in the seawatching hide. I might see something good." He beamed at them, humouring them in their interest. "I'm writing a new story now. I'll have it with me. I'll bring some chocolate. We'll have a picnic."

It was like an invitation to a party and Jerry smiled his acceptance.

Elizabeth served coffee in the common room. Charlie

had gone, but all the observatory residents were there. They were discussing Charlie, his state of mind, his finances, Gillibry and the observatory. They seemed almost to be enjoying the excitement, the pleasure of the gossip. Elizabeth did not join them. She had put the big kettle on the stove to heat the water for washing up and was sitting, waiting for it to boil, when Mark came into the kitchen. It was a large room, impossible to heat and difficult to clean, with a stone floor and dusty corners, but Elizabeth liked it. Mark was the only guest she allowed in, without making him feel like an intruder.

"I've come to help."

She smiled at him gratefully. What a thoughtful boy he was. She threw him a clean tea-towel.

"What are they all doing?" she asked.

"They've decided to postpone the committee meeting, since neither Charlie nor John has reappeared. I suppose that Charlie has forgotten all about it. Pamela says that she's going for a walk, but she's still in the common room now. Jerry didn't offer to accompany her. I think she was a bit put out, but she could hardly change her mind then. The doctor is going through the accounts so that he can convince Charlie that it would be impossible for the Observatory Trust to buy a bag of nails, never mind an island. Jasmine is bringing the log up to date and Nick is staring at the fire and coming to terms with the fact that his world is about to come to an end."

"Isn't that rather melodramatic?"

"I don't think so. Since his mum died it's all he's got."

"He's never mentioned his mother."

"She died a couple of months ago. She wasn't very old. She worked for the Todds too, as a sort of housekeeper in one of the hotels. His dad died not long before she did. Nick's always had a chip on his shoulder, though. He was never popular at school. But he's come out of himself a lot since he's been on the observatory committee."

"Is that why you keep coming here? Because you feel sorry for him?"

"It's one of the reasons. He's always been a good friend to me."

They had finished washing up. Elizabeth wiped over the table top and hung up the cloth. She felt very tired. She wondered if she should look for John, but decided that she could not face his anger or his misery. She wanted to escape from thought of the island sale with an easy book or some music. But first she must bring in more wood for the common-room fire. She felt a sting of resentment. While John was being sentimental out in the dark she was left with responsibility for the practicalities. Mark helped her to collect logs from the generator shed, and she opened the doors while he carried them through the building to the common room. When she first opened the common-room door she thought that no one was there. Then she saw Jerry and Pamela standing by the window. They were not talking but it was clear that they had been arguing. Pamela was dressed in outside clothes—she had changed again into trousers—and she was very angry. Mark murmured something about finding Nick and going to catch some waders. Elizabeth followed him out and thankfully escaped to the flat.

John knew that he should have stayed and stuck it out with Elizabeth, but if he had he would have caused a scene, and she would hate that. He had wanted to shout at them as they sat around the table, their faces long and sallow because of the strange, lemon light of the tillies.

"What does it matter to you?" he had wanted to say. "It's only a weekend retreat for you, a hobby, a game It's our home, our livelihood. It was going to be the home of my child."

His anger was directed as much at the other guests as at Charlie.

"I've created this place," he had wanted to say. "I ring more birds here than the rest of you put together. It's my seawatching that's made Gillibry famous. I don't mind if you take the credit for that, but don't pretend that you care more about the place than I do."

Without thinking he began the walk that he made at least twice a day around the trapping area. It was dark, but he did not need a torch. The path was so familiar that the street lamps on the mainland provided all the light he needed. He walked quickly past the dining-room windows. No one saw him. They had finished eating. He did not notice Charlie's distinctive white hair, and wondered if he had returned to the Wendy House. Poor Charlie, he thought, as he always did when he contemplated the older man's awkwardness and loneliness. The instinctive reaction, such inappropriate sympathy, surprised then amused him, and his anger began to dissipate. He felt happier away from the claustrophobic tension of the dining room. The observatory and outbuildings were surrounded by a high white-washed wall. He walked through the painted gates and he was out on the island. He followed the track to the stile over the drystone wall where the stonechats called in spring, and climbed into the paddock. Mushrooms grew there, skylark and meadow pipit bred there. He had seen his first long-eared owl in the paddock, and still remembered the bright orange eyes, the fine mottled plumage. There was no need to check the trap. It had been shut at dusk. But he walked through the big wire-netting cage as he did when he was trying to flush birds into the glass trapping box, and returned to the paddock through a netting door at the funnel end of the trap. The next heligoland had been built over a gully cut into a rock by a stream taking the shortest cut to sea level. He had caught an aquatic warbler in the gully trap. He had not known what it was until he had taken it from the box. Birdwatchers had come from all over the country to see that. The ground was boggy and the grass was long and coarse. In spring there were orchids. He stepped across the stream and climbed the steep bank on the other side. He was on the high area of the island which they called the Beacon. Further west, down the slope towards the sea, there was bramble and buckthorn, two more traps and a lot more memories. Here there was only dying bracken and a small cairn to mark the highest point on Gillibry.

23

"Perhaps we should keep some sheep," he thought, "to keep the vegetation under control."

Then he remembered again and his anger returned.

He looked down over Gillibry, his island. To the west and north was darkness, the open sea, the wind that brought storm petrels and shearwaters. The island spread beneath him to the south, and beyond the island were the estuary and the mainland lights. A torch light pulled his attention from the horizon to the track only twenty yards below him. He could hear footsteps on the gravel track and the rustle of a waterproof kagoul, and there was a faint perfume. He knew at once who was walking there. He stood very still. He had always been attracted to Pam, but he had never liked her. She was the last person he would have wanted to see now.

"Perhaps she's going to see Charlie to seduce him into changing his mind," he thought.

He had been intending to follow his usual path round the traps: across the track, through the trees in the Wendy-House garden and back along the east cliffs. Now, to avoid meeting Pam Marshall he walked along the ridge of the Beacon, sat under the halfway wall and looked out to sea, letting the flashes of the Lundy lighthouse and the Hartland lighthouse relax him and empty his mind.

Mark found Nick in the bird room. He was mending a mist net, and sat in a tangle of fine nylon line. The bird room was small but well equipped. A worktop ran along one wall. There were bird bags in a pile, a set of scales, strings of rings hanging on hooks to the wall, ringing pliers. The school groups used the room as a laboratory.

When Nick saw Mark he rolled the net up into a rough ball and stuffed it back into its canvas bag.

"Where are Jasmine and the doctor?" Mark asked.

"I don't know. Aren't they in the common room? Perhaps they're making wild, passionate love in kestrel hollow."

"It's a big tide. Do you want to try that wader roost at the north end?"

Nick looked at him suspiciously, like a toddler being

24

jollied out of a sulky mood. "Since when have you been so interested in ringing waders?"

"I'm not, but I can't face hanging around here, listening to people beefing about Charlie all evening."

"All right. We can't use this net, though. One of the guys is missing. I wish that people would put the nets away properly. This one's in an awful mess. I don't know why we can't keep the guys separate from the nets like everyone else. It would make life much easier."

His self-righteousness was cheering him. He loaded Mark with poles and nets and took a handful of bird bags, and they went out.

From her bedroom Jasmine Carson watched them go. They were laughing over some infantile joke. She was tempted for an instant to shout down to them, to ask if she could join them. Her fingers were too stiff for ringing now, but she could help to put up the nets. But she had already changed her clothes and her arthritis was so tiresome that the thought of changing back exhausted her. If the boys had looked up to her window, they would have seen that she was crying.

One of the corners of the common room had been made into a library. High shelves separated it from the living part of the room. Paul Derbyshire was sitting there, turning the accounts into a precise statement of the financial position of the observatory, into an account so simple, he told himself, that even that blockhead Charles Todd will understand it. At first the raised voices in the common room merely irritated him. His powers of concentration were intense and he was able to continue with his work. Occasionally the deep, personal anxiety which haunted him like a recurring nightmare intruded, and then he was miserable, momentarily distracted, but he was not aware of the argument beyond the bookcase. When he had finished the accounts, however, he found that he was in an embarrassing position. He wanted to go to see Charlie. That was immensely important. He was quite sure that he would make Charlie see sense. About everything. Al-

though he had not been listening to the argument outside he had heard enough to realize that Pam Marshall and Jerry Packham were discussing a matter of extreme delicacy. He wished that he had been aware of the nature of the conversation earlier, so that he could have taken more notice of what was being said. If he emerged from the library now, they would wonder why he had not made his presence known before. Now he could only wait for the row to end and the protagonists to leave. This he did with some impatience.

Little of interest was being said. Pamela was hurling abuse and recrimination, and Jerry was fending it off. At last the argument reached a crescendo. Pamela shouted: "You're so bloody spineless, Jerry. If you haven't got the nerve to do it, I have," and he heard the sound of footsteps and the slam of the door. Soon after Jerry left too, and the doctor heard the door shut gently behind him. Paul Derbyshire gathered together his papers, unwilling now to face the task ahead of him, then he sighed and went to find his coat.

Charlie Todd sat in his rocking chair in the tidy, doll's-house living room. He was feeling pleased with himself. His visitors that evening had made him feel important. He supposed that eventually he would have to think about what had been said. He had promised, after all, to think about it. He did not want to be unkind. He remembered the hostile faces around the supper table. He was genuinely surprised by the reaction to his news, but he was determined to have his own way. He would be sorry to leave this house, but his room on the boat would be very similar to this room. He lay back in his chair and fell asleep.

John did not know how long he had been sitting, looking out over the sea, when Elizabeth found him. In her torch light she looked untamed, distraught. Her long hair was tangled. There was mud and sand on her shoes and her jeans. How different she looked, he thought, from that

day when we first met. She's like the lady who joined the raggle-taggle gypsies. Will she leave me, he thought, if I cannot find her somewhere wild and dramatic to live? If I have to get a real job, and a house on an estate and a mortgage, will she still love me?

"I've been looking for you on the shore," she said. "Nick and Mark have put up a net at the North end and I thought that you might be with them."

"Nick did say that he wanted to go ringing. I'd forgotten."

"I've just come up through the Wendy-House garden," she said.

"Oh?" He was still watching the Lundy light. He counted the space between flashes. He seemed overcome by an overwhelming apathy.

"I almost went in to see Charlie. The light was still on. I thought that I might tell him that I'm pregnant. I thought it might make him change his mind."

"But you didn't?" He hardly seemed interested.

"No. I decided that it was better not to. If we leave him alone perhaps nothing will come of it. He's always getting these enthusiasms, but they never last long, and he doesn't usually follow them through. He only bought the island because Doctor Derbyshire organized it for him. All Charlie had to do was sign his name. But if we bully him, he might get stubborn."

"You seem calm." For the first time he turned his attention from the light on the horizon. "You were upset when he told us. You'd been crying."

"That was surprise, I suppose. Shock. And my hormones."

"What are they all doing? Did they have the AGM?"

"They couldn't really, without you, and Charlie went home straight after supper. I don't think that anyone felt that they could concentrate. Mark helped me to wash up, then he and Nick put up a net."

"Have they caught anything?"

"Yes, but nothing special."

"What about the others?"

"Earlier Pam and Jerry were having a row in the common room. I suppose that the doctor and Jasmine had discreetly made themselves scarce. I don't know where they all are now."

"Were they offended that I left in the middle of the meal?"

"I don't think they noticed. Everyone was absorbed in their own worry. They all pretended that nothing had happened."

She turned to him and kissed his forehead. She had a sweet, dark smell, like flowers in a summer night. He wanted to lean against her, to lose himself again in the darkness, but she despised weakness.

"Come on," she said. "Do you want to help Mark and Nick take down the net, or shall we go home?"

"Home."

She went first, sure-footed, down the slope to the track, and she saw the fire first, and began to run. He heard her shouting, but he was still dazed after his dreaming on the hill in the darkness. It took him a while to realize what was wrong, then he was running too, and he found that he, too, was shouting.

The light behind the trees in the Wendy-House garden was too bright; it moved and threw dark shadows. There was a smell of smoke.

They found the fire extinguisher just inside the unlocked door. It must have come with the Wendy House. Charlie would never have thought to buy one. Unbelievably, in the wood-panelled sitting room he was still asleep. He was leaning back on the cushion of his rocking chair, his mouth open, snoring. He was a notoriously heavy sleeper and he did not wake until Elizabeth shouted at him. Inside the fire was not as frightening as it had seemed from outside. One of the curtains was alight, and because the window was open the flames, sparks and smoke billowed outside. Next to the curtain, on a small table under the window, a tilly was lying on it's side. But without the extinguisher they would not have put out the fire. Charlie made no attempt to help them, but watched with a kind of

sleepy excitement as John used the extinguisher and Elizabeth tried to beat out the flames with an orange, woven rug.

It was all over even before the window frame was alight, although the varnish on the frame and the panelling around the window were charred and blistered, and there was an unpleasant smell. John put the extinguisher on the floor and Elizabeth folded the rug. Only then did Charlie stand up. It was as if he were standing to applaud the end of an outstanding play.

"Wonderful," he said. "Most efficient. Now I feel like a drink. You must have one too. I insist. Do sit down."

He poured drinks. Elizabeth guiltily and John gratefully accepted.

"Well, Charlie," John said. "How did you manage it?"

"What do you mean?" He was enjoying his role of host. He had turned up the Calor-Gas fire and was looking to see if he could offer them anything to eat.

"How did you manage to knock over the tilly?"

"Oh no," he said. "I didn't knock it over. I was sitting here, you see, in front of the fire. Even if I had moved in my sleep I couldn't have reached the lamp. It was on that table."

"I can see that. Something must have knocked it over."

"Perhaps it was the wind. Or it might have been Tomo."

Tomo was the island cat. He was supposed to live in the observatory outbuildings and keep down the mice, but Charlie had adopted him.

"I suppose it might have been, although it doesn't seem very likely. Tomo's only a kitten and the tilly is quite heavy."

"All the same," said Charlie, looking at John with strangely blank, blue eyes, "I think that it must have been Tomo. There's no other explanation, you know. And really there's no harm done."

When John and Elizabeth returned to the observatory, in the common room Jasmine Carson was pouring cocoa from a jug, and everyone was there. Cocao at ten o'clock

was an observatory tradition, served usually by Elizabeth. When it had not arrived Paul Derbyshire had become petulant, and had gone to look for her. When he could not find her it had not occurred to him to make the drink. Mark and Nick had returned. Their woollen socks were hanging on the fire guard to dry. They had found the brooding atmosphere in the common room oppressive. Pamela and Jerry were silent, the doctor was muttering trivial complaints and Jasmine had returned to the log, treating the entries with as much scorn as if she were marking a mediocre exam paper. So they had offered to make the cocoa, and on their return with it everyone made some attempt at ordinary, polite conversation.

When John and Elizabeth came in and told them about the fire in the Wendy House, nobody was very surprised. Charlie was appallingly absentminded. Things like that were always happening to him.

3

They woke, next morning, to a storm.
The wind penetrated the building, rattling windows, making the solid-fuel boiler burn so furiously that the water boiled in the pipes. The thick walls could not shut out the sound of the gale, but John was used to the weather, and was woken not by the wind but by the telephone. It was a quarter to seven. He put on Elizabeth's dressing gown and went barefoot to the telephone extension in the sitting room of their flat. As he had expected it was the coastguard with a routine cone message. He stood, shivering. The coastguard wanted to chat. At last he returned to the bedroom, dressed and went out on to the island. The wind was blowing from the northwest, dragging the shore into ridges, driving the surface water into grey and white waves. He pulled the canvas cone from the generator shed. The wind filled it and made it unwieldy. He carried it in to the mast on the Beacon, fastened ropes and shackles and hoisted it: an anachronistic and unnecessary statement of the obvious, a warning to shipping that there was a gale from a northerly direction. The tide was not full in, but already the waves were breaking over the flat rocks at the

31

north of the island, and had reached the stilt legs of the seawatching hide. The flaps of the hide were shut and that surprised him. It should be a good day for seabirds and he had expected Nick and Mark to be there already. When he got back to the flat Elizabeth was being sick.

He wished that he could be outside waiting for the seabirds, but breakfast was at 8:30 and he had promised Elizabeth that he would help her to cook it. Eventually she looked so uncomfortable in the kitchen that he sent her outside for fresh air. He was surprised when she went, without argument, pleased when she came back exhilarated.

"It's an amazing storm," she said. "I can't remember one like it before. The seawatching hide is completely cut off. I hope that Charlie and Jerry managed to get out."

"What do you mean?"

"Jerry arranged to meet Charlie there before breakfast to discuss work."

"There was no one in the hide when I raised the cone at seven o'clock. If they *are* there, they'll be quite safe. They'll only have to wait for the tide to go out."

"I suppose that Jerry might be late for breakfast. Charlie usually has his in the Wendy House."

But when they went to the dining room everyone, except Charlie, was there. They were talking about the weather. It was impossible to ignore it. The windows were streaked with salt spray and there was a background noise of wind and water. Occasionally there was the sharp crack of a slate being lifted from an outhouse roof.

"You cowards," John said to Nick and Mark. "I should have thought that you'd be in the hide on a morning like this. The birds could be pouring up the coast. It's brilliant seawatching weather."

He was rather annoyed. He would have liked to be there—he was doing a special study of shearwaters—but someone should have been counting the seabirds. It was the first big storm of the season.

"We would have gone," Nick said resentfully, "but we thought that Jerry was meeting Charlie there and we didn't want to intrude. By the time we realized that no one was in

the hide, the tide was so high that we couldn't get across. We've done a count from the west cliffs but we must have missed a lot."

Jerry was pale and miserable. "I'm sorry. I don't know what's the matter with me. I meant to get up to meet him, but I overslept. I hope that Charlie didn't wait for me."

John watched Nick and Mark exchange glances laden with schoolboy significance. Jerry had overslept on previous weekends and had been seen to emerge from Pamela Marshall's bedroom. There had developed a story, which had started as a joke and become half-believed myth, concerning Pamela's sexual appetite and her seduction of Jerry. Later, John thought, the boys would snigger together, the myth would become more elaborate. He felt oddly old. Pamela Marshall was ignoring Jerry and the boys. She had brought her own expensive brand of marmalade, and she was spreading it on to the toast. He realized that he was staring at her and turned away. As he did so he caught Jasmine Carson's eye. She had seen him staring. She smiled maliciously. He no longer felt old, but painfully adolescent. He noticed that Jasmine's hair was damp, and to relieve his embarrassment he said:

"Where have you been this morning, Miss Carson?" She looked at him as if he were a fool. "I always take a walk before breakfast."

Mark joined the conversation: "Did you do any seawatching? We didn't see you on the west cliffs."

"What I have been doing, young man, is my own business. Now, perhaps you would be kind enough to give me an accurate account of the birds you have seen."

After breakfast John, Mark and Nick went out to seawatch. John did not stay to help Elizabeth to clear the plates. She understood the urgency. It was his work, his passion. He had missed the best stage of the tide, but it was possible that birds had been blown further into the estuary and that they would fly back past the island, towards the open sea as the tide ebbed. It was not only that he was anxious that he might miss some rare or beautiful

33

bird; it was a matter of principle that everything should be counted and recorded.

His sense of urgency, almost of desperation, made him intolerant, increasingly irritated by Mark's flippancy. As he had expected they were speculating about Jerry's relationship with Pam. Nick's pomposity suited his mood more closely. John had hoped that Jerry would come with them. He took his birdwatching seriously and had a flair for identification which seemed instinctive, but Jerry had said that he must apologize to Charlie and had hurried off towards the Wendy House. There was only enough room in the hide for four people to sit in comfort. This was Doctor Derbyshire's usual excuse for the infrequency of his expeditions from the comfort of the observatory common room, and he had used it again today, saying at breakfast that he was prepared to sacrifice the opportunity of a place in the hide in favour of the younger, more skilled observers. He had waited for the last statement to be contradicted, but it was not. John would have been happy to have had Jasmine Carson as a fourth companion in the hide—she was meticulous, yet enjoyed the birds—but Nick said that she made him feel as if he were still at school, so they had escaped immediately after breakfast.

Although the tide had started to ebb the wind was still strong. They had to turn their heads away from it to speak, and then they had to shout. They were all wearing wellingtons, and on the low, rocky part of the island just south of the hide the water was only calf deep. They waded through. Further out to sea white spindrift was blown across the surface. Nick and Mark stood aside to let John climb the ladder to the hide first because they knew that the door would be locked. John balanced at the top of the sturdy ladder, reached in the deep pocket of his oiled jacket for the key, then tried to fiddle it into the big, brass padlock.

"Damn," he said at last. "It was open all the time. I must have forgotten to lock it last time I was here."

He pulled open the door and climbed in. Despite the light from the door he could not see at first. The glare from the sea had been bright and his eyes had not adjusted

34

to the darkness. He was at home in the hide though, and felt without hesitation for the stiff and rusty bolts of the big, front flap, and pushed it open. The light and a fine wave of sea spray seemed to blow in together. He wiped the water from his eyes. It's like being a part of the sea, he thought. This is what they mean by being at one with nature. He felt intensely emotional, close to tears, and the experience had little to do with the prospect of leaving the island. Then he smiled at his romanticism and thought that they would have to sit well away from the flap, or their binoculars would be covered with spray and quite useless. By now the others were coming up the ladder. He turned to speak to them, to share with them his excitement, and he saw then the body in the corner. Lying on his back on the floor, his legs still hooked round the bench seat, was Charlie. His eyes, pale and blank as when they had last met, stared at John. Charlie was unmistakably dead.

At first John only felt the panic of responsibility. What should I do? Should I call a doctor, or an ambulance? An ambulance would never get here. Should I try to move the body? Because he felt that he should, he felt for a pulse, listened for a heart beat, but he was quite sure before then that Charlie was dead. It was Nick, standing on the ladder, looking into the hide, and watching in bewildered silence, who saw the thin, green nylon rope, like a trickle of green blood around Charlie's neck, so it was Nick who forced him to accept the reality of the scene. His voice was high-pitched with hysteria.

"Somebody's killed Charlie Todd," he said, and in the enclosed space of the hide it seemed to John that he was shouting.

"Somebody's killed Charlie Todd." Nick was gasping for breath as he pointed at the convulsed body. "It's one of the mist-net guys. He's been killed by a mist-net guy."

Then he looked ill, and half climbed, half slipped down the ladder to the rocks. He caught on to Mark's shoulder to steady himself, held on to it longer than he needed for comfort, was stifling sobs. Nick's hysteria surprised John. It occurred to him that the boy was over-reacting, and he

felt suddenly calm, mature and sensible. He shut the flap and bolted it, climbed out of the hide, fitted the padlock and carefully locked it, then descended the ladder to the rock. Nick was already becoming more controlled and began to apologize. John knew exactly what must be done now. There had never, really, been any question.

"I'm going to telephone the police," he said. "You two stay here. I expect that Charlie's key is in his pocket, but you two stay here, just in case. While you're here," he added, partly serious, partly trying to relieve their tension, "you might try to count some seabirds."

As John walked down the island towards the observatory he saw that someone was on the shore, following the tide out towards Gillibry. Although the figure was a long way off, he recognized the tall, thin silhouette and the shape of the old army rucksack which the man carried high on his back.

It's George, he thought, and he felt the relief, the release of shared responsibility.

George Palmer-Jones was not quite sure why he retained his membership of Gillibry, nor why he had allowed himself to be elected to the committee. He had first become involved through his friendship with Jerry Packham. They had met on the Scilly Isles one October. Everyone who was at all interested in rare birds tried to spend some time on the Scillies in the autumn, but George found many of the obsessive birdwatchers tedious and blinkered. Jerry had been quiet, a little over-awed by the fanatics and the number of birds, and the two men, quite different in background and temperament, had become friends. At that time Gillibry had been owned still by an elderly, reclusive lady who had allowed the ringing group to operate from there and to store their equipment in her barn. Soon after, she had died. Charlie, erratically, had been a member of the ringing group, though he had never applied for a full licence. He had been at the height of his success. His accountant had been in favour of him buying the island, but he had been uncertain, uncommitted. Paul Derbyshire, chairman of the ringing group, had asked Jerry Packham to

call in George Palmer-Jones to help to fire Charlie's imagination. George had long been an advocate of a west-coast bird observatory to replace Lundy. George Palmer-Jones was a respected figure in British ornithology. He was a member of the Council of the RSPB, he had once been on the British Birds Rarity Committee, he appeared, occasionally, on BBC natural history programmes. Charlie had listened to George, the island was bought, and Gillibry Bird Observatory Trust had been formed. George had felt that it would be churlish to withdraw immediately. He had paid his subscription, intending to visit the island a few times during the first year, to remain a nominal member for another couple of years, and then to resign: Gillibry was a long way from his home, after his retirement he had become increasingly interested in rare birds and there was little chance of a rarity turning up in North Devon. But he had come to appreciate the autumn weekends on Gillibry, and though he seldom visited the island more than once a year, he had not resigned. He admired John Lansdown's abilities as warden and as a birdwatcher, and there was something sedate and old-fashioned about the committee weekends which contrasted with the frenzy and chaos of hunting rare birds. It was like a return to the days when natural history was the pastime of eccentric gentlemen, of elderly parsons and retired dons. He could imagine Jasmine Carson as one of the Victorian ladies who had founded the RSPB to prevent the import of exotic birds to provide feathers for fashionable hats, and Doctor Derbyshire, with his love of order and meticulous detail and lists, as one of the originators of the theory of taxonomy. Even the young men seemed different from the rest of their generation. They did not bring girlfriends to sunbathe in bikinis in the observatory garden, they did not get drunk on the doctor's whisky, take drugs, sniff glue or decide to become vegetarian. He was not sure that such an *anachronistic* organization was healthy, or that it would survive, but for one weekend a year he could enjoy it.

He was walking out against the wind. It was as if nothing else existed—not the mainland where the people at

work hardly recognized that there was a storm, certainly did not know which way the wind was blowing, nor the island ahead of him. Nothing mattered but the effort of walking against the wind, the sand stinging at his eyes and the surface water blowing around his boots. He stopped once, on his way across, to catch his breath. He turned his back to the wind, almost leant against it to rest. Then he saw the two navy-blue Land Rovers leaving the shore. They were not driven slowly across the sand, as John would have driven the observatory Land Rover to save it from the salt spray, in a fruitless attempt to slow down the inevitable corrosion, but frantically, at speed. He realized that something must be wrong on the island. He turned back into the wind and continued his walk.

As he walked through the gates into the observatory compound John saw Paul Derbyshire coming up the path from the south of the island. It was so unusual to see the professor away from the common-room fire that he almost waited, to find out what had prompted the older man to face the gale. Then he decided that he could not face explaining why he was not seawatching and he hurried in to the ringing room and the telephone. There he hesitated, unsure whether he should make a 999 call or phone straight to the police station in Gillicombe. He was quite certain that Charlie was dead, so there was little urgency, and he decided on the police station. Then he dialled, and he noticed with surprise that his hands were shaking. He wished that George had already arrived. The policeman who answered was slow and calm, and took his name and address, then passed him to another officer, whose name and rank were given, but immediately forgotten.

Superintendent Savage was at home. It was his weekend off. He had slept late and was nursing an unobtrusive hangover. He had spent the night before in the Catholic Club. It was the only place in Gillicombe where he felt really at ease. Most of the members were incomers, Irish, or Merseysiders like himself. His wife never complained

about his evenings out. Her lack of complaint was a kind of repayment. He had moved to Devon because of her. She had always been emotionally frail and had found it impossible to live with his work in Liverpool. If he was late home from a shift he would find her a neurotic wreck, peering through the curtains, waiting for the sound of his car. She had settled well in Gillicombe, and was happy. Despite his boredom he had never regretted the move and wished that she could forget his sacrifice, would stop being quite so grateful. They were having breakfast together when the telephone went. They had no children, and it was a calm, unhurried meal. Mary answered the telephone.

"It's for you," she said. "Graham Connibear." They had been living in Gillicombe for ten years. In another ten he would have retired. Yet he still marvelled at the change. in her. Graham Connibear was one of his detective constables. That meant that the call was probably a summons to work, but there were no tears, no pleas that he refuse to go. He missed the pace, the urgency of city policing, but perhaps it was a small price to pay.

His first reaction to the news of the Gillibry murder was a feeling of well-being, of health. His hangover disappeared. He felt immediately more vital. But his voice was restrained. Mary was listening.

"Sort out transport," he said. "Notify the scene-of-crime team and the pathologist. And I'll want a map of the island and some facts about it. Who lives there and what goes on there. I'll come now. I'll be in the office in a quarter of an hour."

Mary looked up from the newspaper. "Work?" she asked. "Anything special?"

He hesitated. She would hear about it on the radio. "Murder," he said. "Over on Gillibry, that island in the estuary. I expect it'll be straightforward. They usually are. But it should be interesting. It'll take some special organizing. I don't know when I'll be back."

He spoke gently, but she recognized the excitement. She smiled. She had long ago lost the habit of panic.

39

"Don't worry," she said. "I'll look forward to hear all about it when you get home. I'll expect you when I see you."

It was a dismissal.

Connibear was waiting for him in his office. He was flushed and excited, but in a file on his superior's desk, was a large scale ordnance survey map of the island, a typewritten sheet explaining the function of the observatory, and even an old observatory report. Connibear needed a haircut. In any other circumstances Savage would have told him so, but today the superintendent ignored him, sat at the desk and read the notes with a desperate intensity. Savage was very thin, drawn, as if his body had been ravaged by disease, but the flesh had been burnt away not by illness but by a restless, insatiable energy. It had not made him popular in the force. He looked up from the papers.

"Stop dithering, lad," he said to Connibear, who hovered just inside the door. Except for his training, and a holiday to Malta, Connibear had never been outside North Devon, and Savage, with his Liverpool accent, his Catholicism, his passion, was foreign, unpredictable. "Have we got transport?"

"Yes sir, Land Rovers. And according to Mr. Lansdown, the observatory warden, we can drive across now."

"We'd better go, then." He moved remarkably quickly and was out of the door before his constable.

The two men rode together in the first Land Rover. The sand blew in pretty swirls low over the shore and rattled against the windscreen.

"Do we know anything about the victim?" Savage asked. "Todd is a big name in Gillicombe, isn't it?"

"Everyone knows Charlie Todd, sir. He's a character in his own right. But the family is an institution. They employ a lot of people."

"Tell me."

"Old man Todd, Charlie's father, started off as proprietor of the Grand Hotel, on the prom. It really was grand too, in those days. Grand, but old-fashioned. He tarted it

up, put in a few more bathrooms, a swimming pool, encouraged coach trips to stay there. Turned it into a sort of high-class holiday camp. Then he started buying land, before prices really rocketed. He never seemed to have any trouble getting planning permission for the development. He owns all those caravan sites and chalets on the other side of the coombe. Since then the Todds have branched out into gift shops, cafés. I've heard it said that they own half the property in the High Street, but you'd have to check on that. Old man Todd has three sons . . ."

"Is he still alive?" Savage interrupted.

"The old man? I believe so, sir. He'd be nearly ninety now. My gran went to the board school with him."

"Go on. You said he had three sons."

"Sir. Ernest, Laurence and Charlie, and there was one daughter. I can't remember what she was called, but she married another local businessman, called Sandiford. It was seen as a bit of a business merger, but I think that the Todds got the better deal. They still live locally. They had a daughter, and she married . . ."

"All right, lad. We'll skip the detailed family tree for now, shall we? What about the sons?"

"Sorry, sir. Ernest helped his father at the Grand for a while, then he took charge of all the caravan sites and that holiday camp on the hill. They called the business Todd Leisure Enterprises. I suppose that they formed some sort of company. Laurence was involved too, though I'm not sure what he does.

"By all accounts Charlie was always a bit—odd. Not simple exactly, but not quite normal. His mother was quite a few years older than Albert, the old man. They say he married her for her money not her looks, and she must have been well into her forties when Charlie was born. Ernest and Laurence went to school here in Gillicombe and left at fifteen to work for their father. I know that, because Ernest was on the board of Governors when I was at school, and he told us so every speech day. I suppose because he was a bit slow, Charlie got sent away to some private place.

41

"Apparently the old man wanted to make Charlie manager of the Grand when Ernest set up Todd Leisure, but he soon realized that it wouldn't do. When Charlie came back after National Service he was a bit wild. There was a scandal, I think, about girls in the town. One of them was under age. The parents made a fuss. Old man Todd tried to have Charlie locked up in some sort of mental clinic, but the doctors wouldn't certify him. His mother had died by then. Albert gave up any hope of Charlie earning his own living, and offered to pay him an allowance if he promised to keep away from Gillicombe. I don't think it was specially generous, but Charlie seemed to manage on it. He didn't quite keep his part of the bargain, though. You quite often saw him around Gillicombe."

Savage was astounded. Connibear was thirty-five. How could he know what had happened to an unrelated family years before his birth? Even allowing for the curiosity of Gillicombe people, the Todds had made an enormous impact on the folk history of the place.

"But I thought that he bought the island," Savage said. "How did he manage that on a not very generous allowance?"

"Haven't you ever heard of Charlie Todd, sir? He's famous. He wrote children's stories. Smashing stories they are, too. My kids love them. But he only became famous about ten years ago. Before then he had a peculiar lifestyle. I met him once in a pub. I was only a youngster and I thought he was a real character. Every winter he worked as Father Christmas in one of the big London stores. Then he would go to the Cold Research Council place for a few weeks. He had a friend with a smallholding in Cornwall and he'd go and help out there, until the school summer holidays, when he ran a Punch and Judy stall at St. Ives. Autumn was fruit picking in Kent, and then it was back to London for the season as Father Christmas."

"But he settled here when he started writing stories?"

"I suppose so. He had a cottage down the Storr Valley. I think he still did his stint as Father Christmas. He told me that he loved that."

"Who's that?" Savage interrupted sharply. They were approaching the south end of the island. A figure was walking towards them, a scarf around his face to protect him from the blowing sand.

"It'll be John Lansdown, the warden, I should think. He said that he would walk down to meet us. The route on to the island over the rocks is a bit tricky. He was afraid that we'd get the Land Rovers stuck."

Savage said nothing.

John had found Elizabeth in the kitchen. He had still been shaking, but when he told her of Charlie's murder, she had been calm, very practical. She had offered to tell the others the news of Charlie's death, and had sent him out to meet the police. He wanted Elizabeth to go with him, but she refused. She would ring the bell, as if for coffee, and when everyone was gathered in the common room, she would tell them. Then she would go out to meet George and tell him. She would be quite safe. She would feel better for telling George.

In the Land Rover Connibear introduced himself and his superior. Savage remained silent, but John was aware of him, and was nervous of him. He pointed out the track. As they drove past the Wendy House he wondered if he should explain that Charlie had lived there, but somehow he felt unable to speak. He supposed that it was shock.

The Land Rovers stopped at the observatory, but Superintendent Savage went straight to the hide. He sent Mark and Nick back to the observatory. He was curt but not unfriendly. He smiled at them. He did not stay there long. In the hide there was not, after all, much for him to see or do. It was the time for the pathologist and the scene of crime team. In the cramped space of the hide he was only in the way, and he could feel that his restlessness and impatience irritated the other officers. The wind was still blowing hard as he walked back to the observatory. He pulled his mackintosh around him and was conscious of a deep, spontaneous happiness, followed immediately by guilt. By an effort of will he drove the guilt away. Why should he not enjoy the investigation? He had been trained

43

for just this sort of case, and he had so little opportunity now to exercise his skill.

Connibear and John Lansdown were still standing by the Land Rovers. They were looking at a tide table.

"Where are all the residents?" Savage asked.

"In the common room with one of the uniformed blokes."

"So what's the implication of the tide time?"

"Crucial, sir. High water was at 7:46 A.M. so there would have been no access to the island after 5:30 this morning."

Savage turned to John. "What about by boat?"

John shook his head. "Impossible in the sort of wind that there was this morning."

"And what time did you find him?"

"Ten past nine. I'm quite certain because I was hoping to start the seawatch at nine and I realized that we wouldn't make it."

"Gillibry was still cut off from the mainland at that time?"

"Yes. It would be possible to start walking from the mainland then, but you wouldn't be able to cross the gully until nearly ten."

Talking to himself Savage said: "The pathologist should be able to give us a more accurate time of death."

Then to John: "There would have been no reason for Mr. Todd to be in the hide before 5:30?"

"None at all. He was there to do a seawatch. There would be no point in being there before it was light."

"As far as you know, no one left the island after the tide this morning?" Savage looked at the flat expanse of shore and added: "It would be difficult to slip away unnoticed."

John shook his head. "I didn't see anyone, and I think that I would have done, but you should ask George, George Palmer-Jones. He walked over straight after the tide and arrived at the same time as your Land Rovers."

Savage looked up suddenly at the sound of the new name, but did not comment. "Since we arrived I've had two men searching the island and keeping an eye on the

44

shore." He turned to Connibear. "They haven't turned anything up?"

"They're not back yet."

"Have you sorted out about an office?"

John answered. "There's the bird room," he said tentatively. "We do all the ringing there and it holds all the ringing equipment, but I use it as an office too. There's a telephone extension, a desk, even an old typewriter if you needed it."

"That sounds ideal."

"Do you want to see it?"

But Savage felt suddenly impatient with these preliminaries. He wanted to get to the heart of the investigation immediately.

"Not yet," he said. He turned to John and smiled, unexpectedly. "If you will, Mr. Lansdown, you'll show me to the common room. I think it's time for me to meet everyone."

4

In the common room they sat separately, without talking. Occasionally, as if it were some nervous tic, Doctor Derbyshire cleared his throat, seemed about to speak, but never did. Jasmine Carson still read the bird log, but the hand which held the book was shaking, and once she wiped tears from her eyes.

Foolish old woman, she said to herself. You didn't even like him. She knew though that she was not weeping for Charlie, but for her brother, killed in the war. Any sudden death brought back the grief, even a news item on the radio or in the newspaper. Silly old woman, she thought again. What will they all think? And she tried to concentrate on her book.

Paul Derbyshire found the silence constricting and unnecessary. He wanted to talk. Of course murder was terrible, quite terrible. His mouth formed an embarrassing smile and he quickly erased it. Murder was terrible, but there were more important matters now to be decided. He disliked unpleasantness, and he tried to conjure a more agreeable image: the face of a girl, a slim, athletic body, but even to him that seemed tasteless, inappropriate. His

thoughts drifted back to Charlie. What a horrible little man he had been, a threat to all that was important and lovely.

Pamela Marshall caught Paul Derbyshire's eye. She smiled beautifully and enjoyed his response, his pleasure at her attention then his sudden embarrassment. What an old woman he is, she thought. He's just dying to have a good gossip. He doesn't realize the danger at all. We shall all have to be careful about what we say. I must talk to Jerry.

Jerry Packham felt physically ill and wondered what would happen if he asked to go to the bathroom. Would someone accompany him?

Elizabeth was planning lunch. Soup first, then something cold and quick. She supposed that the policemen would cater for themselves.

Mark realized that he would never enjoy coming to the island again, and grieved more for that loss than for the loss of a man he had hardly known. Will Jonathan be pleased, he thought, or will his uncle's death be of as little importance to him as it is to me?

Nick remembered his mother's death. At least Charlie had died quickly. Then all the old bitterness returned and he knew that Charlie's death had changed nothing.

George Palmer-Jones watched everyone, wondered what they were thinking, and tried to suppress a rising and unsuitable curiosity.

When Savage walked in he seemed to bring all the energy of the storm with him. They looked at him with interest. He was impressive enough, though at first it was hard to explain why he impressed. He was only just tall enough to be a policeman, and slight. It was the extraordinary, drawn face which held their attention and the power and self-confidence which impressed them. There was something Celtic about his dark eyes. Palmer-Jones expected him to be Welsh or Scottish, and the Merseyside accent came as a surprise. He was courteous, but they all felt that he found the formalities irksome and that he was impatient to be elsewhere. While he was talking his eyes moved around the room, and the intensity of his stare contradicted the politeness of his words.

"I must apologize for not having introduced myself before," he said, "and for asking you to wait for me here. I'll be asking you to be patient for a bit longer, I'm afraid. I'll explain as briefly as I can what we plan to do. I'm sure that you will co-operate."

He was standing just inside the door, with Connibear on one side of him and John on the other.

"Mr. Lansdown has kindly offered us the use of a room, which we will be using as an office. Throughout the day I shall be speaking to each of you. The interview will be taped, but I can assure you that the conversations will be confidential and that no information will be passed on or used unless it is relevant to our inquiries.

"In the meantime I would like to ask your permission for our men to search your rooms and to take dust and fibre samples from your clothing. Of course you can be present while the search is taking place, but I think that you'd be more comfortable here."

He paused, took the silence as consent to his plans, then continued: "The officers will come to see you here. One of my men might ask you to remove certain items of clothing, so that they can be taken away for tests. I can assume that no one has changed during the morning?"

Once more there was silence.

"The officers will ask you to show them your coats and outdoor shoes, and again I would ask you to be co-operative.

"I understand that you all planned to spend the night here and to return to the mainland tomorrow. I understand that it will be distasteful to you to stay here in the circumstances, but I would be grateful if those arrangements could be maintained. Of course if anyone chooses to leave, he is free to do so, but I'm sure that you can appreciate how much more convenient it will be if we are able to complete at least the preliminary interviews under one roof."

It was as if he had completed a set speech. He relaxed, then, and beamed at them, as if they were well-behaved children.

"That's splendid. Now, are there any questions?"

Elizabeth felt that she should raise her hand as if she were at school, but managed to restrain the impulse.

"I'll need to go to the kitchen to prepare lunch," she said. "That will be allowed?"

"Of course," he said. "But perhaps you could wait until my officers have been in to see you."

She nodded.

"Now Mr. Lansdown," Savage continued, "perhaps you could show me your ringing room. I know that you've spoken to DC Connibear, but I'd be grateful for your help for half an hour or so."

John looked helplessly at Elizabeth and at George Palmer-Jones, then followed the two policemen out of the room.

There was a uniformed policeman in the bird room, and he had rearranged the furniture so that it was no longer familiar to John. Savage sat on one side of the desk and motioned John to sit at the other. The uniformed policeman had disappeared and Connibear stood somewhere out of John's line of vision.

"Right then," Savage started. He leaned forward on the desk and concentrated his attention on John. John found the dark eyes intimidating and turned away from them. "I don't know anything about the set-up here. So you tell me all about it, and exactly where the deceased came into it all."

"Charlie owned it," John said, surprised. "He owned the island and the observatory."

"This place is the observatory?"

John nodded. "There are several around the coast, all owned by charitable bodies. We carry out a scientific study of birds, count them, ring them, and provide facilities for people to stay, and to help us. We have lots of school groups here, especially in the spring and summer. All the people staying here now are members of the observatory committee. They decide on policy. I suppose that they employ me."

"And Mr. Todd was a member of this committee?"

"Yes. A very special member, because he owned the island, and besides my wife and myself he was the only resident. He lived in that wooden chalet down the island."

"Did he live here all the time?"

"No. Sometimes he would stay for months at a time and we would see a lot of him, then he would disappear. He always came back for the committee weekend though."

"That was this weekend?"

"Yes."

"Tell me exactly what happened, from the minute you picked up the party on the shore on Friday evening . . . Just a minute, Mr. Todd was with them?"

"Yes."

"How long had he been away from the island?"

"A week. I gave him a lift off last Saturday."

"Right. Carry on then."

John described meeting the party on the mainland and Savage let him talk uninterrupted until he reached the point in the narrative when he left the table in the middle of the evening meal.

"Why?" he asked sharply. "Why did you walk out like that?"

All the policeman's questions came immediately, aggressively. John was given no time for thought.

"I've tried to explain. I was very upset. If Charlie sold the island, it would mean that I would lose my job and my home."

"A bit melodramatic, wasn't it, walking out like that?"

John's voice rose in anger.

"Elizabeth is expecting our child," he said. "I was worried about the future. Our future."

"I suppose that you'll be in the same position now though, won't you? The island will still be sold."

"I suppose so," said John, then immediately regretted the easy, defensive answer. The policeman was bound to find out about the will. He might even know about it now. He looked up at Savage.

"That's not quite true," he said. "I hope that we'll be able to stay now. Charlie left the island to the Observatory Trust in his will."

Savage raised his eyes but made no comment. "Go on," he said.

John explained that he had been for a walk on the island, that some time later Elizabeth had come to meet him, then described the fire at the Wendy House.

"How do you think the fire was started?"

"I don't know. Charlie thought that the tilly was knocked over by the cat, but it seemed unlikely even then. The tilly's so heavy."

"You say that it was standing by an open window. Could somebody have reached in through the window and pushed over the lamp?"

"I suppose so."

"You suppose so. What does that mean?"

"Yes, someone could have pushed over the lamp."

"Did you see anyone while you were out on the hill, being worried?"

"I didn't see anyone, but I heard somebody walking down the track."

"Towards Mr. Todd's residence?"

"Yes."

"When was that?"

"I'm not very sure. Perhaps three-quarters of an hour before the fire."

"Did you hear them return?"

"No."

"Who was it?"

"I told you. I couldn't see."

He did not know why he lied. Perhaps it was an attempt to maintain some independence in the presence of this dominant man. So powerful did Savage seem that John almost expected him to detect the untruth, but the Superintendent continued:

"Now. Go through the events of this morning."

His memory sharpened by the detailed questioning, by the intense concentration of the man who sat opposite, John relived for Savage the phone call from the coast-guard, the tedium of helping Elizabeth in the kitchen, the conversation at breakfast.

"So while you were at breakfast you learned that Mr. Packham had arranged to meet Mr. Todd in the seawatching hide."

"Elizabeth told me. They had fixed it up at supper, after I'd left."

"Was everyone aware that this arrangement had been made?"

"I don't know. Certainly Nick and Mark were aware of it. That's why they didn't go into the seawatching hide. Charlie and Jerry worked together. Jerry did the drawings for Charlie's books. The boys didn't want to intrude."

"Do you know why Mr. Packham did not keep his appointment with Mr. Todd?"

"No."

But the answer was not as definite as the others had been. Savage stopped the relentless questions, paused, then asked: "Are you sure?"

This time John was unable to lie. "Well, Jerry and Pam Marshall are known to be . . . friendly. They always sleep in adjacent single rooms when they're here." He allowed himself one of Mark's schoolboy grins to cover his awkwardness. "I thought perhaps he'd had a tiring night and had overslept."

"Who else had been outside before breakfast?"

"Nick and Mark had been doing a seawatch from the cliffs. Miss Carson had been out. She was looking very wet and bedraggled."

"What would she have been doing outside?"

"Going for a walk, I expect."

"In that weather? She must be nearly seventy."

"Miss Carson always takes a walk before breakfast when she's staying at the observatory. She wouldn't alter her routine for a hurricane."

"Anyone else?"

John hesitated and Savage repeated: "Anyone else?"

"Elizabeth went out for a while while I was helping her to cook the breakfast. She was only gone for ten minutes, and the hide was already cut off from the island then. She told me when she came in."

"Do you know what the other residents were doing while you were preparing breakfast?"

"No."

"We'll move on now to the time after breakfast. You and your two friends went to the seawatching hide together?"

"Yes."

"What were the other residents doing?"

"I don't know. We went as soon as we had finished the meal."

"When you got there, the door was unlocked?"

"Yes. I was surprised. It's become a habit for us to keep it locked. In the summer we get a lot of trippers on the island. They're not supposed to go to the north end, but they do, and once some kids tried to camp in it."

"How many keys are there?"

"Two. Charlie had one and the observatory the other."

"We found the key to fit the hide padlock in Mr. Todd's pocket. Where was the other kept?"

"It was kept in the bird room, so that anyone could get it when they wanted."

"Did you notice if it was missing this morning?"

"I didn't come in here this morning, except to get the key. That was immediately after breakfast. It was here then. But if Charlie was in the hide, he would have left the door open. It's impossible to lock from inside. Anyone could have got in then."

"So they could, but it's a possibility that the murderer was there first. I understand that you can identify the nylon rope used to strangle Mr. Todd?"

"Yes. It's a mist-net guy. A mist net is a fine net used for trapping birds. It has shelves in it, where the birds are caught. The poles are held steady by guys. Nick told me last night that one of the guys was missing. Most observatories store the guys separately but it's a tradition here to keep them in the mist net bag."

"How did he know that the guy was missing?"

"He and Mark went out last night, ringing waders. One of the nets had been messily replaced in its bag, and the guy wasn't there."

"When was that particular net last used?"

"Goodness knows. It could have been weeks ago. We don't do a lot of mist netting, and we've several nets."

Superintendent Savage smiled, and suddenly the atmosphere in the room changed. Both men relaxed. The policeman's attention was no longer focused solely and intensely on John. John felt exhausted, as if he had completed an important exam. It had been a peculiar experience, exhilarating, almost flattering to sustain the attention of another person for such a long period.

"Thank you," the superintendent said, standing up, holding out his hand. "Thank you. I hope that everyone is as helpful."

Connibear was surprised when Savage asked him to fetch George Palmer-Jones.

"But sir, he wasn't here. We saw him walking over when we were driving across."

"I know what I'm doing, lad. Ask him to come in please. And be polite about it, will you?"

Connibear was polite, and if Palmer-Jones was surprised that he was the next to be interviewed, he did not show it.

When the two men entered the bird room Savage stood up quickly, formally.

"Good morning, Mr. Palmer-Jones," he said. "Very pleased to meet you again, sir."

Palmer-Jones looked at the face. Before his retirement, when he was working for the Home Office, he had met many policemen. The younger man was staring across the desk at him, willing him to remember. Then it came back to him. There had been an important corruption case in the northwest and he had been sent as observer, with no official status, just the requirement that he should report back to the minister. A young detective constable had come to him with information about one of the senior officers conducting the investigation. He remembered the meeting in one of the big, shabbily ornate pubs in Liverpool. It had been very smoky, the light had been poor, and in one corner an old lady sat drinking Guinness, singing. He remembered the policeman's dark, angry eyes, and his resentment that no one within the organization had been prepared to listen. "It's a bloody cover-up," he had said over and over again. "A bloody cover-up." Palmer-

Jones had been able to use the information without implicating the constable. He understood that there had been changes in the Merseyside force after the inquiry which followed. At last the name and the face coincided.

"Superintendent Savage," he said. "Congratulations on your promotion."

"Thank you, sir. It would never have happened without your help."

"How can I help you, Superintendent? I wasn't here, you know, when the offence was committed."

"I know that, sir."

"I don't expect to be consulted, or to be given any special consideration. I have retired. I won't interfere."

"It's not a question of interference, sir. It's a question of helping the police with their inquiries."

"I don't quite understand."

"Well sir, you are in a special position here. You know all the suspects. You share their interest and you've got their trust. I'm sure that they will confide in you, in a way they never would in Connibear or myself. And I'm sure that you would never put personal considerations before the pursuit of justice."

George's immediate reaction was anger. What right had the little man behind the desk to talk in clichés about justice? His tone, however was mild.

"I hope that you're not asking me to spy on my friends, Superintendent."

Savage took the question seriously. "Not that, sir. No. But if you were to be told something which might help, I'd be grateful if you'd pass it on. Murder's not a matter of etiquette. You know that as well as I do."

Do I? thought George suddenly. Do I really care who murdered Charlie Todd? And realized that it did matter, very much. He recognized with some distaste the old relief that something out of the ordinary had happened; at least for a few days he would not be bored. And he recognized the old arrogance: If anyone can sort the matter out, I can. They need me.

"I won't do it secretly," he said. "I won't pretend that

I'm just asking questions out of interest. They're too intelligent to believe that anyway. I will explain that because I know the set-up here, and because of my experience, you've asked me to keep an eye on things. And then I'll pass on anything I learn, or anything that occurs to me.''

"That will do very nicely, sir," Savage said. "What's your opinion to date?"

George smiled. "Superintendent Savage, you overestimate my powers. I don't know anything at all about it."

"I understood that Elizabeth Richards met you on the shore and explained what happened."

"She told me that Charlie Todd had been found murdered in the seawatching hide. She didn't know any details. No one else has spoken to me."

The superintendent rewound the tape on the machine on his desk.

"I've just been speaking to John Lansdown. I'd like you to listen to the interview."

George Palmer-Jones listened, writing occasionally on the back of an envelope with an expensive fountain pen.

"That gives a broad outline of the matter. Did you know that Mr. Todd intended to sell the island?"

"No, though I'm not surprised."

"I understand that he was somewhat . . . eccentric. Still, I don't suppose that it's relevant. It's hardly a realistic motive for murder."

"Perhaps not."

"Except for Mr. Lansdown and his girlfriend. I presume they live together as man and wife. I wonder why they don't get married?"

George did not reply.

"Do you happen to know if anyone gained financially from Mr. Todd's death? Did he have anything else to leave?"

"I'm sorry. I don't know. He had the reputation of being a wealthy man, but I shouldn't think that he had much left after buying the island. It would be different if he'd had a stake in the family business."

"So I believe."

The superintendent looked at his watch. "Lunch will be at one o'clock, will it?"

"Yes."

"Then I've time to see one more. Who do you suggest?"

George hesitated. He was gratified, despite himself, to be given the power to shape the investigation, but disliked being put in the position of informer.

"I was expecting you to talk to Pamela Marshall," he said. Savage was, after all, only doing his job. "Perhaps you don't know. She was Charlie Todd's niece. Perhaps she can give you more information about his financial affairs."

"Thank you very much, sir. That's very convenient. Connibear, show Mr. Palmer-Jones back to the common room and ask Mrs. Marshall to come in to see me."

He hardly looked up. He had taken Palmer-Jones's help quite for granted.

She looked expensive, Savage thought, even in ordinary slacks and a hand-knitted jumper. She was in her late thirties, slim, blond, discreetly made up. She reached out to shake his hand, and she even smelled expensive.

"Good morning, Superintendent," she said. "I don't think that I can help you, but I'll be pleased to try." She had a pleasant, careful voice. He had expected sailing club stridency, but there was still a hint of a Devon accent. She smiled at him.

She's trying too hard, he thought, and asked: "Did you go to see your uncle last night?"

"No," she said calmly. "I had thought about it, before supper, but in the end I didn't bother. Because he was my uncle I felt obliged to go to see him when I was here, to talk about the family, but we didn't really have a lot in common."

"Did you go out at all yesterday evening?"

"Just for a walk in the garden after supper."

"Did you see anyone?"

"No one at all."

"Could you explain your exact relationship with Mr. Todd?"

"My mother Dorothea was his elder sister."

"Did you and your family have much social contact with him?"

"I never saw him, except when I was on the island. As I have explained we had very little in common."

"Do you know the terms of your uncle's will?"

"Only what he told all the observatory members. That he intended to leave the island to the trust. I don't know what was to happen to the remainder of his estate."

"You didn't expect to receive anything yourself?"

"Good God no. I shouldn't think that there was very much left, and even if there were, Charlie would be bound to leave it outside the family. He never really got on with the rest of us. He thought that we were all staid and boring."

"I see. Could you describe your movements this morning?"

"Of course, Superintendent. But as I explained, I don't think that I can be of any use to you. I woke at 7:30, dressed and went down to the common room. I read there until the bell rang for breakfast. Afterwards, the boys went seawatching. I had planned to go with them, but they had gone before I was ready. I was just getting into my waterproofs to go out to join them when John came in. I could tell that something was wrong. I suppose I was curious. I decided to stay in. Later Elizabeth told us that Charlie was dead."

"Can you see anything of the island from the common room?"

"Not really. The windows all look out to the sea and then the shore."

"Before breakfast, was anyone in the common room with you?"

"Not at first. Then the doctor came down."

"Had he been outside?"

She laughed unpleasantly. She's stopped trying to attract me, he thought. She feels safe now.

"Doctor Derbyshire doesn't go out very often. Before breakfast it's unheard of. He treats the observatory as sort of social club."

"Anyone else?"

"Mark and Nick came in next. They said that they'd been seawatching."

"What were they wearing?"

"They'd taken off their boots and anoraks in the hall. Then I heard Elizabeth and Jasmine. The boys had left the common-room door open. They came in almost together. Elizabeth went straight into the kitchen, but I could see Jasmine through the open door. She was shaking out that big waterproof cape which she wears, then she hung it up with the other coats. She was just coming in to talk to us when the bell went for breakfast."

"And Mr. Packham?"

"We were all sitting down at the table when Jerry came in. He muttered something about oversleeping."

"Had he been out?"

"He didn't look as if he had."

"And that was the first time you'd seen him? You hadn't been together earlier in the day?"

"I'm afraid I don't understand you, Superintendent," she said calmly. "I first saw Jerry Packham this morning when he came in late to breakfast."

He seemed about to question her, to make perhaps some teasing comment, then he changed his mind, looked at his watch and stood up to dismiss her.

"Oh well," he said easily. "I'll be speaking to Mr. Packham this afternoon, I expect."

She looked at him defiantly and walked out.

Savage stretched back in his chair and motioned Connibear to sit opposite to him.

"She was lying," he said. "But perhaps she was just worried about her fancy man. How long have we got, before we need to leave the island?"

"Until five this afternoon, sir. Otherwise, it'll mean staying until nearly midnight."

"I'll try to finish by five."

There was a knock on the door and a uniformed constable came in. "The pathologist and some of the scene of crime team have finished, sir. Can they get the body off now?"

59

"You take them off in the old Land Rover. Get some food—you'd better start taking orders—and come straight back. I'll see if I can negotiate for a pot of tea. I expect the local press will be on to the case by now. If there are any reporters on the quay tell them that I'll have a few words at about five-thirty. We don't want them trying to make their way over here. But don't say anything else to them."

"Sir."

For the first time since Savage had arrived they were without a police presence. The constable who had been sitting with them in the common room had not followed into the dining room. Elizabeth ladled out a thick vegetable soup. There was home-baked bread which she had retrieved from the freezer and put into the oven to warm, and cheese and fruit. They all seemed to be hungry and to be enjoying the food. The absence of the policeman had made them all curiously light-hearted, light-headed even. The wind had dropped a little, and that too was a relief. There was a general murmur of conversation, but they all heard the Land Rover start.

"What's that?" John said. "Are they going already? It would have been polite to come and tell us."

"Oh, I don't think they'll be going yet," George said. "They'll be taking off the body. In any event, they'll certainly be coming back. You do understand, don't you, that someone here killed Charlie Todd? The police won't go away until they find out who that was."

5

Albert Todd sat at the table by the window and waited for his dinner. He had always eaten the main meal at midday, and affluence had not altered his habits or changed his use of words. Lunch was a snack which children took to school to eat in the playground. Dinner was what he wanted now. The window was streaked with rain. The lawn outside was littered with twigs, blown from the yews at the end of the garden. There were clumps of overgrown shrubs with dark shiny green leaves. He did not mind much that the garden was a mess. He didn't often go out there now. It did not affect his comfort. The rhododendrons and the heavy velvet curtains at each side of the window shut out the little light that there was. In the room the electric light was on, shrouded by a red plastic shade, and the gas fire hummed. There was central heating, and that was on too. Albert felt the cold. He had moved into the ugly, yellow-brick villa fifty years before, and by now he had things arranged to his satisfaction, to provide for his comfort. He and Alice had bought the house because it was near to the park, for the children. Now he still went to the park to watch the bowling. He would never

move from the house. It had everything that he needed, and he was in charge there. He had been persuaded to go into a nursing home for a month, after a replacement hip operation, but the stay had not been a success. The staff had been as pleased to see him leave as he had been to go. There had been complaints from the other residents, who had said that he was common.

Albert looked at the clock in the bulging wooden frame which sat on the mantelshelf. It ticked so loudly that he could hear it above the noise of the wind. It was only ten to one. At one o'clock Elsie would bring in the meal. Elsie was the wife of his middle son, Laurence. She was always on time. She knew that it pleased him. Albert considered that Laurence had married well. Elsie was big-busted, down to earth, with a barmaid's easy sympathy and more brain than she was given credit for. Her only ambition was on behalf of her son, who was at university and wanted to be a lawyer. Before her marriage she had worked as a housekeeper. At the Laurels her duties were less arduous, her rewards greater, but she was just as conscientious. Albert never understood what Elsie had seen in Laurence; they seemed fond enough of each other.

She came in then, carrying a tray, pushing open the door with a round, tightly covered buttock, which still caught his attention, made him remember other days when he would have done more than look. There was steak and kidney pie for dinner. The kidneys had a sweet, fertile smell, which stirred more memories, made him look again at Elsie, at the rich fullness of her squeezed into the cheap clothes. She did not notice that he was staring, or if she did, she was so used to it that it was not important.

"There's a lovely piece of chuck steak in this," she said. "I told him I didn't want any of the rubbish he sent up last week."

Elsie had cooked the meal. The cleaning lady would wash it up, but she did all the cooking. She sat with Albert at the table, set a plate on each of the cork place mats, and

they began to eat. They were comfortable together. It was as if they were the married couple. They appreciated each other. She never knew, though, what he was thinking. Albert was a great one for secrets. She still did not know how he had first made the money to buy the Grand. Perhaps no one knew. So she waited for him to speak, to tell her how he had taken the news of his son's death. She could not guess what his reaction would be.

"So Charlie's gone before me," he said with satisfaction. He was a big man, broad-bodied, wide-faced, soft and boneless as a cuddly toy. He leaned back in his chair and rubbed his belly. He could have been talking about the food. "I can't say that I'm surprised."

"But murder!" She was naïvely shocked and distressed. She had not known Charlie well. She suffered nothing by his death, yet she felt a real, unselfish, impersonal grief. Her sense of propriety was offended by Albert's complacency, but because he had always believed that he was right about everything, she began to suspect that her distress was inappropriate. She wondered if her sadness were silly.

"I can't say I'm surprised," Albert repeated. "Some people bring bad luck on to themselves."

They continued to eat rice pudding in silence. The wind blew a branch against the window. The lights flickered in threat of a power cut. The clock carried on ticking. Albert cleared his dish with relish and placed the spoon squarely in the middle of it. He looked slyly at Elsie. Perhaps it was to tease her, to shock her, that he said with such boyish excitement:

"I wonder who killed him."

If it was an attempt to shock, he succeeded. She felt a spasm of revulsion. Charlie had been Albert's son. They might not have been friendly, but this should be a day for regret, respect. Then the habit of acceptance returned. He's an old man, she thought. He's eighty-six. What can you expect?

Vaguely, to humour him, she said: "It will have been

63

one of those maniacs. You often read about them in the papers.''

"If Ernest had been killed, I could have understood it,'' Albert continued, as if she had not spoken. "There's a few that would like to see Ernest out of the way.''

"Now Dad,'' she said. "That's no way to talk.''

"It's true though.'' He was certainly teasing her, was laughing at her discomfort and embarrassment. The fleshy stomach seemed to ripple with suppressed mirth. "There was young Nick, Mary Mardle's boy. He threatened Ernest with all sorts when Mary had to leave the cottage. He saw Laurence about it, didn't he? And he came here to see me. He was in a proper temper when he was here.'' The laughter could no longer be contained, seemed to splutter from the round cheeks like a mouthful of food. "More like Old Nick he was then. Like Old Nick himself.''

Elsie fought her confusion at the man's peculiar reaction to his son's death, by treating the matter seriously.

"I thought Ernest was hard on Mary Mardle,'' she said carefully. "She started working at the Grand at the same time as me. That's a long time. And the guests thought the world of her.''

They had had the conversation before, and despite himself, Albert could not make light of it. He had to follow the old argument through.

"Maybe. But that cottage went with the job of caretaker. She understood that she'd have to move if anything happened to Fred.''

"It was wrong to make her leave when Fred died, especially when she was so ill.''

"If she thought it was wrong, she could have gone to the tribunal.''

Ernest knew that Mary wouldn't have gone to any tribunal. She wasn't the sort. And she wasn't the sort to live in a council flat. She looked, with some reproach, at Albert. "You could have had a word with Ernest.''

"I could have done,'' he said, "but it wouldn't have done any good. You know Ernest.''

There was a silence. They both knew Ernest.

"Besides," he said. "It would have been wrong. I made him manager. I had to let him manage."

"What did Nick say when he came to see you?" she said, perturbed but curious. She had never had the courage before to ask him. "Laurence would never tell me."

"He said . . ." Albert spoke slowly, with emphasis. "He said that this family were a bunch of murderers. If ever he thought he could get away with it, he would murder us one by one."

And the old man began to laugh again, rocking backwards and forwards in his chair, until he choked and she had to bring him water.

"Of course," Helen said. "You'll tell the police about the Mardle boy."

"I don't know," said Ernest Todd. "We've got to think about the publicity. All the business about the cottage is bound to come out. There are other things it's best to keep secret. And of course, Mardle does still work for us."

"I told you at the time that it was a mistake to keep him on."

"And I told you that it wasn't my decision. The old man felt very strongly about it."

"The old man!" The contempt in her voice was directed at him as much as his father.

"He does still own fifty per cent of the business, and he can always call on Laurence for support. It puts me in a very difficult position."

"So you're always telling me."

They stopped speaking as the waitress approached. They met most lunchtimes in the restaurant of the Grand. The food was often indifferent, but it was a free meal, and she enjoyed the special attention, the panic of the staff who had to serve the boss and his wife.

Ernest Todd was a heavy man, built like his father. He was in his late fifties with a red, always slightly shiny

face. There was no trace of his native accent. He was one of the ruling members of the golf club, sang with the operatic society. He drank a lot and liked his secretaries to be very young. When he was not drunk, he was shrewd, intelligent. His wife Helen was fifteen years younger than he was. She had been his secretary. She knew his habits. She had worn well, dressed smartly, but she could not compete with his pink-haired, tight-skirted girl Fridays. Her father had been a doctor. She had been privately educated and although she had married her employer and money, it was considered that she had married beneath her. She was a magistrate, enjoyed good works and power, but her power over her husband was limited.

"All the same," she said. "I think that you should tell the police. It's your duty."

Ernest sighed. He did hate her self-righteous mood. She had been to some charity meeting, and looked like a well-dressed schoolmistress in her pleated navy skirt and jacket. He wished she would not bully him.

"I thought that you didn't like Charlie," he said patiently. "You never exactly made him welcome."

"But that's not the point. I wouldn't have strangled him. Do you think that Nicholas Mardle *did* kill him?"

"I don't know." It was the least important point. He had not considered it. "Yes, probably. He was very unbalanced. And he was there."

"In that case, you must tell the police."

It was fruitless to argue. "Yes Helen. I suppose that I must."

"Do we know what was in the will?" She spoke carefully, pretended not to be really interested, but he was not fooled. She was very interested in money.

"Yes," he said. "I know."

"Well?"

"He leaves the island to his friends at the observatory, and the remainder to the children."

"Children? What children?"

"He always called them the children, but they're

66

named in his will. His nephew and niece. Pamela and Jonathan.''

She hid her disappointment with scorn. "Pamela Marshall's got children of her own and Jonathan is in his final year at university. Hardly a child.''

"It's quite logical, you know," he said gently. He still felt a remnant of affection for her. "They are his only younger relatives. If we had had children, I'm sure that they would have been included. Besides, I don't think that he had much to leave.''

"Well, Elsie will be pleased," she said, "although I think that she has already ruined that precious brat Jonathan.''

Then she brought her face and voice under control. She always pretended to have no interest in Elsie and bitchiness did not match her image of charitable benefactor.

"You will go to the police this afternoon, Ernest?"

"Yes," he said. "Yes. I'll go.''

But Ernest did not go straight to the police station. He watched Helen drive away in her car then buttoned his sheepskin jacket and started to walk along the promenade towards his office. He did not walk very often and he found the effort uncomfortable. Helen had offered him a lift, but she would have dropped him at the police station and watched him go in. The wind blew straight along the promenade, scattering summer litter and sand. He walked past the new development on the front and saw with satisfaction that all the flats had been sold. The tide was out and in the poor light the stretch of sand and water looked grey, unattractive. Whoever would want to live here? he thought. When I retire I want a bit of sun in the winter. He did not even glance at Gillibry, would never have understood if Jasmine Carson had explained why she had been persuaded to buy one of his luxury apartments.

He turned into the High Street, which rose steeply away from the promenade. The shops were crowded together, the usual shabby seaside mix: gift shops, cafés, one super-

market. There were no tourists. He recognized most of the people he passed.

The office was above one of the shops which they owned. Laurence dealt with the financial side of the operation and he had insisted on an office away from the hotel. Ernest was responsible for more immediate decisions concerning the business. He appointed the staff, inspected properties, was concerned with advertising, marketing. He did not use the place as much as Laurence. Laurence was always there, even on a Saturday.

Laurence had had his lunch in the office and there was an empty place on his desk. Elsie always made him sandwiches. He had been out once, but only to walk to the paper shop to collect his railway magazine. He was a steam enthusiast. His desk was by the window overlooking the High Street, and he was reading from a computer visual display unit. As he went into the office Ernest switched on the light, and Laurence looked round, blinking. He was a small, dapper man. Helen always said that he looked like a tailor. His face was long in comparison with his body, and Ernest thought he looked more like a character from a children's television cartoon. He had never seen a tailor with such a big head. They had been together in the office when Elsie had phoned with the news of their brother's death.

Ernest cleared a space on Laurence's desk, leaned against it and said: "About Charlie."

"Yes," Laurence said. "I've been thinking about it all morning. I can't concentrate on anything else."

"We've got to decide what we're going to tell the police."

Laurence thought. "Yes," he said. "Yes. I see."

"It wouldn't do for them to find out about our visitor last Friday."

"I've told you," Laurence said, "how I feel about that."

"But you won't mention it to the police?"

"No."

"Helen says that I must tell them about Nick Mardle's threats to the family."

"Does she? I don't think that they were serious, you know. He was very young. But I suppose that we must trust the police to make a proper judgement about that. I don't think we should make too much of it."

"No. Perhaps not. He's an unpleasant young man, all the same. It's not Mardle that I'm most concerned with. We don't want the police looking into our affairs. Or the press. Especially the press. Not yet. And then there's the family. You know that Pamela and Jonathan are beneficiaries under his will."

"Yes I knew. Charlie made no secret of it. There's no reason to keep that from the police. They will see the will anyway. I don't have any anxiety about Jonathan. He wasn't anywhere near Gillibry. He went up to London last weekend. He wanted to have a few weeks to work on his own before term starts."

"But Pamela was there."

"Yes. Yes, I see. Of course, Pamela was on the island."

He was blinking again, very nervously. His lashes were fine and fair.

"And I understand from Marie that Pamela came in to see you yesterday morning."

Marie was their secretary.

"Was she asking for money again?"

Laurence looked uneasy.

"How much did she want?"

"She wasn't specific," Laurence said, "but I gather that it was a substantial amount. She said something about school fees. Sian's not getting on very well at the local school, and they were hoping to send her somewhere with smaller classes."

"What did you tell her?"

"That it wasn't my decision. That I would have to discuss the matter with Father. And with you. I told her that it was unlikely that we would be able to help."

"I should say that it's unlikely. We pay that solicitor

husband of hers a fortune in legal fees, and we've put a lot more business his way. He does criminal work too, and Helen says that there's always someone from his firm in the domestic court. But that's not the point. The point is, should we tell the police that she has been asking us for money?"

"Oh no." Laurence spoke very quickly. He sounded shocked. "Oh I don't think so. It was a private conversation. I haven't discussed it with anyone. Not even with Father yet."

"Nor have I. I'd better have a word with Marie. Tell her not to mention it. I'll call in to her home on the way to the police station."

He winked unpleasantly and went out. The wind caught the door and banged it behind him. Laurence Todd turned back to the computer, but after staring at it blankly, turned it off. He picked up the railway magazine, and only as he became engrossed in an article about a narrow-gauge railway in Shropshire did the nervous blinking stop and his face become calm.

Sian Marshall sat at the kitchen table, surrounded by dog-eared text books, and willed herself to concentrate on irregular French verbs.

"I think I must be dyslexic," she said out loud, watching the words on the page, hoping that she would realize how the conjugations worked with a miraculous flash of insight. "Or just dim," as no miracle occurred.

There was no one to hear her. Her father was playing golf and Edward was in town with some of his friends. Edward always finished his homework on Friday nights.

With a sudden gesture of freedom Sian pushed the books back into her satchel and called to her dog, Tramp, to come out to play. Mummy would be back tomorrow night to help her. Mummy had promised.

Mrs. Derbyshire did not know about the tragedy on Gillibry. She did not take a daily paper or listen to the

local radio station, and her husband had not telephoned her. She did not know that there had been a murder on the island, but she was obsessively worried. She could only allow herself to be worried when Paul was away. When he was at home all her energy was taken with meeting his needs, caring for him. Worry had become an almost pleasant indulgence, the only way she had now of asserting her own personality.

She found the envelope of photographs in the filing cabinet in his study. It was locked, but she knew where he kept the key. She had not known that they would be there, but it had not taken her long to find them. She did not look at them immediately. She made a cup of coffee and sat with it and the envelope in the conservatory. The house was near to the sea, but there was not much to see through the glass—a line of dunes, a bank of marram grass. She was glad that she could not see the water. On such a stormy day, that would have disturbed her.

She sat in the most comfortable chair, which Paul usually took, and opened the envelope. The photographs were all of the same girl, who was still, almost, a child. There was nothing pornographic about the prints. In some, the girl was wearing a swimsuit, but in most a pretty dress and sandals. In two, she was posed self-consciously in school uniform. Mrs. Derbyshire returned the photographs to the envelope. She must remember to replace them in the filing cabinet before Paul came home. It seemed to her that nothing had changed. He had been hiding photographs of young girls since they had married. That was why he needed her so much to take care of him. So why, in the last month, had he been so frightened?

PC David Martindale was in love, wonderfully, neurotically in love. He drove the Land Rover off the island towards the mainland, following the tyre tracks made that morning, and thought about Rachel. It was as if the corpse in the canvas bag, the men talking shop in the back of the Land Rover, were part of a hazy dream. He thought of

work only as an obstacle to seeing Rachel. Savage had told him that he would probably have to stay the night on the island, and he had arranged to take her out for the evening. He would leave a message at her office. She would understand. He was aware suddenly of a small crowd of people on the quay. They were blocking the path and he shouted at them to move. He yelled Savage's message to the reporters without waiting for any response. Ghouls, he thought, and the business which had seemed so exciting when they had raced over the sands earlier in the morning now seemed squalid, a melodramatic nonsense.

Perhaps I'm in the wrong job, he thought, and leaving the others to deal with the body he walked away to find a telephone box and to buy food for his colleagues who were still on the island.

6

Jasmine Carson sat quite calmly opposite Superintendent Savage. She answered his questions promptly and politely, but he knew that he had failed to impress her. She answered because she wanted to, not because she felt at all compelled by him. He had never met anyone like her before. He had known many formidable women, but none with her control, her detached intelligence.

"Could you tell me what you did last night?"

"I had supper with the others. Charles Todd told us that he intended to sell the island."

"How did you feel about that?"

"I was shocked and upset. The island means a lot to me."

"And after supper?"

"I went into the garden for some air, then went up to my bedroom to change into more comfortable footwear. I had been wearing heavy shoes all evening. I have severe arthritis, and I had some difficulty in undoing the laces. I saw the boys going out with the nets, just as I had finished. I was disappointed. I would have enjoyed going with them, but it would have taken too long to change

again. I lay on my bed to rest. As I have explained, I was shocked that Charles could consider selling the island, and I wanted to think about it. He said that he would be prepared to sell the observatory to the trust at a realistic price, and I wanted to think out the implications of that. I decided that it would not be feasible. Some time later I went into the common room, and talked to Paul Derbyshire who had come to the same conclusion. Elizabeth usually serves hot chocolate and biscuits at ten o'clock, but it was not a usual evening. The boys had come back from ringing, and went to make the drink themselves. We were pouring it out when John and Elizabeth came in and told us about the fire at Charles's house.''

"Could you describe your movements this morning? First of all, did you know that Charles Todd intended to meet Mr. Packham in the seawatching hide?''

"We all knew," she said. "Except John, perhaps. He had left the supper table before it was decided. I thought,'' she added, "that it was a rather rude and childish gesture to walk out. Not at all like him.''

"This morning you went out for a walk before breakfast?''

"I always take a walk before breakfast when I am on the island.''

"How long were you out for?''

"Only for fifteen minutes. It was rather windy.''

"Did you see anyone?''

"I met Elizabeth as I was coming in. She too had been for a walk.''

"Did you take the seawatching-hide key from the bird room this morning?''

"No.''

"When did you last use one of the mist nets here? Do you know anything about the guy which was used to strangle Mr. Todd?''

"I come to the island regularly, Superintendent Savage, at least once a week. When I am here I help with the work of the observatory. We catch most birds in the heligoland traps, but we use mist nets fairly frequently. Unfortunately my arthritis prevents me from actually ringing the birds or

removing them from the nets, but I help in any way I can. I can assure you that any nets used in my presence are properly put away. My nets do not have missing guys.'' She was angry.

"Is there anything else you can tell me, Miss Carson, which might help in the investigation?"

"If there were, Superintendent, I should already have told you.''

In the common room Paul Derbyshire looked at his watch. There was no sense of tension or drama now. The wait was just tedious. They could have been going to see the dentist. It was half past two. He thought: What will she be doing now? Where is she now? and he played the old game of conjuring a scene in which he and she were the only actors, a scene of subtlety and tenderness and beauty. He imagined that they were together in a wood in late spring. She was collecting bluebells, armfuls of bluebells to bring for him. Then she sat beside him and began to confide in him, telling him her secrets. Her long hair, white as silver, brushed against his cheek. Then, in the stillness and the shadow, she held his hand. He was not mad. He did not confuse fantasy and reality. He knew that this had never happened and that it never would. But, he told himself, he needed the dream of an innocent beauty to protect him from the pressures, the niggling stresses, which even after retirement continued to depress him. He needed the dream as he needed Gillibry. Now, with Charlie's death, both were safe again.

When Connibear came in he half rose, expecting to be called next for interview. He was not anxious about the interview, because he did not confuse fantasy and reality, and Savage had no means of knowing about his dreams. But Connibear called Jerry Packham, and the doctor looked at his watch again and settled back to wait.

Savage waited, with interest, for Jerry Packham. He had not noticed him in any detail at the first meeting, and he was interested to meet Pamela Marshall's lover. The policeman was surprised, even a little disappointed. This was no sophisticated artist. He had sandy, curly hair and a

beard, thick red fingers. He could have been a bricklayer. Savage watched him walk into the room, sit on the wooden chair at the other side of the desk. All the furniture in the room looked as if it belonged in a classroom. Perhaps it had been donated by the Education Department. The man looked as nervous and uncomfortable as if he had been summoned to the headmaster's room. Then he asked if he could smoke, and lit a cigarette.

Savage waited while Connibear brought an ashtray. There was no view from the ringing-room window. It looked out to the stone wall of the generator shed. They were even sheltered on that side of the house from the noise of the wind. It was like any other interview room. It would have made no difference to Savage if there had been a view. He was beyond distraction.

"What did you want to discuss with Mr. Todd?" Savage asked gently. "Why was privacy so important?"

He had assumed an understated, self-effacing style. Connibear had never seen him work like that before and was impressed by the change in technique. He's showing off, Connibear thought. He's enjoying every minute of it. He wants to prove that he's not lost his touch.

"I illustrated all his storybooks," Jerry said. "I wanted to tell him that I wasn't prepared to work with him again. Not for a while at least . . . I was bored with them. I'd been offered other work and I wanted time to do it."

"How did you think that Mr. Todd would take the news?" The policeman spoke very softly. Connibear could hardly hear the words.

"I thought that he would be angry, upset. That's why I wanted to talk to him privately. He could be quite childish if he didn't get his own way. I wasn't looking forward to telling him."

"Did you go to see Mr. Todd last night to get this unpleasant interview over with?"

"No. I didn't leave the observatory yesterday evening."

"What exactly is your relationship with Mrs. Marshall?" He still spoke slowly, but he looked directly at Packham for the first time. His long, lined face was quite still, intent, as he waited for the reply.

"We are good friends."

"Do you sleep with her?"

The pace of the questions was increasing. Jerry Packham did not reply.

Savage said sharply: "This interview is in confidence. Do you sleep with her?"

"Occasionally."

"Did you sleep with her last night?"

"No."

"Why?"

"I had decided that I wanted no more than friendship from her. I want to be more independent."

"Did Mrs. Marshall leave the observatory yesterday evening?"

"She said she was going for a walk."

"Did she go to see Mr. Todd?"

"Not to my knowledge."

"You arranged to meet Mr. Todd in the seawatching hide early this morning. Did you go?"

"No."

"Why didn't you keep the appointment?"

"Because I overslept. I had set my alarm clock to go off at six-thirty. Either it didn't go off or I didn't hear it. I slept very heavily. When I woke it was almost breakfast time. I felt very guilty to have missed him, especially when I saw how bad the weather was. I presumed that he hadn't waited for me, or that he hadn't bothered to go because of the storm, so I went down to the Wendy House—that's what we call Charlie's bungalow—straight after breakfast."

"Do you know anything about the mist net with the missing guy?"

"No. Although I'm a member of the committee I don't manage to get to the island very often. I haven't got a mist-net endorsement to my ringing licence, so I can't use the mist nets on my own and John is usually busy with school parties."

"Did you take the seawatching-hide key from this room at any time during the weekend?"

"No."

They waited until Jerry Packham had shut the door behind him, and the footsteps had moved away down the stone corridor.

"He's keeping something from us," Savage said.

Connibear said nothing. The superintendent wanted him to act as admiring audience. Connibear did not want to upset his relationship with Savage—his chances of promotion depended on it—but he was not prepared to admire too readily.

The superintendent stood up, stretched.

"Protecting his fancy woman, I shouldn't wonder. He's worried about something. And I don't believe that he overslept. Birdwatchers get up early don't they? They don't oversleep."

"Do you think that he strangled Todd?" Connibear felt that Savage was expecting some contribution.

"I don't know, lad. And I don't speculate." It was a rebuke. "I haven't seen them all yet." He hesitated. "I want to get this right," he said. "Not for them . . ." he nodded vaguely in the direction of the mainland, of the glass and concrete office block which housed his superiors ". . . but for me."

"Which one do you want to see next?" asked Connibear. Now that the first excitement was over, it was just a job, an investigation like any other. He thought that Savage was being melodramatic.

"Go and fetch the doctor for me."

In the common room the doctor had banished his romantic dreams. He was frightened to dwell on them too often in case they lost their magic. He had been considering the ethical problem of whatever he should pass to Savage the conversation between Pamela Marshall and Jerry Packham which he had overheard from the library the night before. He enjoyed thinking about it. He enjoyed teasing out the possible implications of the argument between them. He enjoyed the sense of happiness and security which the awareness of other people's problems can bring. He had come to the conclusion that it would be right to repeat it,

78

but this decision had nothing to do with ethics and everything to do with the power of gossip.

When Connibear came to summon him he felt nervous after all. He fumbled the business of standing up. His hands shook on the door handle. As he walked into the ringing room Savage's attitude immediately reassured him. The policeman was still standing up. He leaned across the desk and shook Doctor Derbyshire's hand.

"Sorry to keep you waiting, sir," he said with an extravagant show of apology. He gestured Paul Derbyshire to sit down, and waited until the doctor was comfortably seated before sitting down himself.

"I understand that you are the chairman of the Observatory Trust."

This recognition of his status gave Paul Derbyshire confidence in the policeman. His nerves disappeared. What did he have to fear? He smoothed his white hair, which was a little long at the back and a little thin on the top.

"I am," he said. "I was elected chairman at our first committee meeting five years ago, and I have remained so."

"So you can explain to me what Mr. Todd's proposed sale of the island would have meant to the observatory?"

"It would have been catastrophic. We could never have afforded to buy the observatory building and if we had done so, the work of the observatory would have been quite changed. You see the most important function of the place is to ring birds. The observatory has a small garden, but most of the mist-net sites are out on the island. The correct habitat is essential."

"Do you do much ringing yourself, Doctor?"

"Not as much as I would like to now, though I maintain my licence, of course. My eyesight is rather poor. My function is predominantly supervisory, you know. I see to the administration."

"So you would not know anything about the mist-net guy which was used to strangle Mr. Todd?"

"No. Nothing at all. Nick Mardle is our keenest ringer. These boys are inclined to be untidy at times. Only the

79

other day I noticed that he had six bird bags in his coat pocket. Six! They should be left in the ringing room, you know.''

"Bird bags?'' Savage was momentarily distracted.

"Small cloth bags with a drawstring. We use them to carry the birds from the traps to the ringing room to process.''

"Now, Doctor, I would be grateful if you could give me a detailed account of your movements yesterday evening.''

"Yes of course. I knew that you would ask me.''

He described the trip from the mainland, the discussion at the supper table, John's sudden absence, in minute detail.

"I was devastated by Charles's decision to sell the island,'' he said. "Since I retired my work here has been increasingly important to me. It does not only have personal importance, but real scientific value. I felt that it was essential that I should persuade Mr. Todd that our work should continue. I had to show him that without his help the trust would not survive. I thought that if I summarized the accounts, so that he could understand the position more easily, he would be more sympathetic. You must understand that I was engrossed in my task. I certainly had no intention of eavesdropping.''

"But you overheard a conversation which you feel may be relevant?''

"Oh no.'' The professor seemed shocked. "I'm sure that it has nothing at all to do with Charlie's death. But I feel that it is my duty to tell you.''

He's enjoying this, Savage thought as Paul Derbyshire repeated the fragment of argument between Jerry Packham and Pamela Marshall. So even distinguished doctors enjoy a good gossip. The thought saddened him. He felt let down.

"You're quite sure of Mrs. Marshall's words?'' he interrupted. "They were having a row, then she said: 'If you haven't got the nerve to do it, I have.' ''

"Quite sure, Superintendent.''

"What do you think she was referring to?''

"As I've explained, I don't know. I really was concentrating on the accounts." There was a strong trace of regret in his voice and Savage believed him.

"What did you do yesterday evening, after Mr. Packham and Mrs. Marshall had left the common room?"

"I decided that I should go to see Charlie Todd to explain to him the enormity of his suggestion."

Savage's face and voice betrayed no interest. "So you saw Mr. Todd last night?"

"No, Superintendent, I did not. If you will allow me to explain. I decided that I ought to see him. I even went upstairs to change into more suitable clothes. Then I noticed that it had started to spot with rain, and it occurred to me that I could just as easily talk to him in the morning. It looked most unpleasant outside. I returned to the common room."

"Did you get up early this morning to go to meet Mr. Todd?"

"I did not." Unnecessarily, he added: "After breakfast I went out for a walk. Just down to the island. To check the traps."

But Savage was not interested in the ornithological routine of the island. He was beginning to feel the pressure of time. There always was pressure, but the incoming tide was relentless, completely inflexible, and that was something new. It was a challenge. He dismissed the doctor with a flash of a smile, but little courtesy.

"Do you want to see Mr. Packham or Mrs. Marshall again?" Connibear asked when the doctor had left the room.

"I don't think so. I've not much time left, if I'm to get off this place before the tide comes in. I want to see everyone. Pamela Marshall and Jerry Packham had an argument, but Todd wasn't mentioned at all. It could just have been a lovers' tiff. Packham admitted that he was trying to cool things with the beautiful Pamela." He gave the matter his full attention for a few seconds then set it aside. "It sounds like a domestic matter to me. Not relevant."

81

He turned to Connibear. "Let's see the keen ringer—Nicholas Mardle."

Nick Mardle looked older than his twenty years, prematurely middle-aged, with a sagging, pear-shaped body, dark, straggling hair. The only remnants of adolescence were his poor skin, his ungainly posture. Savage felt an initial impatience at the slovenly appearance, then restrained himself. The boy would have to be carefully handled.

"I'm sorry to have kept you waiting," he said routinely.

"That's all right," the boy said. "We're used to being treated like dirt. We do all the work here, but they still think of us as kids."

The outburst surprised Savage. He said nothing. The boy did not have the experience to cope with silence. He would continue to talk.

"They treated Charlie in exactly the same way. You would never think that he actually owned the island. They decided where the traps should be built, how often the school parties should be allowed, all the matters of policy. Then they told the rest of us."

"They?" Savage tried to speak mildly, but his impatience was influencing his style. The effect was rather one of controlled intensity, but Nick Mardle was too self-centred to notice.

"Doctor Derbyshire and Miss Carson. They consult Mrs. Marshall and Jerry Packham if they're here, but they're not very often. I come every weekend, and in the spring and autumn I walk over in the evenings if the weather is good for birds, but they only talk to me if they want me to do some maintenance work."

"Doctor Derbyshire did say that you did most of the ringing here. I was hoping to talk to you about the nets, the ringing procedures."

"Did he?" Nick was pleased but suspicious. "John rings more birds than me because he's here all the time, but I do twice as much as anyone else."

"Yesterday evening you and your friend were ringing waders on the shore?"

"Yes. As the tide comes in, the waders come in to

roost. We put a four-panel, sixty-foot net on the strip of sand at the north end. We did quite well."

"So you have different-sized nets to catch different birds."

"Yes. That's right."

"I understand that when you were looking for a net, you found one that you couldn't use, because it had a missing guy. Can I take it that it was one of the kind that you would use for waders?"

"Yes. Sixty foot long, with four gathered shelves to catch the birds in."

"And this net, the one with the missing guy . . . Did you get the impression that it had been put away as you found it, or had someone rifled through it, to pull out the rope? Just a minute, how are the nets stored?"

"In nylon bags in the cupboard over there."

Connibear pulled open the heavy wooden door of a built-in cupboard. About a dozen nylon bags, the sort used for carrying small tents, were piled on the floor. Many bamboo and metal mist-net poles were leaning against the wall at the back of the cupboard. Other pieces of ringing equipment and bird bags were piled on a shelf to one side, and hanging on a nail were several strands of nylon rope of different lengths.

"Why not just take a piece of rope from there?" Savage muttered to himself. "Why bother to open the nets?"

Nick Mardle seemed to be trying to remember how he had found the incomplete net.

"I think that it had been put away without the guy," he said. "The bag was completely closed and the drawstring at the top pulled tight, but the net hadn't been properly folded, just roughly rolled up as if someone had put it away very quickly."

"Do you know when that particular net was last used?"

"No. It would have been some time in the last two months. The waders don't come in until July. Unless of course it was put away like that last season. I know that John has caught some big numbers of waders—redshank and knot—over the summer. Liz helps him a lot with the

nets, and Miss Carson potters around presiding over the proceedings if she's here. On very warm evenings it has been known for Doctor Derbyshire to ring a few birds—as long as someone else is around to identify them, and age and sex them.''

"I see." Through habit, Savage was careful to conceal his disappointment. He turned back to Nick Mardle.

"Can you describe exactly what you did yesterday evening?"

Savage listened to the now familiar story of Charlie's revelation at the supper table.

"Did you go out with your friend immediately after supper?"

"Not immediately. Mark's a gentleman. He went to help Liz with the washing up. I was feeling a bit shattered."

He looked up at Savage. "I like it here," he said simply. "I couldn't imagine not being able to come to the observatory."

"That's when you went to look for the nets?"

"Yes."

"Did you see anyone while you were down on the shore?"

"Liz came down later in the evening, looking for John."

"Were you together on the shore for the whole of the evening?"

"No." Once again he looked at the superintendent and there was anxiety in his face. "I found that I'd left my favourite ringing pliers here, and I came back to fetch them. But I didn't go and set fire to Charlie's house. I quite liked him. He wasn't like the rest of the family."

"You know the Todds?"

"I work for them. I'm assistant manager of one of their shops—the leisure wear and sports equipment shop in the High Street. My family has been working for the Todds for years."

Savage caught the sharp note of bitterness in the boy's voice, but did not follow it up. He was short of time and it was probably not relevant.

"Did you see anyone when you were on your way back to the observatory?"

"No, but someone had been out. Everyone hangs their coats in the hall, just outside the ringing room here. There's a duffel coat that's been here for years. For all I know it was left behind by Trinity House. There was a sharp shower of rain while I was on my way back to the shore after collecting my pliers. When we came into the observatory after finishing ringing, I noticed that the duffel coat was wet."

"Was the coat used by anyone in particular?"

"No. We've all borrowed it at some time, to save having to go upstairs for a waterproof, or if we've come over to the island without a coat."

"Can you tell me what happened this morning?"

"Mark and I went out to do a seawatch. We got up about seven-thirty. I would have set the alarm to go off earlier if I had known it would be so windy. When we got out I wanted to go to the hide, but Mark thought that it wouldn't do to interrupt Jerry and Charlie. We came back in time for breakfast. You know what happened afterwards when we went down to the hide."

"Yes. I know. I'll not keep you much longer. Where did you meet Mark? Were you together all morning, until you went to the hide?"

"We shared a bedroom. He's a really heavy sleeper. I woke him up. We went to the bathroom separately, but apart from that we were together all morning."

"Thank you. Thank you, Mr. Mardle. You've been very helpful."

Superintendent Savage decided immediately that Mark Taylor looked like a monkey. He did not have any prejudice against monkeys, but he did against long-haired, unkempt, bearded young men who looked like them.

"Sit down," he said shortly. "You're a student are you?"

"Yes," Mark answered. "How did you know?"

"You look like one."

Mark, who was considered unconventional by his friends, thought that the policeman's image of a student was dra-

matically out of date, but he said nothing. Superintendent Savage felt that he was being rushed. It was gone four and he still had to speak to Elizabeth. He turned the full force of his personality towards Mark.

"Now," he said. "You're a student so you're a bright lad. We'll have no messing. Do you know who killed Mr. Todd?"

"No," Mark said. "If I knew I would tell you. Without waiting to be asked. I liked Charlie. And not all students hate the police."

Savage allowed himself one short, bark-like laugh.

"No. I don't suppose that they do. Describe in detail what happened to you yesterday evening. Start after the evening meal. Unless anything important happened before that."

"No, there was nothing important, except that everyone seemed more irritable than usual. I had coffee in the common room with everyone else. Everyone except John, of course, and Elizabeth who was in the kitchen. Then I went to help her wash up."

"Why would you want to do that? Fancy her, do you?"

Mark blushed deeply and uncontrollably. Savage pretended not to notice and continued: "Not that that's got anything to do with me. What happened then?"

"I went with her to help her to carry some wood for the common-room fire. Pam and Jerry were there. It looked as if they'd been arguing. Anyway, I felt a bit awkward about intruding. Liz went to the flat and I went to find Nick. He was in the ringing room trying to untangle one of the mist nets. We went ringing."

"He says that he came back to the observatory to fetch some pliers. What did you do while he was away?"

"Carried on ringing."

"You didn't leave the net?"

"No."

"And this morning, did you go out before Mr. Mardle woke you at seven-thirty?"

"No."

Once again Savage looked at his watch. "I've no more questions just now, Mr. Taylor. Thank you."

They went to interview Elizabeth in the kitchen, where she was preparing the evening meal. It would have been just as quick for Connibear to have fetched her into the ringing room, but Savage felt the need to demonstrate his impatience, the hurry. She was carrying a large pan of potatoes from the table to the stove. He took it from her, set it on the gas ring.

"You shouldn't be doing that," he said, "in your condition."

She sat on the stool by the table. She was wearing red. Connibear, looking at her and at Savage, thought how alike they were, with their dark hair and strong features. She could have been his daughter. There was an immediate antagonism between them, more like that between family members than between strangers.

"John told you," she said. The superintendent could tell that she did not like him. "I wish that he hadn't done."

Despite his impatience, Savage was intrigued by her. "How did you come to be living here, Miss Richards?" he asked. He wondered why it seemed so important.

"Mrs. Richards," she said. "I'm divorced. I was married to a BBC camera man. He was working on a documentary film on Bardsey—that's an island in North Wales. I went with him. It was the last attempt to save our marriage. John Lansdown was assistant warden at the observatory there. When Frank, my husband, left, I didn't go with him. John got the job here the following season, and I came too. Though what the hell that has to do with you or with Charlie Todd, I don't know."

"Do you like it here, Mrs. Richards?"

"I love it," she said.

"Do you know who killed Mr. Todd?"

"No."

"I've got a pretty clear picture of what happened yesterday evening throughout the meal and immediately afterwards, but there are a couple of questions I'd like to ask. Were you surprised when your boyfriend left the dining room?"

"No. He always reacts to things emotionally. He's impulsive."

"When you took the wood into the common room yesterday evening I understand that Mrs. Marshall and Mr. Packham had been arguing. Could you hear what was said?"

"No. But I'm sure that they'll tell you if you ask."

"Why did you go to find Mr. Lansdown yesterday evening? Were you worried that he would do something silly?"

"It depends what you mean by silly. I was worried that he would spend all night on the Beacon, brooding. I was not worried that he might try to set light to the Wendy House, or steal a mist net guy with the intention of strangling Charlie."

"What sort of coat were you wearing when you went out?"

"I wasn't wearing a coat. I've got an oiled fisherman's sweater. I was wearing that."

"You went to the shore to talk to the boys who were ringing?"

"Yes. I thought that John might be with them."

"Which way did you walk to find him?"

"There are steps cut into the cliff just below the Wendy House. I climbed those and walked through Charlie's garden."

"Could you see into his house?"

"I didn't look."

"Did you see anyone else?"

"No."

"What time did you wake up this morning?"

"A quarter to seven when the coastguard phoned up for John to hoist the cone."

"Did you get up then?"

"Yes. I was feeling sick. I went to the bathroom."

"You didn't go outside?"

"Not until later, until we were cooking breakfast, and by that time the seawatching hide was cut off from the island."

"You met Miss Carson while you were out?"

"Yes."

"Did you see her leave the observatory?"

"No. She must have gone out before me."

Suddenly his mood changed. He became, almost, fatherly. "I want to leave one of my men here, to keep an eye on you all. Will you be able to put him up?"

"Yes. It'll be in the dormitory, where we usually put the schoolchildren, but he'll be on his own in there."

"That will be fine, fine." He seemed about to say something else, to tell her, perhaps, to look after herself, when Martindale walked in. The young man stood awkwardly, just inside the door.

"The Land Rover's ready, sir," he said. "Connie asked me to tell you."

"Just coming, Martindale," He turned to Elizabeth. "This is the constable who will be staying here tonight."

They walked together to the yard, where the Land Rover was waiting. John was there, talking to George Palmer-Jones. Savage approached the two men, spoke to Palmer-Jones, then shook his hand. He nodded to John and climbed into the Land Rover. Connibear was obviously not used to driving it. The gears grated, it jerked forward and they were gone.

Elizabeth left the group in the yard and went out on to the Beacon. She watched the Land Rover cross the sand, and wished that she were with them.

7

Immediately after lunch George Palmer-Jones went to the Wendy House. The police had finished there, and Savage had given him permission to look around, and a key. The police search could not, he thought, have taken very long. There were only two rooms of any size, with a galley-like kitchen off the living room, and a shower room next to the bedroom. He had decided to visit the Wendy House, not so much because he wanted to see where Charlie lived, as to be on his own. His brief explanation at lunch of police procedure had made him, to the other residents of the observatory, an expert, someone who could relieve anxieties. He had encouraged a discussion about the murder, but now he needed to be on his own, to sort out the information he had gained so far. On such an island privacy was almost impossible, but no one would come to the Wendy House. He would have thought that in such a place it would have been impossible to commit murder, to do anything at all, unobserved. The murderer must have had considerable luck, or the crime had been very carefully planned. Yet would there have been

time for such planning? Charlie Todd had arranged to be in the seawatching hide only the evening before he died.

He stood in the sitting room. It was lined with wood—floor, walls and sloping roof were made of varnished pine panels. There was a small kitchen table by the window. The tilly still stood there. There were no curtains at the window. George presumed that Charlie had taken down the burned remains to throw them away. What happened to rubbish on the island? He would have to find out. Against the middle of the opposite wall stood a Calor-Gas fire, and two easy chairs covered in bright orange folk-weave faced towards it. There was a pine dresser against the third wall with crockery, a few books, some photographs and post-cards propped on the shelves. On the lowest shelf, which was wider than the others, was a wind-up gramophone and a pile of 78 r.p.m. records. From the position of the furniture it seemed inevitable that the fire had been arson. He wondered if Charlie had had any visitors between supper and the fire. Perhaps he had mentioned them to John and Elizabeth. But John would surely have told the superintendent, and all he had described had been some unidentified person walking towards the Wendy House. He would have to talk to John about that.

I wish that Molly were here, he thought suddenly. She is so much better at all this.

Molly was his wife. She enjoyed talking to people. She would have been quite happy, sitting in the common room, listening to repetition and irrelevance, instilling trust, until she noticed a contradiction, a small piece of useful information. He could listen too, but he was not so patient. He knew that the younger observatory members were a little in awe of him, because of his ornithological reputation, yet he would need them to talk freely to him. The tapes of Savage's interviews would give him the background, show him which questions to ask, but he knew that if he were to achieve more than the police, it would be through talking—through asking the right questions and listening to the answers. The police had the advantage in every other field: they had technical knowledge, manpower.

Had it come to this? he thought. Do I have to take part in some competition with the police to prove that although I'm retired I'm still capable of logical thought, that I've not turned into an old gossip like Derbyshire, who can live vicariously through other people's scandal?

Molly would have laughed him out of his mood of self-examination. She would have said that he had agreed to help because he was there, and because he could do it. She would have said that there was nothing wrong in enjoying the intellectual challenge of the investigation. He would help the police anyway, she would say, out of his over-developed sense of duty, because he had been a public servant for so long that it had become a habit, so why not enjoy it?

Why not? he thought, and turned his mind to the facts.

The police would, he supposed, have been given a relatively accurate time of death, but it should be possible to work out an approximate time, because he knew that when Elizabeth went out on to the island at about 8:15 the seawatching hide had been separated from the island, but when John had hoisted the cone just before seven it had not been. He had asked them both specially. Mark and Nick had started their seawatch at 7:45. Because they had decided not to interrupt Charlie they had not noticed specifically if it would be possible to get to the hide, but Mark thought that the gully was starting to fill. In any event, even if they had been engrossed in their seawatch, they would surely have noticed someone wading through the gully from the hide towards the observatory. That put the latest time of death at about 7:35. He had an idea, and went into the bedroom. There was a small alarm clock by Charlie's bed. The alarm was set for six o'clock. How long would it have taken him to get to the hide? George walked through to the kitchen.

It was a thin room, narrow as a corridor, only wide enough for cupboards on one of the long walls. The sink was built in there too. On the wooden worktop he found one dirty cup, empty, a dirty spoon, a jar of instant coffee and an opened packet of biscuits. It seemed that Charlie

had only had a cup of coffee and a biscuit before going out. Presumably he had been expecting to have breakfast in the observatory. Surely he would have reached the seawatching hide by 6:30? Would it have been light then? Just. George Palmer-Jones decided that he could work on the assumption that Charlie Todd had been killed between 6:30 and 7:35. The ease of the deduction pleased him. He looked again at the kitchen. On the draining board by the sink, washed but not dried, were three glasses and three mugs. Who had been sharing Charlie's hospitality? John and Elizabeth certainly. But would he have offered an alcoholic drink *and* coffee? George would have to ask them.

He felt more confident, ready to face the other island residents. At lunch he had spoken generally, asked some harmless questions, and so had encouraged a conversation about the murder. Now it was time to be more direct. He walked through the Wendy House garden towards the track. The mud was very soft there, a muddle of footprints. Almost hidden by the mud was a small bird bag. Automatically he bent to pick it up. It was beautifully handstitched and George saw with amusement that the initials P.D. were embroidered on the edge. How typical of the doctor to have his own personalized bird bags.

He saw that there was a small group of birds on the elder bush over which the heligoland trap had been built. They were goldfinches, bright as clowns, primary painted in red and yellow. He walked into the mouth of the net, making an absurd clucking noise to flush them into the box, caught three and was ridiculously pleased. He felt in his pocket for bird bags, found only two, and put the third finch in the doctor's bag. Back at the observatory, he found John in the generator shed, splitting firewood with a furious, mindless desperation.

"I've just caught these," George said. "I suppose there's no chance of ringing them? Is all the ringing gear in the bird room with the policemen?"

"No. I brought all that I thought I might need out here." John pointed to a workbench made of driftwood,

where rings, pliers, a measure and scales had been laid. In the shed the sound of the wind and water outside seemed very loud. There was a smell of wood and oil. In the corner the generator stood. It was very big and faintly menacing. John wiped his hands on his stained cord trousers. "Do you want to ring them?"

"I wouldn't mind. I need the practice."

George took the first bird from its bag, held it in the approved manner with its head between his second and third fingers, fitted the ring into the pliers, then carefully closed it around the bird's leg. He weighed it, measured its wing, then took it to the shed door and let it go.

"What do you think of the policeman?" John asked.

"I don't know," George answered truthfully. "How did *you* find him?"

"Intimidating. I suppose that he must be good at his job. I wouldn't like to cross him. He fired questions at me so quickly that I didn't have a chance to think. I suppose that's part of his technique, but there are some things that you genuinely can't remember, or that you need time to sort out in your mind."

"Was there anything that you wanted to tell him, but didn't get a chance to?"

"Why do you ask?"

George was holding the second bird, smoothing the feathers with his long fingers so that he could measure the wing.

"Savage recognized me," he said. "You know that I was working for the Home Office before I retired. I had some dealings with the police then. He's asked me to help him, unofficially. He hopes that I'll be able to give him some background information." He fitted the ring, released the bird. "Savage played me a tape of your conversation with him."

"Did he?" John was surprised, annoyed.

"Of course he shouldn't have done that without asking you first."

"You didn't have to listen."

"No, I didn't," George agreed. "But I said that I'd

help. I want to find out who murdered Charlie Todd, as quickly as possible. I presume you've no objection to that."

"Oh, I don't know. I just want them all to go away and leave us alone. I just want to get on with my work." He sounded like a confused, spoilt little boy.

"As I said at lunch, they won't go away until they find out who killed him."

The birds had all been ringed, the numbers recorded. George collected together the bird bags. John smiled, an attempt to relieve the tension. "How did you get hold of the doctor's bag?" he said. "He looks after them like gold. His wife made them all specially."

"I found it by the heli," George said. He refused to be distracted. "Do you mind if I ask you some questions?"

John smiled again, pulled himself up to sit on the workbench.

"No. No, of course not. I'm sorry."

"I didn't realize that Elizabeth was pregnant. Congratulations. I can understand why you were so shocked when Charlie said that he wanted to sell the island."

"Can you?" The anger flared again, then died away. "I'm sorry. Yes. It would be hard enough for me to find another job in the natural history field, but impossible to find one which paid enough to keep Elizabeth and a child or provided the sort of accommodation where you could live with a baby. It's going to be difficult anyway. I've put an advertisement to sell some of my books and my camera in *British Birds*."

"When you left the dining room, you ended up on the Beacon?"

"Yes."

"You told Superintendent Savage that you heard someone walking up the track. Could you really not tell who it was? You know the people here so well. Could you not make a guess?"

"It was Pamela Marshall," he said. "I don't know why I didn't tell Savage. Perhaps because I thought that I

wouldn't be able to explain that I knew it was her. It was, though. I recognized her walk and her perfume.''

"You say that she walked past about three-quarters of an hour before Elizabeth found you and you saw the fire. You didn't hear anyone else after her?"

"No, but I wouldn't have done. I moved down to the halfway wall and sat at the top of the cliff.''

"How long did you stay with Charlie after you had put out the fire in the Wendy House?"

"Not very long. Perhaps twenty minutes.''

"Did you have a drink with him?"

"Yes. He had some brandy.''

"Did you have some coffee?"

"No. He offered some, but Elizabeth wanted to get back.''

"Did he mention if he'd had any visitors before you and Elizabeth?"

"No.''

"You were out on the Beacon at seven this morning to hoist the cone. You would have been able to see anyone who was out on the island then. It would have been quite light. Did you see anyone at all?"

John shook his head.

"But I couldn't guarantee that no one was there. It was very windy. It was difficult enough to stand up. I was worried about Elizabeth and just hurried back into the observatory.''

"Which way did you go into the observatory—the door by the ringing room, or the back entrance by the kitchen?"

"The door by the ringing room. I wanted to make a note of the coastguard call-out. We get paid for the cone.''

"Did you see anyone there? Anyone who looked as if they had been out?"

"No.''

"Did you get the impression that everyone was still asleep?"

"I'm not sure," John said slowly. He was thinking. "No. I did expect to see someone. I thought that one of the residents was up, but I can't remember why. Perhaps I

heard someone moving around in the common room. I'm not sure. I just wanted to get back to Elizabeth. I didn't especially want to see anyone. I *will* try to remember.''

"Did Elizabeth tell you yesterday evening that Jerry had arranged to meet Charles in the seawatching hide?"

"No."

"What sort of season has it been so far?" The polite, conventional question seemed strangely out of context.

"Very good. We had a lot of school parties in the summer. More recently there've been a couple of ringing groups—one from Edinburgh and one from Worcester. That's why I can't be certain who used that mist net last. Everyone who comes uses our nets."

"Yes. I see. Have there been any strangers hanging round the observatory? Anyone trying to camp?"

"Campers are always a problem in the summer, but there's been no one recently. And in the summer they were only kids."

John said hopefully, uncertainly: "Do you think that someone from outside might have killed him?"

"No. It's a possibility I suppose, but really very unlikely."

"Have you any idea who . . . ?"

George interrupted: "No. Not yet."

"I was just going to the kitchen to get a cup of tea," John said. He seemed restless. He wanted to get away from the generator shed and the questions. "Will you come?"

"No thank you. Not just yet. Will all the ringing records be in the log in the common room?"

"All except last week's. They're on the day sheets in the ringing room."

"Did you catch any waders last week?"

"I didn't, but the Worcester Ringing Group who were staying did."

"You didn't go out with them?"

"No." He grinned. "I wanted to get the place tidied up for the committee weekend."

"Were any of the committee over?"

"Nick came for a couple of evenings. The Worcester lot have been here before and he's quite friendly with them. I think they did more drinking than ringing, though. Jasmine spent all day Tuesday here. I picked her up in the morning and took her back after the tide. I don't know if she did any mist netting, though she had a tremendous seawatch. She saw Sabine's gull. I remember it very well, because I need it for the island."

George allowed John to escape, and waited until he had disappeared through the kitchen door. Then he walked to the observatory, went in through the main entrance and stood looking at the familiar hall as if seeing it for the first time.

On the opposite wall to the ringing-room door was a long row of coat hooks, underneath them a row of outdoor boots and shoes. He recognized Miss Carson's massive waterproof cape and her shoes, so sturdy and high round the ankle that they looked like surgical boots. Perhaps they were. Nick and Mark had identical anoraks of an oiled canvas, Pamela Marshall an expensive down kagoul, and Jerry a disreputable parka. His own coat was there and his boots, and the old duffel coat and wellingtons which belonged to no one, were used by everyone and had been there since he had first visited the observatory.

He walked on through to the common room. Mark was there, still waiting to see Superintendent Savage. He grinned nervously, then retreated again behind his Tom Sharpe novel. He did not seem to be reading it. The log book was on the table in the library. The majority of the entries were in Miss Carson's hand. The writing was very strong, as if she could only control the pen by pressing hard against the paper. The rest were in Paul Derbyshire's spiky scribble and John Lansdown's sloping, left-handed print. On each page there was a record of the weather, the birds that had been seen and ringed, and a list of observers. The first waders of the season had been caught on 20 July, and the observatory had been ringing about twice a week since then. The most recent entry was for Friday, just over a week before. Charlie had left the island for his week away.

They had caught three redshank and a dunlin. The only ringers had been Packham and Pamela Marshall.

George Palmer-Jones found Pamela on the west cliffs. She was looking at the seals which were lying in one long line, as if in a bus queue, on a sandbank which was exposed only at low tide. The wind had dropped a little, but the sky was overcast. She was wearing designer jeans and a tight-fitting sweater. She heard him approaching, turned round and smiled.

"I'm sorry," he said, "about your uncle."

"So am I," she said. "I rather liked him. At least he was better than the others."

"Was he? What are the others like?"

"Oh, rather boring, you know," she said lightly. "Only interested in making money."

"Why did you go to see Charlie last night?"

"I didn't. I know that I was talking about it before supper, but I decided not to go in the end. I just went for a breath of air in the garden. I explained all that to the superintendent."

"John Lansdown says that you went down the track yesterday evening."

"Well, he was wrong. It wasn't me." She was quite confident. Then, more cautiously: "Did he tell the policeman that he'd seen me?"

"No."

"Well, he can't have been very sure then, can he?"

"Why did you and Jerry Packham come to the island last Friday?"

For the first time she looked scared. "Why? What's that to do with anything?"

She was stalling, trying to decide on her response. He said nothing.

"Who told you that we were here?" she asked.

"Nobody. I looked in the log."

"Why are you interested?"

"I was wondering if perhaps you were using the mist net from which the guy was taken, the guy used to strangle Charlie."

99

"Oh." She was relieved. She did not question his interest in the murder. "Oh, I see. I shouldn't think so. You know how meticulous Jerry is, and he put the gear away."

So something else had happened on that Friday to frighten her, but now she realized that he was ignorant of it, and she would not be persuaded to talk. Again he regretted that Molly was not with him.

"Did you see Charlie that day?" he asked. "How did he seem? Did he mention where he was going?"

"I had coffee with him that day," she said. "He was very mysterious about his trip. I presume now that he was going to meet the people in the canal-boat theatre to discuss the project with them."

"He didn't drop any hints about selling the island?"

"No. Not at all like Charlie." For a moment her mouth stiffened as she said, "He was very bad at keeping secrets."

Then the impression of anger was gone. She smiled at him, took his arm, and they walked together back to the observatory.

That night they sat for the meal much as they had the night before, but PC Martindale took Charlie Todd's place. He was embarrassed, preoccupied, took refuge from his awkwardness in dreams of Rachel. There was the same hiss of the tillies, the same movement of the tide, the same prints on the walls of birds and shipwrecks, but everything was quite different. Because of Charlie Todd's death, and because of the presence among them of a murderer, they were all different. In the shadowed light, with a policeman at the table, they could no longer pretend that this was just another meal. They ate in silence. Then Jasmine Carson spoke to George. He was sitting next to her and she did not speak loudly, but they all listened.

"John tells me that you intend to help the police to find the murderer."

He emptied his mouth, answered slowly and calmly. "I've told them that I'll help in any way I can. I'm in a special position, I suppose, because of my work, and because I wasn't here when the crime was committed." He smiled at Martindale, who had not been listening and

was confused by the attention. "But I'm sure that the police are competent."

"Are you?" she said crossly. "Someone broke into my flat six months ago and they never found the thief on that occasion. I want this matter sorted out quickly. We don't want it hanging over the observatory. It will ruin our reputation, stop the serious work of the place."

She spoke in sharp, staccato phrases, looked scornfully at Martindale, then continued. "I'd rather trust you than the police, P.-J. If there's anything I can do I'd be pleased to help."

George could think of nothing suitable to say. Doctor Derbyshire broke in nervously:

"Of course we all want to help, that goes without saying. But I don't understand. Do the police really believe that one of us . . . ? Does that mean that they'll be poking and prying around the place . . . ? His voice faded. He became flushed and agitated. His reaction was so severe that George wondered for a moment if he had some medical complaint. His hand was shaking. "It's intolerable."

"It's quite logical," Palmer-Jones said mildly, afraid almost to provoke the elderly man to further hysteria. "It would have been just possible for someone to get here to commit the murder, but I really don't see how they could have got off the island afterwards. The police searched very thoroughly when they got here."

"Quite, quite," the doctor muttered. His indignation had disappeared. He wanted the subject quickly disposed of. "I must apologize. Shock, you know. Shock."

They finished eating and Elizabeth took the plates to the kitchen. She returned and they all lingered over the glasses of wine, waiting for someone to move from the table first.

John looked at Elizabeth, then said: "There's something that we wanted to tell you. We weren't going to say anything just yet, but I've had to tell the police, so of course we want you all to know too. We're going to gave a baby."

He was nervous and upset, but still managed to sound very proud. Elizabeth was suddenly overwhelmed with

affection for him, an easy pleasing affection, as one might feel for a pet, or someone else's child.

Jerry Packham was speaking. "That's terrific," he said. "I am so glad for you both. I'm sure we all are. Thank you for telling us. At a time like this we all need some good news."

There followed a clamour of congratulation, but George Palmer-Jones, as he looked around the table, noticed that Mark Taylor's smile was forced, that his voice as he shouted his best wishes across the table to John was unusually harsh and that he avoided looking at Elizabeth who was sitting next to him.

Elizabeth and John went to the kitchen then, to make coffee, and the others moved towards the common room to wait for it. George helped to gather the glasses together and was the last to leave the dining room. Pamela Marshall was waiting for him, just outside the door.

"Can I talk to you later?" she said. "I should have told you earlier. I've been thinking about last night."

"You did go to Charlie's?"

She nodded.

"Did you see anyone?"

"It's not what I saw, it's what I heard."

Elizabeth caught them up then. She was carrying the pot of coffee. George opened the common-room door for her, and said to Pamela:

"I'll see you later perhaps."

Palmer-Jones drained his coffee quickly. He felt impatient, not just to speak to Pamela, but to be outside, away from the other people in the room.

"I'm just going up to the Beacon for a blow," he said. "Does anyone want to join me?"

"Yes," Pamela Marshall said quickly. "Yes, it does seem very stuffy in here. I'll come if you don't mind."

She was walking across the room towards the lobby to fetch her coat when Paul Derbyshire said: "Would you be kind enough to bring my mackintosh with you, my dear? I believe that I'll come with you."

She stopped, surprised. "You," she said almost rudely. "But you never go out if you can help it."

"Oh come, my dear, you're exaggerating." His voice was spiteful. "But of course, if I'm intruding . . ."

"No," she said sharply. "You're not intruding."

They went out together, and although George Palmer-Jones and Pamela Marshall walked briskly the doctor managed to keep up with them. He had a strange way of walking with his hips thrust forward and his shoulders back, so it seemed that he must eventually tilt backwards and fall, but despite his reputation for laziness he showed no sign of being out of breath. He stood with them on the Beacon and the wind blew his long white hair away from his face and there was no trace of his previous tension. He seemed to be aware that they wanted to be alone, and to enjoy their discomfort at his presence.

George Palmer-Jones returned to the observatory without having had the opportunity of talking to Pamela Marshall. He could perhaps have made more effort to do so, but his walk had relaxed him. It did not now seem so important. There would be time enough on the following day.

8

When Superintendent Savage reached the mainland it was almost dark, but a small group of men still waited. They were reporters who stared across the estuary as if they would get their story just by looking at the island. He made a brief statement of the facts, refused to speculate about motive or suspects. The interview took place through the Land Rover window, and soon he ordered Connibear to drive on, leaving the men there in a useless bedraggled heap, like driftwood washed up by the tide.

The police station was brightly lit and cheerful. It had been built in the sixties, was square and concrete. Connibear opened the door to the central heating, the smell of cigarettes, disinfectant and fried food from the canteen. The smell was so familiar that he did not usually notice it. But the day had seemed very long and he felt that he had returned from a foreign country. Savage was not bothered by such fancies. He went straight to his office and sent Connibear to check what had been happening in their absence, and to bring coffee and food. Then he phoned his wife. When he told her that he would be late, she was

concerned that he might be tired, told him to look after himself, but there was none of the old panic of the Merseyside life. She had been deceived into believing that things really were different here. Connibear knocked just as he put the phone down, came in backwards, pushing the door with his body so that his hands were free to carry a tray with two mugs of coffee, a pile of bacon sandwiches and a file.

"Well, lad," said Savage, eyes bright with frantic, nervous energy. "What have they been doing while we've been out on that bloody island? Solved the case for us, have they?"

"Not quite, sir."

Savage motioned Connibear to sit down, pushed the plate of sandwiches towards him.

"Go on then, lad. Tell me what they *have* been doing."

"There's a copy of the will, sir. That's quite interesting."

"Well?"

"The island, with all its buildings, the Land Rover and the dinghy that's kept there goes to the Observatory Trust."

"We knew that. Go on."

"The remainder is to be divided between his nephew and niece, Jonathan Todd and Pamela Marshall."

"How much is the remainder?"

"About £1000 in bank and building society accounts, and there's a cottage towards the Storr Valley, which has been valued at about £30,000. He lived there before he bought the island, still used it in the winter and let it out to holiday-makers in the summer."

"So Pamela Marshall was lying. Or could she really not have known what was in the will? Did the rest of the family know the contents of it?"

"Albert, the old man, did. I don't know that they've spoken to the rest of the family."

"Well, they should have done. Is there anything else?"

"They've checked Charlie Todd's movements in that week when he was off the island. He was up staying with those young people with the narrowboat in the Midlands. He promised them the moon, apparently. I gather that they

thought he was just a bit of a loony. They didn't think that he would really come up with the goods. They were quite surprised to know that he really meant it."

"He didn't seem worried, frightened at all?"

"Quite the opposite, sir. Very enthusiastic. They say he enjoyed every minute."

"When can we expect to hear from forensic?"

"Preliminary report first thing in the morning."

"Good. Anything else?"

"Mr. Ernest Todd has been in, apparently, asking to see you. He wouldn't talk to anyone else. There was no one of sufficient superiority available—or so he said. He did say that he'd be in all evening, if you want to see him."

"I do want to see him. Have you got the address there? Come on then. We'll go."

The address was in a village just inland from Gillicombe. They drove down the narrow roads with a controlled frenzy. Savage was driving—just a little too fast. The lanes were lined by trees, and leaves blew in drifts across the road and were piled against the banks in a brown, soggy mess. The Todds had a flat in a white, square house at the end of a well-kept gravel drive. Expensive cars were parked outside. The Todds' flat was on the ground floor and they used the original front door at the top of a short flight of white stone steps. A woman answered the knock. Connibear recognized her. He had often seen her in court, though he had not connected her with Ernest Todd. She invited them in. Savage looked around him with eager and undisguised curiosity. There was a wide, carpeted hall, a table with a copper bowl of flowers, then the woman opened a door into a big room, conventionally, comfortably furnished. The place was stuffily centrally heated, and Ernest sat in his shirt, slippered feet in front of him, watching the television. Helen switched it off. Ernest tried not to mind and stood to greet them. A large whisky was on a coffee table near his chair, and he smelled faintly of alcohol.

"Hello. Good of you to come." His voice was rich, mellowed and deepened by whisky and cigar smoke. They sat on a settee. Connibear sat awkwardly. Savage leaned

forward, his hands on his knees, and stared expectantly at Todd. He was unmoved by his surroundings, and waited like a child hoping for a treat.

"It's a delicate matter," Ernest said. "I didn't want to discuss it with one of your constables."

"You think that you might be able to help us? You have some information about Mr. Todd's death?"

"Not exactly," he said. "I'm not sure that it's relevant at all, but I've always believed in helping the police. I thought that I had better tell you . . . You must decide whether it's important or not . . . I can take it that our conversation will be in confidence?"

"Certainly, sir." Savage grinned encouragingly. He was becoming impatient. "Now, what is this information?"

"It's about a boy called Nicholas Mardle."

"He works for my husband," Helen Todd interrupted. She too was becoming irritated by her husband's inability to come to the point. "Ernest wanted to tell you that he has made threats against our family."

"Has he?" Savage spoke without emphasis, but the child had received his treat, patience had been rewarded. "What exactly did he have against Mr. Todd?"

"That's just it," Ernest said. He felt more comfortable with an indirect approach. "He didn't have any grudge at all against Charlie. It was the rest of the family he disliked."

"Why?"

Ernest took a drink from the glass. His words became smoother, but he was obviously uneasy.

"His parents both worked for us. They were excellent employees and worked for us for many years. His father was caretaker and gardener and his mother began as chambermaid and eventually became housekeeper at the Grand. Because of Mr. Mardle's position, they were given a cottage converted from some of the stables at the back of the hotel. Unfortunately Mr. Mardle had an accident—a road accident, nothing to do with his employment. He was in hospital for a number of weeks and then he died. We were in a very difficult position then. Mrs. Mardle hadn't worked for us for some time because of ill health. Al-

though the son, Nicholas, worked for us he was only an assistant manager and didn't warrant being given the tenancy of one of the cottages. And of course we needed a new caretaker, and we would have had to compensate him financially if we couldn't provide accommodation.''

"So you threw Mrs. Mardle and the son out of the cottage.''

"We asked them to leave. Of course we followed the letter of the law, gave them adequate notice. We even made a generous ex gratia payment for their inconvenience. Mrs. Mardle was quite happy.''

"But Nicholas was not?''

"He's unbalanced,'' Mrs. Todd said decisively. "He's always been a surly, bad-tempered boy. I'm surprised not to have seen him in court.''

"Yet you decided to employ him, Mr. Todd. Why was that? Because you felt some responsibility for him?''

"Only partly,'' Ernest said. "Laurence—my brother— felt that he might be useful to us. He didn't get very good O-level grades and he failed his A levels, but Laurence thought that he had a very good grasp of figures. We decided to start him off in the shop to see how he got on. We thought that we might be able to move him then to help Laurence with wages and accounts. One of the boy's O levels was in computer science, and we've recently installed a computer. Of course we could take on a qualified programmer, but . . .''

"That would have cost you more.''

Ernest nodded. He did not recognize any criticism in the detective's words.

"When did you ask the Mardles to leave the cottage?''

"We gave them notice to leave at the end of February. They moved at Easter.''

"Where did they go to?''

"They were rehoused by the council.''

"So all these threats were made six months ago?''

"Nicholas did come to see me then to ask me to reconsider my decision, but no, the actual threats were made at the end of July when his mother died. He was very upset,

naturally. He had some fanciful notion that the move had contributed to her illness and her death. It was all nonsense. I only listened to him because I felt sorry for him. He's never had many friends. His mother spoiled him. Her death obviously hit him hard.''

"What exactly did he say?''

"He blamed the family for his mother's death. He talked about vengeance. He said that he would do the same for us. He said that he would like to kill us all.''

"But you can't have taken him seriously? You would never have continued to employ him if you'd thought that he meant it.''

"Of course I didn't take it seriously. He was so upset that he didn't know what he was saying. He even apologized the next day. Not a proper apology, but he was much calmer. I must admit, though, that I was in favour of dismissing him. Not only because of the outburst against the family, but because I thought he might be a disruptive influence in the shop. Father asked me to keep him on.''

"Your father still has an interest in the business?''

"He never stops interfering.'' Helen Todd immediately regretted these words and tried to soften their impact. "He's a very old man. I'm afraid his business sense isn't as keen as it was.''

"Did Nicholas Mardle discuss the move from the cottage, and his mother's death, with your father?''

"He made rather a scene there, after his mother died,'' Ernest said. "He actually went to the old man's house, started shouting and screaming at him. I would have called the police, but I didn't hear about it until afterwards. Mardle went to see Laurence too, but I don't think that he threatened him. He broke down completely, apparently. Said he didn't know how he would carry on without his mother.''

"The boy hasn't made any threats since then?''

"Not to me.''

"And his work has been satisfactory?''

"Yes.'' Ernest Todd was grudging. "I've had no complaint about his work.''

Savage stood up, walked over to the window. It was not a signal that he wanted to go, he just needed to move. He felt no constraint. It was as if he were in a friend's house. They were all aware of it. Even though he was not speaking, he was still the centre of attention. They were all quiet, waiting for him. He turned to face them.

"I'd like to talk to your father. Do you think that he'd be willing to see me this evening?"

"Oh, I don't think that would be wise," Helen said quickly. "As I explained, he's a very old man."

"Goes to bed early does he?" Savage said. "Doesn't matter. We can call first thing in the morning."

Ernest laughed. It was a deep throaty chuckle and ended in a cough.

"It's no good, Helen. They'll see him some time. One of Superintendent Savage's men talked to Father this morning. You're better going this evening, Superintendent. He doesn't go to bed early, but he does lie in until midmorning. It's become a habit of Helen's to prevent our acquaintances from meeting my father. She thinks that he's vulgar."

"Nonsense," she said, dismissing him, refusing even to be offended by him. "I'm concerned for your father's health. But if you think that he's fit to see the police, of course you must go, Superintendent. Would you like me to telephone to tell them that you'll be visiting?"

"That would be very kind," he said, walking towards her, overwhelming in his gratitude.

Connibear, who had said nothing and had been ignored by both Todds, stood up, and this was a sign that they should leave. Now that the interview was reaching its end, Todd and his wife were gracious. They apologized for not having offered food and drink and stated that of course if they could help at all in the future, Savage should not hesitate to be in touch.

Then they were outside in the dark. The wind had changed to the west and was damp and sweet, and smelled of the wet leaves, and salt. Connibear felt very excited and alive. He was exhilarated by Savage's driving, by the

feeling that they were moving forward, physically and in the task which they were performing.

Albert was thrilled to learn that the superintendent wanted to see him. Elsie took the telephone call. Laurence was in the attic with his model railway. She went to tell him first. He listened to her carefully: he knew that it must be important for her to disturb him when he was in the attic. Carefully he switched off the power, put away the engines and followed her downstairs. Albert was watching a western on the television. He was a little deaf and the sound was turned up loud.

"You mustn't be upset, dear," she said when she got his attention. "Helen's just phoned up. Superintendent Savage has just been to see her and Ernie. He's in charge of the case, you know. In charge of the murder inquiry. He's on his way here. He wants to talk to you."

"About time too," Albert said. "Why did he go to see Ernie before coming here?"

Laurence blinked. "Ernest went to see him," he said. "He thought the police ought to know about Nicholas Mardle. He went to tell them."

"I suppose that was Helen's idea," Albert said. "Ridiculous anyway. Nicholas Mardle wouldn't have murdered Charlie. Charlie didn't have anything to do with the business. Young Mardle liked him as far as I know. Did she say what this detective was like?"

"No. Not really." Elsie was apologetic, as if she should have gained more information. "She said that he wasn't local."

"Perhaps he's from Scotland Yard," Albert said, becoming even more excited. "I wonder what he wants."

"I don't think he wants anything especially," Elsie said. "Just a general conversation."

"Of course he wants something. He wouldn't come here if he didn't want something."

Connibear immediately felt at ease in the house in Laurel Avenue. Elsie bustled them out of the wind and began talking at once about tea. There was a print in the hall

111

which he recognized. His aunty had had one like it on her mantelshelf for twenty years.

Albert Todd sat in a high, straight-backed chair in one corner of the living room. A walking frame stood against the wall beside him, but there was no other indication of his age. He did not look very old. Savage took the chair next to him. Laurence had turned off the television as soon as he heard the knock at the door, and was hovering nervously, uncertain whether he should stay or go, bothered about where he should sit. Elsie was in the kitchen making tea.

Savage and Albert looked at each other. Neither was too concerned with the conventions of politeness and did not hide the mutual appraisal.

"It's good of you to come and see me," Albert said with a touch of sarcasm. "I was expecting to see you earlier."

"We've been on the island all day," Savage said. It was a kind of apology.

"I've never been there," Albert said. "Don't suppose I will now. Do you know who killed Charlie?"

"Not yet," Savage said.

"Well, it wasn't Nicholas Mardle. I knew Fred and Mary very well. They wouldn't have had a son who is a murderer."

"What do you think, Mr. Todd?" Savage turned to Laurence. Laurence was surprised by the question. He hesitated, stammered briefly before speaking.

"No," he said. "No, I don't think that he killed Charlie. He was very upset, very upset, but I don't think that he could have done that."

Savage dismissed Laurence as a waffler. He turned back to Albert.

"When young Mardle came to see you, what exactly did he say? His mother had died?"

"Yes," Albert said. "It was the day after the funeral. You mustn't take any notice of what was said then. It was only natural. I wouldn't have mentioned it. It doesn't show the business in a good light."

"All the same," Savage insisted. "I must know what was said."

Albert repeated the phrase he had used to Elsie earlier in the day. "He said that we were bunch of murderers and that if he could get away with it, he would kill us one by one."

Connibear was discreetly taking notes, watching the protagonists. There was a sudden flash of surprise and fear, on Laurence Todd's face, which he hid immediately behind his blinking eyes and blank expression. It occurred to Connibear that Laurence had not known before what Mardle had said to his father.

Savage made no comment on Albert's words and changed the subject. "Charlie left the island to the Observatory Trust and everything else was to be split between Pamela Marshall and Jonathan Todd." He looked briefly at Laurence. "That's your son?" Laurence nodded, but Savage's next question was directed once more towards Albert.

"Did that surprise you?"

"Yes it did. I wouldn't have thought that he would have bothered much with the family."

"Mr. Todd?" Laurence was asked, but it was obvious that Savage did not expect much from his answer.

"I didn't know what was in Charlie's will. Not until . . ." He hesitated. "No. I didn't know what was in Charlie's will."

Elsie came in then with a tea tray. She was concerned with the policemen's comfort, pointed them towards the easy chairs, poured out the tea for them.

Savage smiled at her, thanked her warmly. "We're just discussing Charlie's will," he said. "I expect it will come in useful for the boy. Expensive business now, being a student."

"Yes," she replied. "Wasn't it nice of Charlie to remember Jon? Not that it will mean much to him now. He says that he's not into materialism. We offer him money of course, but he won't take any more than he needs to make up the grant, so he never has more than the other boys.

He's so independent. I sometimes think that he doesn't eat properly. But we're very proud of him, aren't we Laurence?"

"Yes," Laurence said softly. "Very proud."

"What about Mrs. Marshall?" Savage asked. "Is she into materialism?"

"She's into materialism all right, that one," Albert said sharply. "I've never known anyone spend money the way that she does."

"Got money problems has she?" Savage asked conversationally. No one was deceived by his tone.

"No," said Elsie, shocked. "No, of course not."

"She's got no debts if that's what you mean," Albert said. "Nothing substantial anyway. She always seems to have the problem of never having enough money, but I daresay she's not the only one."

Elsie offered another cup of tea. Savage refused it, watched impatiently while Connibear drained the dregs from his cup, then stood up with a jerk. Before leaving the room he looked directly at Albert.

"Thanks for your help, sir," he said. "If you think of anything else you know where to contact me."

He took Elsie's hand in both of his, briefly acknowledged Laurence's presence, then walked out. Connibear followed.

"What did you make of that?" Savage asked when they were in the car. He had allowed Connibear to drive.

"Not much," said Connibear. He was disappointed that they had achieved so little. His exhilaration and optimism had disappeared. He felt that the interview which had promised so much had been an anticlimax. It had been over so quickly. "They didn't tell us much more than Ernest."

"Oh, they did. They told us that Mardle threatened specifically to murder each of the family members. That makes a big difference."

"But it's not logical. Charlie had no part in throwing his mother out of the cottage."

"Of course it's not logical, lad. It's crazy. But murder isn't logical, and most murderers are mad. The courts

don't admit it very often, but it's true. It's not logical to want to kill every prostitute in Yorkshire but it happens."

"So you think it was Mardle? The old man wasn't very convinced."

"The old man hasn't met as many murderers as I have. I don't think anything yet. I'll want to get some more information from the scientists before I think anything. But I wouldn't be surprised if it turned out to be the boy. I wouldn't be surprised."

"So you don't think that the financial motive is important?"

"No I don't. The amount isn't big enough. For someone like Pamela Marshall it's peanuts. And that boy Jonathan could get anything he wanted out of his parents. They obviously dote on him. If he wanted money, he only had to ask for it. Besides, he wasn't there, and I know that whoever killed Charlie Todd is still on that island."

Connibear drove through the town toward the police station. The orange street lights were reflected in the wet pavements. In the summer it was a shabby, tatty town. The gift shops sold cheap and shoddy souvenirs, the amusement arcades were brash and noisy. There was nothing classy about it. There were no good restaurants, no smart boutiques. Now that all the holiday premises were closed it had a quiet, derelict dignity. The pubs were just closing. Three people waited in the fish and chip shop, but towards the harbour the streets were deserted.

Connibear pulled into the car park behind the police station. It could have been anything from a town hall to an insurance office, but no other building in the town was so obviously open and alive. Connibear switched off the engine, waited for Savage to make a move. He sat for a moment.

"There's no need for you to come in," Savage said. "I won't be long. You go home if you like. We'll have to go back there tomorrow morning."

He nodded into the darkness towards the sea.

"That's all right. I'll come in with you, if you don't mind. I'm in no rush to get home."

It was his first important case. He did not want to miss out on it.

Savage seemed pleased, pushed the door open aggressively, paced impatiently while Connibear fumbled to lock the car, then they walked quickly together towards the building.

"Any news?" Savage shouted at the officer at the desk, but he did not stop moving. The policeman had to call up the stairs after him that there had been no news.

They both sat down. Connibear took out his notebook, so that they could discuss the interview with the Todds in some detail. The phone rang. Connibear answered, waited for the call to be put through. Savage drummed his fingers on the desk crossly, as if Connibear were wasting time unnecessarily. The call came through and Connibear listened. Then he said:

"You'd better speak to the boss."

As he handed the receiver to Savage he said: "It's Martindale. There's been another murder on the island. He's arrested young Mardle."

9

George Palmer-Jones returned to the observatory with Paul Derbyshire and Pamela Marshall at about the same time as Savage was beginning his interview with Ernest Todd. Elizabeth was serving cocoa. Constable Martindale took a cup, and ate the cakes she offered with enjoyment. Everyone was there. Everyone was quiet, exhausted by the drama of the day's events and the wind. Elizabeth collected the cups, John carried them to the kitchen for her. They returned briefly to say goodnight, then disappeared to the flat. The other guests started talking about bed and, led by Jasmine Carson, went upstairs. Pamela lingered, hoping perhaps for another opportunity to talk to George, but Martindale had moved into the seat next to his and showed no sign of leaving them alone.

She said, "See you in the morning," and followed the others up.

"Would you like to hear the tapes of the other interviews, sir?" Martindale said. "Superintendent Savage said that I was to ask you."

"Did he?" George felt tired. Savage's ability to bully

him, despite his absence, was oppressive. He felt inclined to refuse, but curiosity overcame him.

He looked properly for the first time at the policeman. He seemed very young, shy, not as arrogant as young policemen often seemed to be. "Are you local?" he asked.

"Not quite," Martindale said. "I went to school in Bideford."

George smiled. Bideford was only twenty miles away.

They went together to the ringing room and listened to the tapes. George made notes in his bird notebook. Martindale sat very still and listened with concentration. He must have looked like that when he was revising for O levels, George thought. When the tapes finished Martindale looked anxious, as if he were to be examined on their content, but George said:

"I'm too tired to take it all in now. Perhaps we could discuss them tomorrow morning when we've had a chance to sleep on it."

They walked to the entrance hall where the coats hung, and up the narrow stone stairs. John had switched off the generator, and Martindale showed the way with a torch. He went into the dormitory and Palmer-Jones into his cell-like single room. There was a small bed, an old dining chair and his rucksack; there was just room for him to stand. He was tired, but he did not feel ready to sleep. He lit a candle. The place seemed full of small noises, of the plumbing, soft footsteps, the creak of beds and the rustle of clothes. It was as if everyone had been tired in order to avoid the company of others, but now they could not sleep. He wondered if he should find out where Pamela was sleeping. He could see if she was awake and talk to her. But although he was not sleepy he felt a kind of lethargy, so that the idea of any action intimidated him. He sat on his bed and looked at his notes, but the words spun before his eyes and he was left only with a series of impressions, visual images of the kind that usually came to him when he was over-tired. He saw Savage, sitting in the ringing room, intense and competitive, defying the murderer to outwit him, determined that by will alone he could

know what had happened. He saw Jasmine Carson offering her help as if it were a donation to some worthy cause, and Doctor Derbyshire's spiteful, smiling face turned to the wind. He saw fear in young faces, and triumph, because the island had been restored to them, and because the young cannot sustain a pretence of mourning. But he could not be sure if the visions were true, or the distortion of truth, caused by his own interpretation and prejudice. It occurred to him then that he might write to Molly. He began the letter in his mind, and the words comforted him, gave some sense to the situation. He was thinking that he might undress and sleep, when somebody screamed.

It was not a loud scream. It was stifled and could have been man or woman or child. He took the candle, opened the door and walked quickly into the corridor and towards the noise. As he did so other doors opened. The screaming continued. Mark joined him and they ran together towards the sound. Jerry Packham was in front of them. Both were fully dressed. The noise came from the room next to Packham's and he opened the door.

It was another single bedroom, like the one which George had just left, whitewashed, with a hand-painted print of sea-pinks on the wall. The scene was lit by a tilly lamp hung from a hook in the ceiling. Nicholas Mardle was kneeling by the bed like a child at prayer. His hands were red and sticky with blood and as he rubbed his eyes with his fist the blood smeared on his face and hair. He was screaming. On the bed Pamela Marshall lay. Her nightdress had been white starched broderie anglaise. The sheet and blanket had been pulled back from her, carefully and neatly, so that an exact triangle of white sheet had lain against the quilt. Now the nightdress and the sheet and the quilt were crimson. Blood still oozed through the cotton weave of the nightdress and because the cloth was wet, the outline of her breast showed through it. She looked at them with blank-eyed horror.

Nicholas Mardle's screams turned to sobs. He could speak for the first time.

"I didn't mean it," he said. "I didn't mean it."

"It's his knife," Mark whispered to George. "There on the floor. It's his."

Next to the boy's knees, the blade and metallic handle dulled by blood, was his knife.

It had all happened very quickly—the scream, the dash from the bedroom, the assimilation of the scene. They froze for a moment to take it in, then with Mark's words the action started again. PC Martindale pushed through the three men at the door. He must have been following quickly behind them down the corridor. He checked competently that the woman was dead. He seemed unsure, then, what to do. It was obvious that Nicholas Mardle was not dangerous. Martindale took refuge in formality. Hardly looking at Mardle, he told the boy that he need not speak, but that anything he did say would be taken down and might be used in evidence against him. Nicholas seemed not to have heard him and continued to sob.

George Palmer-Jones broke away from the group of spectators and ran down the corridor. The corridor cut the upper storey of the building in two. On one side was the Lansdowns' flat, although there was no access to it from the corridor, only from an outside fire escape and a private flight of stairs from the kitchen. On the other side were the guests' bedrooms, in a row, each with its own door leading directly from the corridor. The dormitory was right at one end, next to that the double room shared by Nick Mardle and Mark Taylor, then his own room, then Jerry Packham's, then Pamela Marshall's. So all the people with rooms to the north of Pamela Marshall's were accounted for. He opened the next door to the south. It was a bathroom and empty. The next was an empty double bedroom. Blankets were folded in piles on a metal-framed bunk bed. There was no possible place to hide. He walked on, tapped at the next door and opened it. Jasmine Carson lay on the bed. Either she was an extremely skillful actress or she was asleep. Even in sleep she looked stern. On the chair next to the bed were a glass of water and two bottles of tablets; one contained pills for the relief of arthritis, the other a branded pain killer and sedative. That's why she's

breathing so deeply, he thought. She was breathing heavily as if she were drugged. At the foot of the bed her clothes were folded carefully on top of a leather holdall. She stirred and he could see that she was wearing pyjamas, buttoned up the front like a man's. They were made of striped winceyette. George shut the door carefully behind him. He knocked at the next door, pushed it open, looked into a small dormitory, four beds close together and a chest of drawers. He did not bother to knock at the next room and pushed open the door. Paul Derbyshire was sitting on the bed, combing his hair. He was wearing a pale blue nightshirt. He had removed his false teeth and when he looked up at George his surprise and horror were made ludicrous. His smile of embarrassment was as pink and gummy as a baby's.

"George," he said. "George, my dear man, what is the matter? You look ill."

He turned away and when he faced George once more, he had replaced his teeth, but the ghost of the toothless face remained and George could not recognize him as quite the same person.

"How long have you been here?" George asked suddenly. "Have you been in here since you came upstairs?"

"Why do you want to know? Has something happened?"

"Yes, something's happened. Have you been in your room since you came upstairs?"

"No. I had a shower and washed my hair. But I didn't want to go to bed until it was dry, so I've been reading."

"Did you see anyone else?"

"No."

"Which bathroom did you use?"

"There's a shower room next door. That's why I like this room. It's most convenient."

"Thank you," George said. "Thank you." He shut the door, pretending not to hear the doctor's questions, his gabbled demands for explanations.

The shower room next to Paul Derbyshire's bedroom was the most southerly room in the corridor. George turned back. Martindale was in Pamela Marshall's room with

Nicholas Mardle. The door was open. Jerry Packham and Mark were sitting together in Mark's room. They were talking quietly together. George walked down the stairs, through to the kitchen and back up to the Lansdowns' flat. He banged on the door. Almost immediately Elizabeth answered. She was wearing a nightdress and a thick brown dressing gown with a hood, like a monk's habit.

"Where have you been?" George asked. "Have you been out?"

"No," she said. She seemed bewildered, a little angry at the interruption. "I couldn't sleep. I didn't want to disturb John, so I've been listening to the radio in the living room. Why?" she asked. "Why? What has happened?"

"Has John been in bed all that time? Are you sure?"

"Yes," she almost shouted. "I'm sure. Do you want to see him?"

But there was no need to call John. He emerged from the bedroom, naked and tousled, demanding to know what the noise was all about.

George stood on the doorstep and explained quickly and precisely that Pamela Marshall was dead, that Nicholas seemed to have confessed, that Martindale was talking to him.

"Nicholas!" Elizabeth said. "Does that mean that he killed Charlie?"

George dismissed the question as if he didn't have time to consider it properly. He looked at his watch. It was half past midnight.

"The police will be able to get over now," he said. "I expect Savage will want to see everyone. But I don't see why you shouldn't stay here until then. Try to get some sleep."

He went back to the landing. Martindale was in the corridor, with Nicholas beside him. He was shutting Pamela Marshall's door. Paul Derbyshire had joined Jerry and Mark. George presumed that Jasmine Carson was still asleep. Martindale looked at Palmer-Jones with relief and a little reproach.

"There you are, sir," he said. "I was wondering where you'd gone to. I was thinking I should telephone the superintendent. Could you keep an eye . . ."

He nodded towards Nicholas, who was standing dazed, silent except for a stifled sob. He was leaning back against the wall as if he did not have the strength to support himself.

"Of course," George said. "Do you think I could clean him up? There isn't any doubt where the blood came from."

"Yes," the policeman said gratefully. "Yes, I think you could do that."

It occurred to Palmer-Jones that the two young men were probably of the same age, that they might even have known each other socially.

"Did you know him?" he asked.

"Yes sir. Played rugby against him at school."

Martindale turned, as if he were going down the stairs to the ringing room and the telephone, then faced Palmer-Jones again.

"I haven't been able to get any sense out of him," he said. "He doesn't seem able to hear me. But perhaps I'm not very good at it. I haven't got the experience. Would you try to get through to him? Before Superintendent Savage gets here."

He spoke gently as if the boy were a patient, a victim. He was very upset. George nodded and the constable went downstairs. George took Nicholas by the arm and led him to a bathroom. He took a flannel, left behind by some forgotten visitor, from the bath, soaked it, and washed the boy's hands and face. Still he did not respond. He allowed himself to be washed, moved when George told him to, but gave no sign that he was aware of what was happening to him. He was shaking. George began talking to him calmly and firmly, trying to break through the barrier of shock and hysteria.

"This has been very upsetting," he said. "But it won't help to behave like a baby. I will help you. Now breathe deeply. Breathe now . . . And now . . . And now . . ."

The boy did as he was told. The shallow breathing, the

123

sobbing calmed. He was standing without support and the colour had returned to his face. At last George said: "Do you feel better?"

The boy nodded. "I'm sorry," he said. "It was horrible. Like a nightmare. I couldn't face it."

"Don't talk now," George said. "We'll go downstairs and find Martindale. Then I'll ask you some questions. Did you hear him explain that you don't have to say anything?"

"Yes," Nicholas said, "and that makes it worse. He thinks that I killed her. Doesn't he? You all do."

"Not now," George snapped, curbing the returning hysteria. "I don't want you to say anything now. I want the policeman to hear everything that you say."

They walked together down the corridor to the stairs. The three men in the tiny bedroom watched them through the open door. Mark seemed about to say something, to approach his friend, but George shook his head slightly, and he did nothing. When they reached the ringing room, Martindale had finished talking to Savage. He was sitting at the superintendent's desk, staring blankly in front of him. He was able to control his panic better, thought Palmer-Jones, but he was probably nearly as worried and shocked as Nicholas.

"They'll be about three-quarters of an hour," he said. "There's some problem with the Land Rover."

"Nicholas is ready to answer some questions," George said. "But if you prefer, we can wait for the superintendent."

"No," Nick said. "No. I want to talk now. I want to talk to you."

George looked at Martindale. He nodded his consent and switched on the tape-recorder. George and Nicholas were sitting on the same side of the desk. The tilly on the desk threw strange shadows over their faces. George wondered if he should go to start the generator, so that they had proper light, but Nicholas was starting to talk.

"I hated the Todds," he said. "They killed my mother. Morally they killed her. Not by stabbing her with a knife, but by exploiting her, then deserting her when she needed

124

them.'' He spoke the melodramatic words as if they were familiar, as if he had repeated them often to himself. ''They exploited her all her working life, then when she wasn't any use to them, they got rid of her. I've dreamed about killing them. When it's quiet at work I plan ways of murdering them, and if I can't sleep at night I lie awake and think about it. It became a sort of game, planning how to kill them without getting caught. I never did anything about it. I suppose that I never really meant to do it. It was just something to stop me having to think about my mother's death. I made all sorts of threats about it, but I never meant to do it. I'd even stopped thinking about it quite so often. Then Charlie threatened to sell the island, and it brought everything back. It was as if it was happening all over again. He'd bought the place, exploited it, made us dependent on him, then because he got fed up with it, he just decided to get rid of it. It never occurred to him to consider anyone else, to wonder what we might feel.''

He had run out of indignation, and sat quietly.

''Nicholas,'' said George Palmer-Jones, ''did you kill Charlie?''

''No,'' he said. ''No. I'm trying to explain. I dreamed about it. I thought about it. But I didn't kill him. That's why I was so shocked to see his body. To see him actually dead. It was as if I had killed him just by thinking about it. But when I saw him dead, I realized how terrible it was. I was sorry, really sorry. And guilty that I could ever have wanted it in the first place. Do you understand?''

''I think so,'' George said.

''That's why I went to see Pamela. I wanted to tell her that I was sorry that Charlie was dead. I'd threatened her family. I wanted to tell her that I hadn't meant it, that I didn't really want anything to happen to them.''

''And what did she say?''

''She didn't say anything, you fool.'' He was screaming. ''She was already dead. Someone had killed her with my knife. It was like a nightmare. I went in. The tilly was lit over her bed and I saw straight away, but I couldn't believe it. I tried to wake her. I did try. I took the knife

out. I suppose it was an instinctive reaction. But it just made more blood. I didn't know what to do. I had wanted to tell her that I was sorry, and she was dead.''

George Palmer-Jones spoke very calmly and quietly: "If what you say is true, she must have been dead for a very short time when you found her. Did you see anyone?"

"It was dark." Nicholas Mardle's voice was still high-pitched. "I left the candle with Mark. I didn't see anyone in the corridor, but someone could have been there. I wouldn't have been able to tell. If her room had been dark I wouldn't have gone in, but I could see the light. The door wasn't properly shut."

"Did you knock?"

"Yes, but only quietly. I didn't want anyone else to know that I was there. Then I just looked in."

He took a deep breath.

"Did Mark know where you were going?"

"No. He wasn't there. He'd gone to the bathroom."

"Did you start screaming as soon as you'd got there?"

"I don't know." He was crying, quietly. "I don't know."

"When did you last have your knife?"

"I had it last night when I was ringing. Sometimes, if a bird gets very tangled, you have to cut it out of the net. I expect I left it in the ringing room. I don't remember having it today."

Palmer-Jones looked at Martindale, inviting him to put a question. The young policeman spoke awkwardly.

"Why did you touch the knife?" he asked. "It must have been obvious that she was dead."

Mardle's eyes flickered towards him before he answered. "You don't understand," he said. "I wasn't acting logically. I wasn't thinking rationally. It was so horrible there. The knife had hurt her. It just seemed that if I took it out it might make her better. It seems insane now, but perhaps I was insane."

"When we found you, you said that you didn't mean to do it. Why did you say that if you didn't kill her?"

"No." Nick was shouting again. "I didn't say that. I

said I didn't mean it. I didn't mean the threats. I hadn't meant that I wanted them all to die."

They sat in silence. In the distance there was the faint rumble of the Land Rover. It approached like thunder. Then there was the flash of torch light and Savage arrived in the room. Outside they could hear the sound of heavy boots on the stairs.

"Can we get any proper light in here?" Savage asked cheerfully as soon as he entered. "They'll need it upstairs."

"I'll go and put the generator on," Palmer-Jones said, relieved to have an excuse to leave. Savage was looking at Nicholas with an air of triumph and success. If George stayed he would feel tempted to interfere.

When he returned Martindale and Nick were alone again in the ringing room. Savage had gone to Pamela Marshall's room.

Martindale was talking quietly to Nick: "You understand what the superintendent said, don't you? He wants to take you to the police station to talk to you."

"I understand," Nick said. "I'll be helping the police with their inquiries. Is he going to charge me?"

"You'll have to talk to the superintendent about that," the young policeman said.

Savage came in then, rubbing his hands, full of energy, as if he were at the start of a working day. George thought that he must have shaved before coming to the island. He looked very clean, very healthy. George suddenly felt tired and grey.

"Could I have a word with you, Superintendent," he asked, "before you speak to Mr. Mardle?"

They went into the common room. The embers of the fire were still glowing. Savage poked them restlessly while George was talking.

"Pamela Marshall came to see me," he said. "She thought she had some information about Charlie's death. She admitted that she'd been to see Charlie last night, though she wouldn't say why."

"Oh. What was the information?" He was listening as intently as ever, but only out of courtesy. It really wasn't

127

relevant now. He wanted to get the boy at the station, the formalities over with.

"I don't know. I didn't get the opportunity to speak to her again alone. I was waiting until the morning to see her."

"Too late then," the policeman said, obviously and callously.

"The boy won't admit to it."

For the first time Savage took a serious interest. "I thought he already had."

"No. Not exactly."

"The murder weapon was his knife."

"Yes."

"Well then." Savage looked cheerful. He didn't like things to be too easy. It was a challenge. He had enough evidence to charge the boy. They could be in court on Monday and he could get a week's remand to the police cells for further investigation. He'd get his confession in that time. "I'll be on my way back to the mainland."

"Don't you want to talk to anyone else?" George was starting to become frustrated by the policeman's blinkered interpretation of the case.

"No," Savage said. "That'll do in the morning. We can take statements then."

Palmer-Jones's surprise registered with Savage. "You won't know," he said, "but the boy threatened to do away with the whole bloody family. We've got witnesses. I would have had him in anyway. This . . ." He nodded his head towards the stairs. "This is just the icing on the cake."

Palmer-Jones was no longer useful to him. He dismissed the older man from his thoughts as he had dismissed all the other suspects. George followed him through to the ringing room.

"Come on then, lad," the policeman said to Nick. "Let's get you back to dry land." He left the room and waited just outside the door.

The boy stood up to follow. He did not argue. He was still very pale, but quite calm.

George went to the desk, took the cassette from the tape-recorder and gave it to Martindale, who nodded.

"I'll give it to the superintendent," he said.

Nick spoke to George. "I didn't do it. I don't know if I can make them believe me."

"Don't worry," George said. "Don't worry." Then he realized how ridiculous that was. But it seemed to comfort Nick. He walked out, between the two policemen, to the Land Rover.

10

After Savage had gone George Palmer-
Jones went back to his room. He still did not feel ready to
sleep. There were muffled sounds in the corridor, voices.
Eventually everything went quiet. Presumably the policemen had finished. He undressed and got into bed, but still
he did not sleep. Previously his commitment to the investigation had been limited. His involvement had been selfish.
It had been a personal challenge. He had wanted to find
out who had killed Charlie Todd, but there had been no
urgency. It was not really his responsibility. It had not
mattered because the police would succeed even if he
failed. Now it mattered a great deal. He did not believe
that Nicholas Mardle had killed Charlie Todd, and he was
quite certain that the boy had not killed Pamela Marshall.
In many ways Savage was a good policeman. He was
determined, energetic and honest. But he had too much
faith in his own judgement. He believed that Nicholas
Mardle was a murderer. Unless he was faced with an
obvious, a very obvious fact which contradicted the theory, he would interpret all the evidence to strengthen his
belief. Now George Palmer-Jones *did* feel responsible.

Savage was stubborn. George had no faith that he would be able to persuade the policeman that Nick might be innocent. So he had to find a fact, a very obvious fact, with which to confront him. Or the murderer.

The next day was horrible, muddled. Savage did not appear. Connibear arrived very early, before the tide, took desultory statements. At breakfast John and Elizabeth bickered spitefully and incessantly. Jasmine Carson was furious that she had not been wakened in the night.

"I should have been told," she stormed. "I am one of the original trustees. I should have been consulted."

"So you should, my dear lady. So you should." The doctor's easy agreement only increased her anger. He seemed to be taking a delight in her discomfort. "But really," he continued, "this isn't the time to cause a fuss, now is it?"

He tried to talk to everyone. Later, when George Palmer-Jones looked back on that day he remembered everything against a background of the doctor's words, meaningless and intrusive. And he remembered the sharp, spiky rain, painful as sleet, which clattered against the windows and jangled the nerves.

No one was willing to listen to Paul Derbyshire. Jerry Packham, usually invariably gentle and polite, had been horrified into rudeness. Although he sat next to the doctor at breakfast he ignored the older man. He might have been sitting there alone. Jasmine Carson, after the first outburst, expressed her disapproval, her feeling of having been left out, in silence. Mark's soft and funny face was expressionless. There was no movement in it. He too seemed very frightened and lonely.

George did not have much time to talk to the other residents. They were planning to leave immediately after lunch and the police had agreed to this arrangement. After breakfast he looked for Jerry and found him in his bedroom, packing.

"I want to talk to you," George said. "Get your coat. We'll go to the seawatching hide."

"No," Jerry said. "Not there."

131

"Yes, there. It's one of the only places on this damned island where we can be sure of not being overheard."

They went out into the rain. It was icy and seemed to pierce the skin. They bent forward to shield their faces from the rain and because the rocks were slippery and they needed to watch where they were walking. They did not speak. In the hide they set up their telescopes, but they did not use them. Jerry looked over the sea occasionally with his binoculars, but George Palmer-Jones made no pretence at birdwatching. He talked.

"I know that you had an argument with Pamela. I know that she wanted to see Charlie. I need to know what it was all about. She told me that she'd been to see him on the night of the fire."

"Did she?" He seemed hardly to have heard. "I still can't believe that she's dead. I saw her there last night, but I still can't believe it. It was different with Charlie. He was always so strange and eccentric, it seemed almost natural that he should die in that melodramatic way. But she was quite ordinary. She seemed self-confident and self-possessed, but underneath she was rather unhappy. When Charlie died I could think: At least it wasn't a complete waste. At least the island's safe. I suppose that it was wrong to think like that, but I kept imagining the observatory turned into a luxury hotel, yachts moored out here by the hide. It could have happened so easily. Then Charlie was killed and it was horrible, but there was a relief too. Because we'd still be able to come here. But with Pam it was a complete waste. She had two children, you know . . . ."

Palmer-Jones felt that he had let Jerry ramble for long enough.

"What was the argument about?"

"We had been ringing on the Friday, the Friday before Charlie went away for the week. It was early in the morning, just as it was getting light. We'd walked over very early, some time before the tide. We were sheltering in the cove, just below the Wendy House. I had my arm round Pam. We must have looked very . . . intimate. Then

Charlie appeared. He had come down the steps and was on his way over to the mainland. We were surprised. He didn't usually walk. I suppose he didn't want to disturb John so early in the morning. He said: "My, my, what a naughty girl you are, Pamela. What would my big brother say?" in that joking, high-pitched voice of his. Then he walked over the shore. Pamela was worried that he really would tell her family."

"Do you know where he was going?"

"I assume that he was going to see Ernest or Laurence. Because of what he'd said about his big brother. That was the impression I got."

"I still don't understand what the argument was about."

"Pamela wanted me to go to see Charlie to ask if he had talked to the family about seeing us together. It was the sort of thing he might have done. He would have thought that it was amusing. He came back to the island on that Friday evening, and she went to see him then, but he only teased her. He said that he'd had a very important conversation with her uncles. 'What an immoral bunch the Todds are, to be sure.' That's what he said to her, but she didn't know what to make of it. She was always concerned about what the family thought of us." His voice was resigned. "They pass a lot of work on to her husband, who's a solicitor. And they were always reasonably generous when she needed money."

"Did she need a lot of money?"

"Yes," he said. "It seemed to me that she needed a lot of money. I suppose that was why she would never leave her husband for me. I didn't have a secure enough income."

He spoke without bitterness.

"But you refused to go to see Charlie?"

"I didn't think that it would do any good. He had probably forgotten all about it. Talking to him would only remind him."

"Do you know what happened when she did go to the Wendy House after you'd argued on the night of the fire?"

"It was as I'd thought. He'd forgotten all about it. He

was so excited by the canal idea that he hardly knew what she was talking about.''

"Did she mention seeing or hearing anyone while she was out?''

"No.''

"Did she say if Charlie had given her anything to drink?''

Jerry thought. "She didn't say, but Charlie would have offered her something. He was very hospitable.''

"Did you hear anything last night? You were sleeping next door to Pamela. You must have heard something.''

"I know,'' Jerry said. "I've been trying to think. I'd drunk quite a lot of Prof's whisky. It was a pretty awful evening. It was the only way I could get through it. I didn't hear voices. I'm sure that I would have remembered if there had been voices. I heard her moving about. And I heard her light the tilly. You know, the sound of it being pumped to prime it.''

"But wouldn't it have been lit already?''

"I suppose so. Perhaps she put it out, then decided she couldn't sleep, so she put it on again to read.''

"Perhaps. When did you hear the sound of the tilly?''

"I don't know. Perhaps a quarter of an hour before Nick screamed, perhaps a bit longer. As I say I was a bit drunk.''

"You didn't seem drunk. You got to her room pretty quickly.''

"A sight like that would sober anyone.''

George left Jerry in the seawatching hide and walked back to the observatory. There was a pile of bags and suitcases in the entrance hall. The residents were obviously eager to leave. He felt ambiguous about going. The island was not a pleasant place to be now, but if he were to go he would lose all touch with the investigation. He saw Mark Taylor in the common room and was about to talk to him when Jasmine Carson came down the stairs. She was carrying her leather holdall. The joints of her fingers were swollen and distorted. George reached out to take the bag from her. As he took it, he wondered if there were strength

enough in those hands to pull the nylon rope which had strangled Charlie, if they had the power to stab a woman. But what motive could she have? She would not be squeamish about murder, but she was a scientist. She would need to be sure that such a risk was worth taking. She cared passionately about the island. Perhaps she was unreasonably attached to it. But she knew Charlie. His enthusiasms came and went like the tide. It was only through Paul Derbyshire's persistence that Charlie's dream of buying the island had become a reality. George was not convinced that, even if Charlie had lived, the island would ever have been sold, and he credited Jasmine Carson with the sense to realize that too.

She thanked him, ungraciously, for carrying her case, and they stood together by the pile of luggage.

"This is a bad business," she said. "Nicholas could be an aggressive young man, but he was always completely honest. And a very good worker. It's all very upsetting. I know that you have faith in the police, but I suppose that there is no possibility that there could be a mistake?"

She could have been in the staff room, discussing some policy decision by the board of governors.

He hesitated, then unconsciously adopted the same tone. "I think," he said, "that there may have been an error of judgement."

"I see," she said. "In a way I'm disappointed. I had hoped that perhaps the whole matter was over, but of course that's not the right attitude at all. We must get it right. Even if the police can't manage to. My offer of help still stands, then." She turned stiffly and walked slowly back up the stairs.

He went into the common room. Mark Tyler was sitting by the fire, absorbed in his own unhappiness. He still had an adolescent's lack of defences. His clowning was natural, not a barrier against pain. Palmer-Jones sat beside him.

"Where were you last night when Nick started screaming?" he asked.

"In the bathroom."

"That's not true, you know. It can't be. You told Nick that you'd gone to the bathroom, but you came along the corridor behind me when we heard the screams, as if you'd just come out of your bedroom, or from the stairs. The bathroom is further down the corridor, past Pamela's bedroom. So where were you?"

Mark stood up. There was no colour in his face. "That has nothing to do with you," he said. "It has nothing to do with you, or with the fact that two people have died, or with the fact that my best friend is a murderer."

He walked away. George Palmer-Jones followed slowly into the lobby, but by then the boy was outside. As he watched Mark go, a Land Rover pulled through the gates and stopped in the yard. Savage got out. He lowered his head against the rain and strode towards the building. He pushed open the door, and George felt the cold wind and the rain, then the door swung back and the two men were together. Savage just stood, looked intently at Palmer-Jones.

"How's the boy?" George asked.

"He's not a juvenile, you know," Savage said, not unkindly. Then: "He's all right. I let him sleep last night, gave him a chance to think. We had a chat this morning, before he went to court." He looked at George sharply. "You're right. He'll not admit it. But I reckon that we've got enough for a conviction. They remanded him in custody to the police cells."

"Did you listen to the tape of our conversation last night?"

"Yes."

"What do you think?"

"I think that he's clever. And frightened. And I think he's got you fooled."

"So you still think he did it?"

"Of course he did."

The policeman laughed, not because he wanted to hurt the old man's feelings but to make light of the differences between them. He could not reject Palmer-Jones completely just because of his silly ideas. He opened the door of the ringing room.

"Come on in. I've got the first forensic report, and I can fill you in on what we found last night. Come on. I've no hard feelings."

George restrained his anger at this patronage, and followed the policeman into the ringing room. Savage sat at the desk, Palmer-Jones opposite.

"Did you get a good look at the body last night? Did you notice anything unusual?"

"No, I didn't look. I left all that to your officer."

Why did he not explain that he had rushed away to check the whereabouts of all the other residents?

"Martindale didn't notice either. Can't blame him, I suppose. He's a young bloke. Inexperienced." His tone implied that nevertheless he did blame Martindale. "The scene-of-crime chaps noticed though. Chloroform. There was a faint smell of it around the face. And a cloth that had been soaked with the stuff on the floor, by the bed." He pointed to the pile of bird bags on the bench. "One of those things."

"So that's why she didn't cry out."

"Yes. She may even have been asleep when he went in. If she woke at all, it would only have been for a second."

"No," George said, "she couldn't have been asleep, because she relit the tilly." He explained that Jerry Packham had heard the sound of the tilly being pumped. "Unless," he continued almost to himself, "it wasn't Pamela who lit the tilly. But if it was the murderer, why bother? A torch would have done just as well. And we all have torches."

He turned to Savage. "Did Nicholas have a torch with him?"

"Yes. A small one in his jeans pocket." He was not really interested, but waited patiently while George thought, tried to work out the solution to the puzzle. He found none and shook his head.

"Did you find the jar? That held the chloroform?"

"No. That side of the building is right by the water. I reckon he threw it out of the window and into the tide. We'll find it washed up in a couple of days. There were no fingerprints on the window frame or the catch, but if the

window was already open, he wouldn't have needed to touch it."

George did not pursue the matter.

"Would you mind telling me what is in the preliminary forensic report?"

"They've identified some fibres found on the bench seat of the seawatching hide and on Charles Todd's clothing. It's a navy-blue material, a rough felt. It came, they say, from a duffel coat or a donkey jacket."

"Yes," George said. "Yes. It would be."

"You know where it came from?"

"Oh yes. There's a duffel coat out there in the hall. It doesn't belong to anyone. It must have been left behind and it's used as a spare. The murderer was bound to use it, because it wouldn't identify him. It's very big and shapeless—from the back it would be hard to tell who was wearing it. It would act as a disguise."

He hesitated, remembering the tapes he had heard the night before, the conversation between Savage and Nicholas Mardle about the arson at the Wendy House.

"Didn't Nick mention to you that he noticed that the duffel coat was wet, when he came back after ringing waders on the night of the fire at Charlie's house?"

"Yes," Savage said, impressed by George's memory and by Nick's apparent duplicity. "He's not daft, is he? He must have set fire to the house when he pretended to come back here. He probably wore the coat then, too. The timing would be right. He knew that we'd find traces of the coat in the hide, so he mentioned it first. He's too clever by half."

George ignored him. He was writing in his field notebook. When he finished he looked up. "Any fingerprints in the hide?"

Savage shook his head. He had given enough information. Now he needed George's help. He had not invited Palmer-Jones to join him simply to spare his feelings.

"Would there have been chloroform on the premises?" he asked. "And if so, where would it have been kept?"

"There may have been," George replied. "The obser-

138

vatory is used regularly by local schools in term time as a field centre. They use this room as a lab. I suppose it could have been used by the biologists in their experiments. But John would know."

"Of course. I'll have to ask him. Is this room never locked?" It was an accusation of carelessness.

"No," George said. "There's never before been any need to lock it."

"I'll go and speak to Mr. Lansdown, then. I expect he'll be in his flat. Do you want to come?" But the generosity was too obvious, and George answered sharply.

"No. No thank you. I've done enough talking for today. I'll go outside, I think. Get some fresh air before lunch."

As he went out he noticed that the duffel coat was no longer on its peg. The police, he supposed, had removed it. Without it, the hall seemed unusually bare, like a room when the curtains have been taken down to be washed.

While he was on the Beacon George decided that he would not leave the island with the others. He would have to stay and see the case through to the end. He would not let time, or Savage with his boyish enthusiasm and his platitudes, defeat him. He had not bothered to change his shoes, and the soggy bracken drenched his trousers, but he did not mind the discomfort. Now that the decision was made he was happier. He would telephone Molly, ask her to join him. It began to rain again and he walked back to the observatory, where the others were gathering in the dining room for lunch.

There was a cold meal already laid on the table, and they were taking their seats when Elizabeth noticed that Miss Carson was not there.

"She was upstairs, I think," she said. "I'll just go and call her."

"I'll go," George said. He was still standing. He went up the stairs and walked along the corridor. Jasmine was not in her room. He felt suddenly anxious and walked quietly on. All the doors were open, and it was with relief that he noticed that she was in the room that had been issued by Paul Derbyshire. She had her back to him, and

139

did not realize that he was there. She was bending over the waste-paper bin. She stood up suddenly.

He moved quickly out of her line of vision, walked back to the stairs, then called: "Miss Carson, lunch is ready."

He went back to the dining room and waited for her to follow. She came in soon after. She gave no explanation for what she had been doing. He presumed that she had not seen him. She took her seat and joined in the general conversation. He did not speak to her about it.

They were all so preoccupied at lunch with their preparations to leave that when George said, diffidently, that he thought he might stay for a few days, no one showed much interest. John said that it would be useful to have somebody else around to help with the ringing. George followed them out to the Land Rover to see them off. They hovered there, not sure what to say to each other. They so much wanted to leave, and now they seemed almost frightened to go. They seemed to envy George. Even after two murders, Gillibry seemed a place of security compared with the unknown of the mainland. They went in the end. George walked up to the Beacon to wave them off. He almost felt sorry for them.

11

George had arranged to meet Molly on the mainland, in the afternoon. She had been pleased to be invited to join him. He decided, though, to go out in the morning, before the tide. There was little that he could learn now on the island. He needed to know where Charlie Todd went on the Friday before he left to look at the canal project. George's impression of Charles Todd had been of a physically lazy man who exerted himself as little as possible. Yet on that day he had been up early, he had seen Jerry Packham and Pamela Marshall together on the shore, he had walked to the mainland, and he had walked back in time to see Pamela that evening, and to tell her that the Todds were an "immoral lot." George felt handicapped by his ignorance of Charlie's family and the business dealings of Todd Leisure Enterprises. He was sure that for some reason Charles had been to see his brothers that day. And he was sure that the visit was relevant to the inquiry.

It was a beautiful morning, calm and clear. Soon, on mornings like this, there would be a frost. As he walked down the tracks near to the Wendy House he met John.

The younger man's hands were filled with the ties of moving bird bags and they were strung round his neck. He was on his way back from the traps to ring the birds he had caught.

"The island's crawling with birds," he said. He was excited. "It's going to be a really good day. I can't ever remember it being as good as this. Isn't it lucky that you're here? I'd never be able to get through them all on my own. I was just coming to wake you."

George was tempted, for a moment, to stay. He could follow the tide out later to meet Molly. But he shook his head.

"I'm sorry," he said. "I'm on my way to the mainland. I want to meet Charlie's brothers. I don't want to leave it until tomorrow. I can't get any further without talking to them."

"But why? The police aren't bothering us any more. I'm sorry about Nick, but it must have been him, mustn't it? Or they wouldn't have arrested him. Why can't you leave it alone? You don't know what you'll stir up with all your questions."

It seemed to George that John was over-reacting.

"No, I don't know what I'll stir up. That's why I must go, you see. I *am* sorry that I can't help with the ringing."

But John had walked away, sulky because his day had been spoilt, a fantastic figure clothed in the squirming bird bags. Thoughtfully George continued down the track. He waded across the gully and on to the sand. After the rain all the colours seemed very bright and the detail on the mainland was very sharp. It was good, after all, to be away from the island.

He drove into Gillicombe and parked his car on the sea front. It was just nine o'clock. Jasmine Carson saw him through her kitchen window, and thought for a while that he was coming to visit her. She was disappointed, and suddenly lonely, when he walked past the flats towards the High Street. What was he doing in Gillicombe anyway? she thought. There was a light wind, it had been a clear night, so it should be a perfect ringing day. He should be

on Gillibry, helping John. Yet, despite her disappointment and her censure she watched him with affection. Just by being there he had brought the island closer to her.

Before climbing the hill into the town, George hesitated. He had planned to visit Todd Leisure Enterprises first, to talk to Charles Todd's brothers, but he turned now towards the police station. He had been devising a theory which might explain Charlie's visit to the mainland on that Friday and the comment that the Todds were an immoral lot. Savage might help him to confirm it. He walked through the glass doors, gave his name to the duty sergeant and asked to speak to Savage. He sat on an orange plastic chair and waited. He waited for ten minutes, then Connibear appeared. The policeman looked slightly embarrassed, but he spoke easily enough. His skill at deception would, George thought, improve with experience.

"I'm so sorry, sir," he said. "Superintendent Savage has asked me to see you. He's tied up all morning. Some administrative meeting, I believe. Can I help you? Do you want to see Nicholas Mardle?"

Do I? George thought. No. He has told me all he can. It would only be a distraction. He felt no anger at Savage's refusal to see him. How pathetic he must seem to the superintendent, an interfering old buffer who could not accept that he might be wrong.

"I'd be grateful for half an hour of your time," he said. Connibear sensed no irony in Palmer-Jones's apparent humility. "Of course, sir. I'd be glad to help in any way. Superintendent Savage has told me all about you. But look, this isn't a very comfortable place to talk. I generally go out for a coffee in the morning. There's a little place round the corner. It's better than the canteen. It'll be quiet now. We can talk there."

So, George thought, Savage has told him to get me off the premises. But he smiled and said that he would be glad of a coffee after his walk from the island.

The café was run by Italians, who served them then took no notice of them. A trickle of workmen came in for bacon

sandwiches to take away, but no one else sat at the stained tables. The coffee was hot and very strong.

"I wanted to talk to you about the Todds," George said. He had dropped his pose of subservience. "The business. Todd Leisure Enterprises. You've never had any dealings with them?"

"Professionally sir? No, I don't think so. Ernie Todd was done for drunk driving a couple of years ago, but I can't recollect anything since."

"As far as you're concerned it's a legitimate business? You've heard no rumours of any tax fiddle, VAT fraud, anything which Charles might have used to blackmail the family?"

"I wouldn't put it past them, but I don't know how Charlie would have got to hear about it."

"Charles seems to have had a nose for a secret."

"So he does, sir. Would you like me to make a few discreet inquiries?"

"Would you mind?" George was a little surprised at the offer of help.

"Well sir, Superintendent Savage said that I was to help you in any way I could. I can see what you're getting at. It would be very interesting wouldn't it, if there was anything of that sort?"

Connibear was tactful. He was very careful not to hurry away. It was George Palmer-Jones who looked at his watch and said that he must go. He was satisfied with the interview and walked quickly up the hill to the High Street. He found the Todd's office very easily. The sportswear shop over which it was situated was smart, the clothes were expensive. There was a separate entrance to the office beside the shop. Inside the stairs were carpeted. At the top of the stairs a secretary sat behind a modern desk. She seemed to be good at the job. As soon as he pushed open the door she smiled at him and said "Good morning." She was blond. Her hair was short and well cut in a fashionable sort of way. She sat upright behind her typewriter. There was no bottle of typex in a prominent position on the desk. She had an air of competence and

144

good humour, and she seemed to be very young to have such self-confidence and efficiency.

"Good morning," he said. "I'd like to speak to Mr. Todd."

"Yes sir," she said. "Mr. Ernest Todd or Mr. Laurence Todd?"

"I'd like a word with them both if I could."

"I'm afraid Mr. Ernest Todd isn't in yet. I'll ask Mr. Laurence if he can see you. Could you give me your name and some idea what it's about?"

"Yes," he said. "My name's Palmer-Jones. I'm representing Gillibry Observatory Trust. As perhaps you are aware we were major beneficiaries in Charles Todd's estate. There were some technical matters I needed to discuss."

"Of course," she said. "I'll just see if Mr. Todd's free."

She took him for a solicitor or an accountant. She was about to go into one of the offices. He called her back.

"Before I see Mr. Todd, perhaps you could help me. I'm trying to trace Charles Todd's movements in the few weeks before he died. Did he come here at all during those weeks?"

"No," she said, without hesitation. "He very rarely came to the office. I would have remembered if he had."

She knocked on a heavy wooden office door and went in, shutting the door behind her. When she had asked for George's name, she had written it in a big desk diary. Very quickly he turned the pages of the diary to 7 September, the Friday before Charlie had gone north to look at the canal boats. At the head of the page was written C. Todd. Underneath, she had written a large question mark. When the girl returned, the diary was back in its right place on the desk.

"Mr. Todd doesn't think that he'll be able to help you," she said doubtfully, "but he says that he'll see you."

"Thank you. And you are quite sure that Charles Todd had no meeting with his brothers in recent weeks?"

"Quite sure," she said firmly.

The writing in the diary had been in her hand. She had been told to lie. He wondered who else had been to see the Todds on that Friday.

Laurence Todd was obviously nervous. He was not used to dealing with strangers. He was not sure what to do.

"I really don't think that I can help you," he said immediately. "Perhaps we had better wait for my brother, Ernest."

He had risen from his seat as George entered, and remained now awkwardly leaning against the desk. He did not offer a seat to Palmer-Jones, who stood just inside the door, more at home in the room than its owner. George said nothing and Laurence continued, stammering slightly and rushing his words.

"You see, our solicitor deals with all the legal details."

"I understood that William Marshall was your solicitor. I hardly liked to disturb him at a time like this." In contrast to Laurence, George's words were incisive, reproving.

"No, of course, I see." Laurence was apologizing. He blushed. "But Ernest consulted with Mr. Marshall. I'm expecting him at any time. If you don't mind waiting I'm sure that he'll talk to you as soon as he comes in. I'll ask Marie to make you some coffee."

But George seemed not to hear. He pulled up a straight-backed chair and sat on it. He smiled reassuringly at Laurence, who sank into the lower chair behind his desk. Anxiously Laurence blinked at him.

"I'm glad of the opportunity to speak to you, while we wait," George said. "I wanted to tell you how grateful I was, how grateful all the observatory members were, to Charles for his generosity. We would never have been able to establish the observatory without his help."

Laurence seemed confused. He muttered incomprehensibly. Finally: "Thank you," he blurted. "Thank you very much. I'll tell Ernest."

"We will miss Charles so much," George continued. He was beginning to feel sorry for the little man floundering behind the big desk, but he had only a limited time and

Ernest might not be so easy to intimidate. "Unfortunately I didn't get to the island in time to see him this weekend, but I was in Gillicombe last week, on the Friday, and I saw him then. Perhaps he had come to see you?"

"No!" There was no stammering or hesitation now. He blinked, took out a handkerchief, wiped a damp nose. "No," he repeated. "He didn't come here. He didn't like us very much."

George lied convincingly. "I'm sorry," he said. "I must have been mistaken. I got the impression that he'd been here."

"You saw him? That Friday?"

George ignored the direct question. "Charles and I were always such good friends," he said. "I felt that we always understood each other so well. So when I last met him, I could tell that something was worrying him. That was one of the reasons that decided me to come to see you."

"Why? Why should you want to see me?"

"Not you personally." George spoke smoothly, kindly, in response to the little man's rising panic. "I wanted to speak to someone in the family, in the business."

"Why? Why?"

"Because I gained the impression, the very clear impression I must say, that he was concerned about some aspect of the family business."

The small, dapper man crumpled behind his desk. George leant back in his chair and waited. He knew that he must be right. Charlie had been in to see the Todds on that Friday and it was clear that the visit had frightened them. He noticed, as he waited, that Laurence's feet were very small, like a girl's, and that the shoes were highly polished. He waited because he was quite sure that Laurence would tell him what he wanted to know. He might make excuses, might even lie, but George thought that he would learn enough to guess at the information Charlie had used to blackmail his family. Laurence seemed to be having problems in finding the right words, so George leaned forward and made prompting, sympathetic noises. Laurence's stammering was reaching the climax of speech,

147

when the door was thrown open and Ernest strode into the room. Laurence seemed uncertain whether to be scared or relieved. Ernest, however, did not notice the drama of the situation, failed to recognize any tension in the room. George composed himself quickly and stood to meet the other man. The brothers were as different as Laurel and Hardy. Ernest was large and blowzy, expensively but a little untidily dressed. He was wheezing after the exertion of climbing the stairs, but he tried for a hearty friendliness. George held out his hand in response. Ernest's was flaccid, hot and slightly sweaty.

George made some conventional statements of condolence. Laurence had given all responsibility for the interview to his brother. He sat and warily watched the two standing men.

"It's good of you to come," Ernest said. "We want to keep in touch with the island, don't we Laurence? As Charlie was so fond of the place. Besides, we never know when we might be able to help each other, do we?"

George looked up sharply. So Ernest had designs on Gillibry. He hoped that Charlie's will had been properly drawn up. He had given up all hope of gaining the information he had been about to receive from Laurence, and began to make excuses to leave, but Ernest would hear nothing of it. He shouted out for coffee, pushed George's chair into a corner and dragged in a more comfortable one from his own office. It took George a little time to realize what Ernest wanted, but it became evident before the coffee arrived. He wanted information and a promise of discretion.

"I heard on the local radio news that Nicholas Mardle has been arrested," he said. He made no attempt to disguise his interest. "Do you know what's likely to happen now? I suppose that the police have closed their investigation."

"I suppose that they have."

"And then poor Pamela. She was my niece of course. Terrible business."

"Yes," George said seriously. "It was quite terrible."

"I suppose that there's nothing that we can do to limit the publicity? For the sake of her children, you know . . . And my father. He's a very old man."

"I'm afraid not," George said. "Nicholas is not a juvenile you see, so the case must be held in open court. Of course if he pleads guilty it will all be over quickly."

"Do you think that he'll plead guilty?"

"No, I don't."

"Oh well, I suppose that the business will survive it." He hesitated, then said: "There's no question that the boy did commit the murders, I suppose? It's not some trick of the police to give the real culprit a false sense of security?"

Ernest spoke in the same tone of detached interest. George could not tell how important the answer would be to him. He spoke lightly.

"I think you've been reading too many novels, Mr. Todd. The police aren't allowed to arrest innocent men, not knowingly."

"Ah well, you never know." He was pleased all the same by the answer. He made polite excuses to leave.

Laurence suddenly came to life. He muttered that he, too, must go out. He had to go through the account at the shop. Without Mardle there had been serious discrepancies. Suddenly George found himself alone with the secretary in the outer office. She smiled at him, but seemed bemused by her employers' disappearance.

"Oh dear," George said. "There was one more question I had to ask Mr. Todd. Perhaps you could help me?"

"Of course sir, I'd be glad to help." She seemed more relaxed, more inclined to chat with both her employers away from the office, and continued: "I went to the island once, on a field trip. Do you know Miss Carson?"

"Jasmine Carson?" George said. "Yes. She's a member of the observatory."

"She was my biology teacher. I still bump into her sometimes. She likes to keep in touch with her old girls. But how can I help you?"

"I believe that you had a visitor a week ago last Friday. Friday the seventh."

"I explained that Mr. Charles Todd hadn't visited us for some months."

"So you did. But I'm not talking about Charlie. Did anyone else come into the office that day?"

She was about to question his right to ask, but the habit of politeness was too strong.

"Yes, someone did call in, but I'm afraid I don't know who it was. She refused to give her name. She saw Mr. Ernest."

"Could you describe her?"

The secretary had obviously been offended by the strange caller. "She was in her late twenties, I suppose. She might have been a bit older. Tall and thin, with long, dark, curly hair. A bit scruffy."

Elizabeth, George thought. Why should Elizabeth want to speak to Ernest?

George went down the stairs without speaking. The secretary watched him go, then composed herself behind her desk, crossed her legs at the ankles and returned to her typing. Just as he was reaching the bottom of the stairs, the door which led out into the street opened. Mark Taylor peered at George through a wild and unmanageable fringe.

"Hello," he said. "I didn't expect you to be here. You're staying on at the obs, aren't you?" He was friendly. There was no indication of his previous anger.

"Yes, I decided to stay on for a few days. Molly, my wife, is joining me."

The boy did not seem disconcerted to see George. He stood at the bottom of the stairs, making no move to go up to the office.

"What are you doing here?" George asked.

"I live in Gillicombe. I don't go back to college until the end of the month."

"Here. In the Todds' office."

"Oh, I've come to see Charlie's brother, Laurence. His son, Jonathan, is one of my mates. I'd lent him a load of records and I wanted to ask when I could go to the house to collect them."

"Couldn't you ask Jonathan?"

"No. He's at college in London, and he went back suddenly without telling me that he was going. His mum says it's to do some work, but I know that he gets fed up very quickly at home. I expect that he had to escape."

"Laurence Todd has just gone out. Didn't you see him?"

"No."

Mark looked at his watch. "The pubs are open," he said. "Come on. I know all about civil servants' index-linked pensions. You can buy me a drink."

Mark took him to a tiny, decaying pub in a road behind the High Street. The bar was like the parlour of a small terraced house. There were family pictures on the walls, and two fireside chairs with threadbare upholstery and crocheted runners faced an unlit electric fire. Only the high stools in the corner turned it into a public house. The landlady, who sat behind the bar drinking stout, was small too. She had a cockney accent and bright, acquisitive eyes. She acknowledged Mark as a friend. George Palmer-Jones felt a sense of unreality. All the protagonists were linked by more than their membership of the Observatory Trust. There was a web of relationships, and he felt he was in danger of being trapped in it. He was afraid of being stuck with the tangle of small emotions and of losing the true perspective of the case. But how could he tell what was the true perspective if he did not explore the relationships? He settled, with his drink, in one of the chairs.

"Did you know that Jonathan benefited from Charlie's will?"

"Did he?" Mark was hardly interested. "He'll be pleased. He's got a very expensive taste in girlfriends."

"What's he like?"

"Oh, very respectable. A chip off the old block. Ambitious in his own quiet way. But independent too. He wants to make his own way, without the help of the family."

"But he's got expensive tastes?"

"Only in girlfriends."

"Will you tell me now, where you were when Pamela was murdered?"

"Yes," Mark said. "I'm sorry that I didn't tell you yesterday."

He went to the bar, bought himself and George a drink. "I was in the common room."

"What were you doing there?"

Mark seemed sheepish, embarrassed. "Brooding, I suppose . . . Grieving."

George Palmer-Jones marvelled at young people's interest in their own emotions. Mark was so concerned to describe his feeling accurately.

"Grieving for Charlie?"

"Oh no, not for Charlie."

He paused.

"It seems ridiculous now." He looked resolutely at George. "It was Elizabeth. I always had a thing about her. I kept coming back to the island because of her. There was nothing in it. I never said anything to her. I knew, I suppose, that it was hopeless, but I was always desperately attracted to her. I've had girlfriends at college, girls of my own age, but Elizabeth was different, special. I like John very much, but they always seemed to be arguing. I suppose I dreamed that eventually they might separate, and I wanted to be there if they did. Then John told us that she was pregnant, and I realized that I'd been daft to consider anything like that. I saw the whole thing for what it was—just an infatuation."

He smiled at George, inviting understanding.

"I see," George said. "How long were you in the common room . . . brooding?"

"I don't know. Half an hour. Not more. It started getting cold and I felt a bit silly and melodramatic."

"Where were you when you heard Nicholas screaming?"

"On the stairs."

"Did you hear anyone moving about in the ringing room, while you were in the common room?"

"No. But someone could have been there. I was preoccupied."

"Did you ever meet Elizabeth on the mainland?"

"Why do you want to know?"

"I'm interested."

"I never did meet her. I wish that I had done."

"Did Elizabeth have anything to do with Ernest Todd?"

Mark looked disgusted. "I hope not. Ernest has quite a reputation, but I should think that she had better taste than that. Besides, I don't believe that there's anyone else. She's really very fond of John."

They sat without speaking. It was very quiet in the room. Then they collected the glasses and walked out into the sunshine. As he went through the door the old lady behind the bar gave George a drunken, lopsided wink.

They stood together on the pavement.

George asked: "Do you think that Nicholas killed Pamela?"

Mark hesitated.

"On Saturday I would have said that it was impossible. But I saw him there, in the room, covered in blood, and I just don't know. I don't know what to think."

"He's a remand prisoner. It should be possible for you to visit him. He'd appreciate that."

"Yes," Mark said. "I could do that, couldn't I? Thank you." And he hurried away.

12

George knew where Jasmine Carson lived. He had given her a lift home once, after one of the Gillibry weekends. He had time still before meeting Molly. He was haunted by the image of Jasmine Carson bending painfully over the wastepaper basket in Paul Derbyshire's room on the island. What could she have been doing there? He rang the bell at the front door of her flat and waited while she came to open it. She welcomed very few visitors to her flat and at first felt a rush of panic. She had never entertained a gentleman there.

She invited him in, then left him almost immediately in her living room, while she went to the kitchen to make coffee. He stood by the large window and admired the view of the island. He was intrigued by the different perspective.

"How strange it looks from here!" he said as she came in, awkwardly carrying the coffee tray. "What a wonderful view."

She was proud, as if he had complimented her skill at interior design. The flat was bare and impersonal. Much of the furniture had been provided by the developer. Only the

view expressed any individuality. It was as if she owned the view and the island.

"Would you pour the coffee?" she said. "I'm afraid that I might make a mess of it. My hands are very stiff this morning." She had set the tray on a dining table, and sat on a high, hard-backed chair.

"Do take a more comfortable chair, if you prefer. I find it so much easier to stand up from here."

He sat with her by the table by the big window. The tide was beginning to come in. The sandbanks beyond the island were covered. He poured coffee for her. Her hand shook as she was adding sugar and she spilled it over the table and floor. He sensed her anger and frustration. He had not realized how disabled she was.

"I have come," he said, "to take up your offer of help."

"How can I help you?" She seemed surprised, but very pleased.

"What did you find in Paul Derbyshire's room yesterday?"

She did not speak. He could not tell at all what she was thinking.

"You did take something from his room?"

She seemed to make up her mind. "Yes," she said. "I don't know how you know, but I did take something from his room. I'm sure that it has nothing to do with the murder, but I felt that if it were to be found by someone else, it might be misinterpreted. Especially by the police. I am sure that Superintendent Savage has many qualities which would suit him to his profession, but he did not seem to me to be an intelligent man."

She levered herself carefully to her feet, walked to a wall unit of veneered plywood which had obviously come with the flat, and from a drawer took a piece of paper. It had previously been torn and had been stuck back together with Sellotape.

"Before I leave the island," she said, "I check that the bedrooms are tidy. Elizabeth is a good worker. I do not believe that she is adequately paid for what she does, nor sufficiently appreciated by the residents. We should not

presume on her good nature, especially now that she is expecting a child. So I go into every bedroom, once the guests have finished, and fold the blankets neatly, empty the waste-paper basket. I repeated this procedure on Sunday. I saw no reason to behave differently because of the outrages which have occurred. In the doctor's bedroom I found these scraps of paper in the waste bin.''

The paper was a letter or, George thought, the draft of a letter, because certain parts had been rewritten, words had been crossed out.

''My dearest Sian,'' it began. ''You will never receive this letter. None of the letters I write will ever reach you. I know better than to hurt you like that, especially now. You must not miss your mother too much. When you are older you will realise that she was not worthy of you. But I am writing, my dear, to tell you that we are safe. Charlie Todd is dead, and I have retrieved from him that which he would have used against us. So remember, my dear, that I will always be your fond friend, Paul.''

''I knew of course about his affection for young girls,'' Jasmine Carson said. ''I have seen it before. I worked with children for forty years. Before he went into general practice he worked in the hospital in Gillicombe. He made a fool of himself with some of the younger nurses, but they were able to look after themselves. Sian Marshall is only a child. I had not realized, I admit, how deeply he cared for her.''

''Sian is Pamela Marshall's daughter?''

''Yes. Her youngest child.''

''How old is she?''

''Thirteen, fourteen perhaps, but rather immature for her age. Pamela always said that she worried about the girl, but I saw no evidence of her concern. She was always happy enough to leave her alone to go off on her conferences and committee meetings.''

''What made you look at the pieces when you were emptying the basket?''

''One of the larger pieces included the words 'Todd is dead.' I was curious and put the pieces in my pocket. It's a

156

habit. From my schoolmistress days, I suppose, when it was my duty to take an unnatural interest in my charges' behaviour. When I got home and saw Sian's name on the paper I felt no guilt in piecing the thing together.''

''Why didn't he burn it? It would have been safer.''

''The only fire was in the common room. He may have been reluctant to take it there.''

''Do you think that the doctor had actually made any advances towards Sian? Did Pamela know about his infatuation?''

''I'm sure that she did not. She was supposed to leave her children with anyone who would look after them. Sian went occasionally to spend an afternoon with Paul Derbyshire and his wife. I doubt whether he has done or said anything at all improper. He's a weak and foolish man, and that nonsense . . .'' She pointed at the letter ''. . . is nothing but fantasy.''

''You know that you must tell the police,'' George said.

''What would they do? Take him to the police station for questioning. They might frighten him into saying something, but I doubt it. He's stubborn.''

''He could not deny the letter.''

''It could all be quite innocent.''

''Yes. It could be.''

''While we've been talking, I have been thinking,'' she said. She was unused to asking for help. ''It has occurred to me that *you* might see him, talk to him, make up your own mind about it. Then, if you think that there is anything suspicious, take the letter to the police. But find out first. The police will not get to the truth of the matter. If he is innocent all the publicity would destroy him, and his wife. If he is guilty, I have no faith in the police's ability to bring him to justice.''

George did not answer directly. ''I wonder,'' he said, ''what it is that Charlie would have used against him. Do you have any idea?''

''I thought perhaps another letter. Paul Derbyshire doesn't seen to have taken great care to destroy the evidence.''

''Charlie would hardly have been in position to check through the waste-paper bins in the observatory bedrooms.''

"You obviously did not know Charlie."

He changed the subject quite suddenly. "Did you know that there was chloroform in the ringing-room cupboard?"

"Yes. Everyone must have seen it there. Some of the teachers who bring school groups to the island seem to be extremely careless about equipment. It would not have happened in *my* school."

He stood up and looked again out of the window.

"I'll do as you say," he said. "I'll go and talk to Derbyshire. It won't be an easy interview. Then, if I feel that it's necessary, I'll go to the police."

She smiled. "Thank you," she said. "That will do very well."

"I want to get everyone on to the island again," he said. "Perhaps on Friday. Do you think that they will come?"

"*I* will come," she said. "You must ask the others."

"I'll ask John to meet you with the Land Rover."

"And I'll be hoping for a north-westerly gale."

George was late for the meeting with Molly at the quay, but he was still there before her. Usually he was irritated by her lack of punctuality, but now he was glad of the opportunity to be alone. Besides, he had waited for her so often that he would have been disappointed if she had been on time. The late-afternoon sun was warm. He sat, like a boy, on the edge of the quay with his legs dangling over the mud. Waders were feeding on the shore in huge numbers, and as he watched them through his binoculars, he emptied his mind of the island and of questions and suspicions and fear. It had always been the only way he could force himself to unwind. While he was counting the birds there was a movement across the mud. The birds started to call, rose in a group in alarm. A peregrine dropped from the sun, took one of the foolish, flapping creatures and flew with it across the estuary to the hills. The incident was over in seconds, but for George it was a joy, a reward to sustain him.

Then Molly arrived. He recognized the engine sound of

her car, the erratic gear changes, the violent braking, before he turned to see it stop, next to his van, by the quay. She climbed out easily and quickly. She did not seem to him to be old. She was grey now of course, and a little plumper, but not very different from when they had married. She had the same energy.

She could tell that he was disturbed because he allowed himself to show that he was pleased to see her. He even kissed her, briefly. They had led self-contained working lives long before such partnerships were common, and his telephone call the night before had been unusually demanding and uninformative.

"Can you come down to stay for a few days?" he had said. "Do try to come."

"I *am* pleased to see you," he said.

She looked surprised, but did not say anything. It was one of her qualities, he thought, that she knew when there was nothing to say.

She had been wearing a pair of old plimsolls for driving. She dressed in baggy trousers and strange, loose jerseys, but for comfort, not for effect. Her appearance had never bothered him, even when he had had to mix socially with men whose wives were smart and sophisticated. Now he did not notice it. She changed into a pair of wellingtons, put on a plastic mac, and they began to walk.

"You didn't say much last night."

"No, I was using the observatory phone. There's an extension in the warden's flat. I was afraid of being overheard."

"I heard about it all on the radio," she said. "It said that someone was helping the police with their inquiries. Does that mean that the police know who committed the murders?"

"They think that they know." He had spoken more sharply than he intended, and added: "I suppose it's inevitable that they should have arrested the boy. But the policeman in charge of the case, Savage, is unimaginative, stubborn. I believe that there's more to the investigation than he realizes, but I can't convince him. I worked with

him once before when I was with the Home Office, so he asked for my help. Now, because I can't agree with him, he doesn't want me involved at all.''

''Tell me what happened,'' she said. ''The man was already dead when you arrived on Saturday?''

''Charlie Todd. Yes.''

So he described the events of the weekend to her. As he answered her questions, tried to help her to understand what it was like to be there, he brought some order to the chaos of his memory. He remembered important details, unconnected snatches of conversation.

''Tell me about the people,'' she said. ''What were they like? How did they all get on?''

''I don't think that they have anything in common, except the observatory. John, the warden, is quiet, conscientious, a bit weak. I should think that Elizabeth is the stronger. You'll meet them on the island. You'll be able to judge for yourself.''

''What about the boy they arrested?''

''Nick Mardle. He seems lonely, a bit disturbed. Perhaps a little immature. I don't think he has many friends, except Mark, who was there too. Mark Taylor. He seems quite harmless. You'd like him. He's a student. He had a crush on Elizabeth, but I think her pregnancy brought him to his senses . . . I don't know how to describe Jerry Packham. I always liked him, but now I think perhaps I didn't know him very well. He was having an affair with Pamela Marshall.''

''Charlie Todd's niece?''

''Yes. And that has confused the case. Because they were both members of the same family, Savage has the theory that it was some sort of psychopathic revenge killing. I'll tell you why I don't believe that, later.''

''All right,'' she said. ''Who else is there?''

''Jasmine Carson. A retired schoolmistress. So much the stereotyped schoolmistress that I wonder sometimes if she has anything to hide. She's efficient. She's the one who really runs the observatory. Doctor Derbyshire thinks that he does, but he's a ditherer. He's good with figures,

160

with abstracts, but he isn't any good at making decisions. I can't quite work out why he still comes to the observatory. He hardly does any ringing now, and doesn't even go out on to the island much. I think, when he was younger, he was quite a keen ringer. I've seen very sound papers by him in some of the more academic natural history journals. He was always specially interested in seabirds. He used to go ringing on sea cliffs in Scotland and the Hebrides, but you can't imagine him dangling at the end of a rope now. And today I've learned that he has other, rather more sinister, interests.''

He described his meeting with Jasmine Carson, the contents of the letter she had found in the doctor's room.

Molly stopped. George had set a brisk pace and she was hot. She felt very exposed. They were alone. The sand and the mud stretched for miles, and no one else was on the shore. The sun was very low and reflected in the water all around them. Only the island broke the line of the horizon. They were close enough to see the detail of it, the white wall around the observatory, the fissures in the low, crumbling cliffs, the sycamores around the wooden frame of the Wendy House. She took off her rucksack and did not object when George picked it up. Then she took off her mackintosh, rolled it roughly into a sausage and tied it around her waist. She turned her face to the breeze. She was recovering her breath.

''What's worrying you?'' she said. ''Why don't you think that it was the boy?''

He walked on more slowly, and she followed him.

''Partly it's the boy,'' he said. ''He's mixed up, but he's not a psychopath. I believe him.''

''Would they let me see him?'' she asked. She was remembering other lonely, mixed-up young people. They had been her livelihood. When she had worked as a social worker she had befriended, been hurt by so many.

''I suppose so. I don't expect he has many visitors.''

''So,'' she said, ''partly it's the boy. But it can't only be that. We both know that boys can be convincing liars.''

''No. It's not only that. I think that Pamela Marshall

161

was killed because of something she heard on the evening of the arson. I don't think it was an insane, motiveless crime. I believe that Charles Todd had discovered some irregularity in his family's business and that he was trying to exploit it. I'm not sure how that fits in, but I'm sure that it's relevant."

They had reached the rocks at the base of the slipway. Molly wished that he would walk more slowly. She had a hole in one sock and the wellington was rubbing a blister. She spoke, as much as anything, to stop his relentless pace.

"Well," she said. "Which of them do you think murdered Charles Todd and Pamela Marshall?"

"I don't know," he said quietly. "I should do. I've talked to them all. I'm afraid that the boy will be convicted. They've almost proof enough. He made the threats. He had the opportunity to set fire to the Wendy House, and to strangle Charlie. He knew that Mark Taylor was a deep sleeper. He knew that Charlie would be in the hide. He could have woken early, realized that Jerry would not wake in time to keep the appointment, then he could have killed Charlie and been back in bed before his alarm went off. On Saturday night his knife was used to kill Pamela and his fingerprints will be on the knife. He was found in her room, covered in blood. When we found him, his words could have been taken as an admission. If we don't find out who is the murderer, Nick Mardle may well be convicted."

He stopped and turned to her. "You don't mind?" he said. "You don't mind coming here and helping? I didn't really ask you, did I? The phone call last night was a bit like a royal summons."

She tried to concentrate on more than the blister and her aching legs.

"I'm pleased," she said in a matter-of-fact voice. "I trust your judgement. If you say the boy is innocent, then we must prove that he is."

13

The next day the sun was shining still, and there were still birds for John and George to ring. They all had breakfast together, in the kitchen. George and John were talking about the birds they had caught. Elizabeth was quiet and preoccupied. Molly listened and watched.

"I'd like to go over to the mainland tomorrow," George said. "I have something to discuss with Paul Derbyshire. But I won't need to go out until later, so I'll be able to help with the ringing again."

Elizabeth looked up. "I'm going out tomorrow, so I can give you a lift if you like."

"Where are you going tomorrow?" John asked sharply.

"Just to Gillicombe."

"Why?"

"To do some shopping, go to the library."

The bitterness in the exchange was embarrassing. There was a silence.

Then, changing the subject, John said: "I meant to tell you before, George. I told you that I thought somebody was up before me on Saturday morning. I remember now what made me think so. It isn't much. There were muddy

footprints on the hall floor. Just one set of wet footprints. I came in after hoisting the cone and I noticed them then."

"Can you visualize where the footsteps went?"

"Oh yes. Only as far as the coat rack. They were made by that spare pair of wellies. You know, the ones which went with the duffel coat that the police took away."

"Are you sure?"

"Yes. The boots were lying on their sides, on the floor. I can remember quite clearly."

"Did the police take the wellingtons with them?"

"I don't think so."

"Let's go to see."

The boots were still there. George looked at them carefully, without touching them. The size number had been worn from the inside and from the tread, but they were big. He could have worn them, and he had larger than average feet. The boots were lying on their sides, so he could see the soles. They were worn smooth and nothing clung to the rubber but the red sand of the track.

"At least the murderer had the decency to take his boots off here," John said, with an attempt at humour, "which is more than Doctor Derbyshire bothers to do. On the morning of Charlie's death he walked up the stairs and left half the garden on the floor."

"Did he? I wonder where he had been. There's not a lot of open ground on the island. What time was it?"

"I'm not sure exactly. It was when I was on the way back to phone the police."

"Did you tell Superintendent Savage about the wellingtons?"

"No. I only remembered this morning. Do you think I should?"

"Yes. You see, nobody admitted to being up before you. So it is important. The boots were probably worn by the murderer."

The men wandered, through habit, into the ringing room. Molly followed them. They did not explain what happened there, but she had been in observatories with George before. She walked around reading the notices of ringing

164

recovery pinned on to the notice board, the old school timetables, the rotas for washing up and cleaning. She was not bored. She was listening. John was showing George some photographs of birds in the hand.

"I suppose Savage asked you about chloroform," George said.

"Yes. He made me feel a bit guilty that it was here, but I didn't bring it on to the island. The teacher of last term's A-level group was using it, I think. The schools have the run of the place while they're here. I've seen the jar in the cupboard, but it never occurred to me that it might be dangerous. People here are usually responsible."

"Did you know what was in the jar? Was it labelled?"

"I knew what was in it because the teacher told me. I can't remember if it was labelled. I suppose it must have been."

"Would everyone have known that it was in the cupboard?"

"Everyone would have seen it. It was on the shelf with the bird bags. But unless it was marked, no one would have known what it was."

There was a silence, comfortable now, as John spread out more photographs, then George said: "You knew Charlie as well as anyone. You've been his neighbour for nearly five years. Would he be capable of blackmail, do you think?"

John was not surprised by the question, but he hesitated while he thought.

"Not blackmail. Not really blackmail," he said. "Charlie would never have tried to make money out of other people's problems, but he enjoyed finding out about them. He was really nosy, a bit like a kid. He was childish in lots of ways. He'd throw incredible tantrums if he didn't get his own way. And I suppose he might try to use the information he'd discovered to get his own way. It didn't always work, but he usually managed to persuade people to his point of view."

"And what was his point of view? What did he persuade people to do for him?"

"Oh, there were silly things. He wanted to have an observatory New Year's Eve party. No one else was very keen. I suppose the lads wanted to be out with their own friends, and Pam wanted to be with her family, but everyone turned up for the party in the end. I don't know how he managed it. But he wasn't always selfish. Once he conned the doctor and Jasmine to allow a bunch of deprived kids from Birmingham to have a free holiday here."

"How did he do that?"

"I don't know. He was very clever, quite subtle. He probably just appealed to Jasmine's better nature. She's so fond of the island that she's quite happy to share it with everyone. Doctor Derbyshire would have been more difficult to persuade, but there are probably some skeletons in his cupboard."

"Any idea what they might be?"

"No. I don't know him very well. I only ever see him here."

"Did he try his form of blackmail on you?"

"He didn't get any opportunity. I made it quite clear before we came that Elizabeth and I weren't married. He didn't mind. He wasn't at all prudish. It wasn't immorality that attracted him as much as secrecy. He tried to find out all about Elizabeth and Frank, Elizabeth's ex-husband. Frank's quite famous in his own field. You see his name on the credits of TV documentary programmes, but again there was nothing to find out. Besides, Charlie was rather frightened by Elizabeth. She intimidated him."

It occurred to Molly that John was speaking rather glibly about the lack of secrecy in his relationship with Elizabeth. From the short conversation at breakfast, it seemed that Elizabeth, at least, had secrets from him. Had Charlie been aware of that?

The men were still standing by the table. They were looking up an identification feature in a field guide. Molly was aware of a movement outside the open door. Elizabeth was standing there. She was, to Molly, still a girl. She looked almost Mediterranean in colouring and features. Her hair was thick and very curly. She made no attempt to

hide, but she was standing quite still. She must have heard what John had said. She caught Molly's eye. Molly smiled, was about to speak, when Elizabeth turned quickly and walked away. Her face had been passive, but it seemed to Molly that she had been pleased by what she had heard.

After lunch Elizabeth found herself talking to Molly in the kitchen. She was not sure, exactly, how it came about. The older woman did not ask questions, hardly spoke at all. With her shabby, ill-fitting clothes, her round spectacles held together with sticky tape, she looked like a grown-up, rather jolly schoolboy. She listened intently, occasionally offered an opinion which was different from Elizabeth's, but there was no element of judgement in her comments. Her opinion was different, not right or better.

She never talked about Frank. She would never have discussed him with John, and there was no one else here with whom she had any intimate conversation. Except perhaps Mark, but somehow he did not count. Yet now she was explaining about Frank. She supposed that George's wife had said something which reminded her of Frank, and which had prompted the discussion, but she could not remember exactly how the conversation had started.

"It seemed so exciting when we first met," she said. "I was a mousy little student at teacher's training college, and he was a lecturer. He wasn't a lecturer for very long. It wasn't his scene at all. He hated having to face all the students."

It was hard to believe Elizabeth was ever mousy, but she continued:

"He was working in the BBC by the time we were married. We had to move to Bristol, so I never had the opportunity to finish my course. I didn't mind. Not at the time. Frank came from Northern Ireland, and had a very conventional idea of what he wanted a wife to be. He didn't mean to be unkind. My dad was a real waster. He moved from job to job, drank too much. Then there weren't any more jobs to get. So the security of a nice house, and money in the bank, and a husband who came home every night, was a real treat. But I started to get so bored."

She stressed the last word dramatically, and stretched to emphasize the yawning tedium of married life.

"He was doing very well at the BBC and for a while that was fun. But he didn't really want me to be involved. He was a very strong character, very organized, a bit rigid. Then I got pregnant. Frank started taking a bit of notice of me then. He was thrilled to bits. He wanted a daughter, to be a doll and to love him. He would have hated it really if there had been a baby. He would have hated the mess, the disruption to his routine. But I had a miscarriage. He was very kind. He said that he was sure that next time everything would be all right, but I knew that I'd never have his baby. I didn't leave him then. I didn't have the energy somehow. He went to Bardsey to do some filming and I persuaded him to take me with him. He wouldn't have taken me usually, but he was still feeling sorry for me."

"I've been to Bardsey," Molly said. "I *did* enjoy it there."

"It was wonderful," she said, with a naïve and joyful intensity. "I was born and brought up in the city. I'd never been on an island. We stayed at the observatory. Frank was out all day, filming. He thought that I would be bored, but just being there was enough for me.

"John was assistant warden there. It was early summer. He showed me round. He was shy, but he did love the place. When the time came for the film unit to go, I asked John if I could stay."

She laughed affectionately. "He was so surprised. I could tell that he liked me, but he would never have had the nerve to ask me to leave Frank. It was a real pleasure to make him happy. I'd never had that effect on anyone before."

"And now you're pregnant again," Molly said. "Are you pleased?"

"Oh yes. Very pleased. But of course it does make a difference."

"Yes. It must do."

"For one thing, I've started worrying about money for

168

the first time. And then John has certain expectations. Of me. I don't want to disappoint him.''

"You won't disappoint him.''

"No? He doesn't disappoint me, though he believes that he does. We seem to have lost touch with each other lately. Even after five years there still seem to be misunderstandings.''

"There will always be misunderstandings. The investigation will have made things worse.''

"I suppose so. I wonder . . .''

She broke off. She had been going to explain. The woman was so easy to talk to. She would have to be more careful.

"Yes?'' Molly asked.

"Oh nothing,'' she said. "Would you like some tea? John and George will be coming in for some soon, I expect.''

The men did come in then. The afternoon was a quiet time for ringing. Most of the migrant birds came through in the early morning. John was asking George's opinion of a paper he was preparing on seabird passage. George made a number of suggestions and John was excited. He wanted to go, right away, to look up the references in the books. Elizabeth said that she would go to rest for a while, and went to the flat. Molly and George were left alone in the kitchen.

"I don't think that Elizabeth has a lover,'' Molly said. George found the term old-fashioned, amusing, but let Molly continue. "I think she's hiding something from John, though.''

"Do you? Any idea what it might be?''

She shook her head.

"I want to go to have another look at the Wendy House,'' George said. "I've still got the key. I only went in, once before, to get an idea of the place. I didn't do a proper search. There were some papers, some correspondence. There may be something which would give us a clue to Charlie's interest in the family business. It seems that Paul Derbyshire has already found whatever Charlie

had which frightened him, but there may still be something there.''

The Wendy House was as it had been, when he had last visited it, though in the kitchen the glasses and mugs had been put away. Presumably Elizabeth had been in to clean.

They went into the bedroom first, and George looked carefully through the pine chest of drawers. There was nothing to see. Each drawer contained a messy and random pile of clothes. Checked shirts and fair-isle sweaters were mixed with odd socks and grey underwear.

"It's almost as untidy as yours," George said. Molly ignored him. She was looking at a framed photograph which hung beside the bed. It was a posed wedding photograph, a family grouping around the bride.

"Who is this?" she asked.

George joined her to look at the picture. "The bride is Pamela Marshall," he said. "I should think it was taken sixteen or seventeen years ago, but she hadn't changed much. The old man must be Albert, Charlie's father. He's still alive. I'd like to meet him, but I'm not sure if I'll be able to make the opportunity. The two couples are Ernest and Laurence, and their wives." The women were wearing the unbecoming short skirts of the late sixties. One of them was carrying a plump baby. "I suppose that's Jonathan, the other beneficiary of the will," George said. At the edge of the group, looking bemused but grinning widely, was a round-faced, middle-aged man.

"And that," Molly said, "must be Charlie." She was studying the photograph intently.

George by this time had moved into the sitting room. On one of the dresser shelves a sheaf of papers had been propped in an old toast rack. He sat at the small table and sorted through them. Most of them were unpaid bills and demands for payment. Many referred to the cottage in the Storr Valley. There was a strongly worded letter from the council about rates, and final demands from the South-West Electricity Board and British Telecom. There was a letter from a hire-purchase company threatening court action because only one payment had been made towards the

170

purchase of a motorcycle. These bills seemed to be in no order and there was no indication that they had been paid. Mixed with them were a number of programmes of the Canal Theatre Company and an entrance ticket for Alton Towers.

"No wonder he wrote such good children's stories," Molly said. She had come into the living room and was looking at the mess spread across the table. "He never really grew up, did he?"

"He must have had an accountant to deal with all this," George said. "But perhaps he just refused to accept financial advice."

He collected the papers together and put them back in the toast rack. He felt disappointed, frustrated. He had learned that Charlie had owed money, but there was nothing about Todd Leisure Enterprises. His only hope now was that Connibear, with his privileged access to official information, would make the vital discovery. Molly sensed his disappointment, took his arm and led him out of the building.

When they returned to the observatory John and Elizabeth were in the middle of a violent row. George had expected to see John in the ringing room. He had wanted to ask if his suggestions for the seabird paper had been helpful. But John was not in the ringing room or the library.

"We'll walk through to the kitchen," he said. "It must be nearly supper time."

They could hear John when they were still in the dark, dusty corridor which led from the dining room. He was shouting.

"Something's going on," he said. "I must know what it is. You must tell me, Lizzie."

"Of course something's going on." Her voice was bitter, scornful. "Two people have been killed. One of our friends has been arrested for murder."

"Not that," he said, as if that did not much matter. "Not that. It's you. You lied to me. Last week you told me that you'd been to the ante-natal clinic, but there

171

wasn't a clinic. Not on that Friday. I looked at your card. Please Elizabeth, don't shut yourself off from me. Not now. I must know.''

"What bloody right do you have to be checking up on me?'' She was beside herself. "I don't belong to you. I'm not even your bloody wife.''

"Is there someone else?'' He was making a great effort at self-control. He spoke gently. "You're right. You don't belong to me. I wouldn't want to restrict you in any way. I just want to know what's going on. You owe me that.''

"Oh, stop talking in clichés,'' she said. "You're making yourself ridiculous.''

They heard a door slam. George presumed that she had gone to the flat. When they got to the kitchen, it was empty.

They prepared their own supper that night. John explained that Elizabeth was ill, and asked if they would mind getting their own. Molly enjoyed it. She liked cooking. They invited John to join them, but he refused. He went to the flat without starting the generator, and they sat in the kitchen, discussing the case and eating their meal by the light of a tilly.

"We don't seem to have moved forward very far today,'' George said. "We know that Charlie needed money, but I'd gathered that anyway.''

"I don't understand why he needed money. He must have had oodles of it. At one time you saw the characters from his stories in every comic and on everything from pencil cases to fizzy drinks.''

"I think he just spent it all. He doesn't seem to have been very organized about finance.''

"So that would have given him a motive for blackmail.''

"That, and the kind of moral blackmail he seems to have gone in for. He wouldn't have thought of it as blackmail. As I see it, he found out that perhaps the family hadn't been quite open in its business dealings, told them that he knew about their misdemeanours, then suggested, for example, that they gave a donation to the Canal Theatre Company.''

"Surely the fact that he was planning to sell the island would suggest that the Todds weren't prepared to give in to the blackmail. He still needed the money."

"I suppose so. It's all conjecture."

"But how would Charlie know of their business fiddles, if he never went near the family?"

"That had occurred to me. Maybe Nicholas Mardle talked to Charlie. He could have passed on staff gossip, and Charlie might have investigated it, and saved it for future use."

"Do you think that the policeman will tell you if he finds anything suspect in Todd Leisure?"

"Oh, I think so. Just to humour me. It won't mean anything to them."

They washed the dishes.

"I think," George said, "that we'll both go to the mainland tomorrow."

As they went to bed, early, they heard the sound of sobbing from the flat. They could not tell whether John or Elizabeth was crying.

14

Elizabeth drove them both across to the mainland the next morning. At breakfast John had been carefully affectionate. He had not asked her where she was going and he had not touched her. She had been gentle with him, but she had given nothing away.

It was another clear and sunny day, but there was a wind, which had blown the sand into hard ridges so that the Land Rover jolted and rattled across. Elizabeth did not speak to them. Molly was never very aware of what people were wearing, but she noticed that Elizabeth looked smart. On the island the girl usually wore jeans, long shirts, John's jerseys. Now, in a skirt and a jacket, wearing shoes instead of trainers, with a handbag by her side, she seemed to Molly sophisticated, frightening. Even driving the Land Rover across the shore she was an elegant professional woman. It was not the new image itself, but the ability to change so dramatically that intimidated. It seemed to Molly that she was a different woman. John must have noticed that she had dressed up, Molly thought. How can he have felt? She wished, almost, that she had stayed on the island, so that he would have had something else to think about.

He would have felt obliged to entertain her. The thought of him there, lonely and jealous, imagining Elizabeth's betrayals, moved her. She passed no judgement on Elizabeth's behaviour, but she wished that things had worked out differently.

At the quay George got out quickly and drove away in his van.

"He has some business in Gillicombe," Molly said in explanation. "I thought I'd take my car to explore. Do a bit of sightseeing."

"Yes," Elizabeth said vaguely. "It is very pretty."

Molly pretended to fumble with her car keys while Elizabeth drove off. In the country lanes that led from the quay the Land Rover was easy to follow. It was high enough to show above the hedges and the lane was so winding that Molly could stay close to it without being seen. As the road widened and they approached Gillicombe, Molly allowed three cars to overtake her, but the Land Rover was still visible ahead of her. It drove along the promenade, turned into the High Street and parked neatly outside the office of Todd Leisure Enterprises. Molly turned into a side street and parked. She had presumed that Elizabeth had intended to go into the Todds' office, and was surprised, when she walked into the High Street, to see that the girl was still there. She was standing on the kerb at a zebra crossing, waiting for the traffic to stop. Luckily she seemed to be daydreaming. Certainly she did not see Molly. A car driver had to sound his horn before she started over the crossing, and she gave a wave of apology to him as she ran across the street.

The High Street was busy in the way that small towns are busy on weekday mornings. There were women with prams and pushchairs and howling children dragged by one hand. They were all laden with shopping and all in a hurry. Even the elderly ladies who pushed trolleys or carried nylon shopping bags and wore gloves walked quickly, with purpose, and the shouted greetings to acquaintances were lost as they moved on up the street. Only the men seemed leisurely, prepared to stand in shop doorways watch-

ing the street. Elizabeth looked at her watch, then went into a boutique and began to look at the dresses and skirts on the sale rack. The shop doors were open, and from the other side of the street Molly could see her. The girl did not show any real interest in the clothes. It was as if she were early for a date and was killing time. Molly, looking in a gift-shop window, could see the boutique reflected in the glass. Jostled by busy, hurrying women who had dinners to cook, washing to put out, she felt that her inactivity, her passive watchfulness made her an outsider, not a true representative of her sex. She was relieved when the girl came out of the shop and began to walk briskly. Molly stayed on the opposite side of the street and kept some distance behind her.

Then Elizabeth disappeared, as if by some conjuring trick. One moment she was there. Molly's vision was blocked by a large woman on the pavement and a delivery van on the road. Then, when she could see the opposite side of the road again, the girl had gone. Feeling a little bewildered Molly crossed the road and the apparent magic was explained. There was a narrow archway between two shops. A flight of steps led through it to a cobbled path. Molly just glimpsed Elizabeth following the path round a sharp left turn. Feeling like an elderly Alice, she followed. It was, in fact, like leaving the real world behind. As she turned too she walked into sunlight and what could have been the set for a film about the middle ages. Ahead of her was the parish church. There was a grass bank, and trees. On the right of the cobbled path was a small courtyard of almshouses, unchanged for three hundred years. The cobbles of the path spread into the courtyard. There was still a pump and trough in the middle of it, and two old ladies dressed in black chatted in the sun. The path led past the church to a terrace of houses, then through a pair of wrought-iron gates to another busy road. But in the churchyard and its surroundings there was no sense of the hurry and noise and female frenzy of the shopping streets. Even the weather was different. Enclosed by the high, soft stone walls, it was sheltered from the sharp sea breeze, and it

seemed that the warmth of the summer was trapped there. Elizabeth walked past the church and into one of the terraced houses opposite. She did not knock at the door.

Molly savoured the place. She forgot for a moment the urgency of the mission. Then she went to investigate. It was an office. A tasteful brass plate on the wall was inscribed Thompson, Lessing and Marshall Solicitors. Next door there was a second-hand bookshop, and Molly waited there. The shelves near the window contained cookery books. Molly browsed through them happily while she watched the churchyard outside. The elderly shopkeeper took her for a connoisseur as her interest did not move to the other books in the shop, and they had a pleasant conversation about English food for more than half an hour. Molly was just beginning to think that she should move, should explore the church perhaps, when Elizabeth appeared. The girl stood still in the sunshine. Her long hair had been pinned back from her face by wooden slides. Deftly she pulled out the slides, put them in her bag, and shook her hair loose. It was a curious gesture of freedom.

Elizabeth walked immediately back to the Land Rover, then drove away. Molly did not follow her. She felt that the purpose of the visit had been achieved.

George went to the police station. He asked to speak to Connibear, but was told that it was Connibear's day off. There was no message for him. He did not ask to speak to Savage, afraid that the superintendent's tact and gratitude had reached their limit. It was an anticlimax.

He had arranged to meet Molly in the Italian café near the station, and as he waited he grew more irritable. When she arrived he was drinking coffee from a tiny cup. It was thick and strong as medicine, but she wanted food, and George had to wait while she went to the counter, exchanged greetings with the proprietor, found out how many children he had, how long he had been in Gillicombe, how business was. When she returned she began to describe the churchyard, the almshouses, her enchantment at having

found it, and he had to interrupt to ask where Elizabeth had been going.

"To a solicitor's office."

"What were the names of the solicitors?"

"Thompson, Lessing and Marshall."

"William Marshall, the solicitor, was Pamela's husband."

She was quiet for a moment, considering the implications of this, then: "I don't know that she saw him. It's surely unlikely that he's at work again so soon after his wife's death."

"It depends, I suppose, how distressed he was by it."

"She could have been there on business."

"What business would Elizabeth have, with a solicitor?"

She did not answer.

"I don't understand," he said, "how it all fits together—Elizabeth's visit to the Todds' office on the same day as Charlie, the week before his death, and now this. What does she have to do with the Todds?"

"Perhaps," Molly answered facetiously, "Charlie went in to blackmail Ernest and Laurence. They knew that John and Elizabeth were hard up, so they hired Elizabeth to kill Charlie. Pamela heard her on the way back from setting fire to the Wendy House, so Elizabeth had to finish her off too. Today, she's been in to the Todds' solicitors (I presume that they are the Todds' solicitors) to collect the money."

But George did not laugh. "Are John and Elizabeth hard up?" he asked.

"I don't know. I get the impression that they don't have much money. Is it important?"

"I don't know. It might be."

"We're going to see Doctor Derbyshire next, aren't we?" she asked. "I wonder if we'll get anything interesting out of him."

She bit into her second ham and tomato roll.

She's not shocked by anything, he thought. She worked with people who were in pain for so long that she detached from it. He found the doctor's taste for young girls unpleasant, even disgusting.

"I wonder if the wife knows," she said, and her voice did express some emotion now. "How dreadful if she does, and she still cares for him. She must be so frightened for what he might do."

"Might he be dangerous?"

"I suppose he might. It all seems to be confined to the realms of fantasy, though. So long as it's all a sort of glorified daydream, I should think he'd be safe."

"Yes," George said. "But the difference between fantasy and reality might not be so obvious to someone else."

"What do you mean?"

"Well, suppose that Charlie found a letter, or a diary, full of the doctor's ramblings, he couldn't be expected to know that the events described were only make-believe. Charlie liked children too. He wrote stories for them. Besides his curiosity about other people's personal affairs, it might have occurred to him that he should have done something about his discovery of the doctor's predilections."

"So he threatened to go to the police, and the doctor strangled him."

"The letter which Jasmine found could certainly be read like that. He could have arranged to meet Charlie in the seawatching hide very early, before Jerry was due to arrive, to discuss it."

"But how could he be sure that Jerry wouldn't suddenly arrive and surprise him?"

"The flaps of the seawatching hide open on all sides. It's possible to see someone as soon as they leave the observatory."

"'Do you think that's how it happened?"

"No, but we must see him anyway."

From the start Molly was intrigued by the tone of the conversation between Paul Derbyshire and his wife, Marjory. She was a tall woman, calm and slow-speaking, with an air of assurance. She was polite, but distant, as if her mind were elsewhere. They lived in a big house, near to the shore, at the end of a long straight road of similar houses. It was out of the town, near the golf course. There were no trees, and the wind blew up the bleak, straight

street and around the ugly brick houses. The house was separated from the water by a stretch of dunes, and as George and Molly got out of the car, sand blew in sharp swirls around their ankles and stung their eyes. Sand was piled like a snowdrift outside the boundary fence.

Marjory opened the door to them. She did not speak, but stood, patient and serene, waiting for them to announce their business. She was dressed in expensive, conventional, nondescript clothes. Her hair was grey, permanently waved. George, whose temper had not improved, stated their business shortly. She invited them in and called to her husband:

"There are some friends to see you, dear."

Although they were ordinary words, they seemed to Molly wrong, out of context. It's as if she's calling to a child, Molly thought. She struggled to place the tone exactly. But she doesn't sound like a mother, more like a nanny or a kindly, elderly aunt.

The doctor emerged from a door at the back of the house. They were still standing in the hall.

"How nice to see you," he said. "How very nice. Marjory, this is George Palmer-Jones. You will remember that I've talked about him very often. And this must be Molly." He hardly acknowledged Molly's presence, and continued quickly. "You must be stranded by the tide, of course. What good fortune that you've come today, George. I've just received *Finches of the World* from the publisher. I put in my order some months ago. I'd be glad of your opinion. There are one or two points that I'd question, but I haven't your experience in the field."

He talked George back into the room from which he had appeared and the women were left together. There was no sense of awkwardness. Marjory smiled sweetly and indulgently after her husband, and offered tea. She showed Molly into a small, rather cold sitting room, but Molly followed her into the kitchen, and she seemed not to mind.

"My husband has a passion for books," she said as she filled the kettle. "But then he was so bored when he retired that I was glad when he developed an interest."

180

"Does he have any other interests?" Molly asked. "Apart from birdwatching, of course."

"I don't think that he *is* especially interested in birdwatching. Not any more. But he does enjoy going over to the island. It's good for him. I do hope this unpleasantness doesn't spoil it for him."

"It must have been a great shock."

"Yes. Although he has taken it better than I would have imagined. Of course shock presents itself in many forms."

Molly said nothing.

Marjory continued: "You see, we knew them both quite well, the . . . victims. Charles was a great character and Paul worked with him very closely when he was buying the island. They had their little arguments, but really they got on so well." Again she could have been talking about children. "And of course Pamela was one of Paul's receptionists. That was just before we were married and I never met her then. Unfortunately she left the practice soon after, and they didn't bump into each other again until they met on the island. We have become very fond of her children, Edward and Sian. You see, we were late marrying, and we never had children. I think, in many ways, that it was fortunate. Paul doesn't find it easy to mix socially. But he did enjoy the company of the children. Perhaps he was a little foolish—he did tend to spoil them so, especially Sian—but there was no harm in it."

So you know about his infatuation, Molly thought, but you indulge him in it, as you indulge him in everything else.

"How did you meet him?" she asked, too curious to be concerned by the impudence of asking.

"I was a matron of a rest home for the elderly," she said. "A small, private home, my own business. His mother was one of our residents. He visited her regularly. When she passed away, he asked me to marry him."

That's it, Molly thought, identifying at last the nature of the relationship between Paul and Marjory Derbyshire. She treats him, not like a child, but like a very old, slightly

demented gentleman whose fantasies must be humoured and who must be protected from his own mischief.

Paul Derbyshire had taken George Palmer-Jones into a small room. It must, George thought, be very similar to his surgery. There was a desk with a card index, and on the walls rows of books. Half of them were medical academic, half of them concerned with natural history. A large, glossy book lay on a sheet of brown paper on the desk. They discussed it briefly.

George did not want to frighten the doctor into immediate denial.

"I believe that Charlie had something which belonged to you, when he died," George said carefully.

"How do you know?"

"I don't wish to tell you that. I want to know how it was returned to you."

But Paul Derbyshire did not answer the question.

"Did he talk about it to anyone?" he said wildly. "How could he understand? He never cared for anyone but himself. Well, it's too late. I've burnt it. No one can prove anything now."

George tried not to show, not to feel, distaste. "I don't think," he said, "that it's a matter of proving anything. But I need to know how it was returned to you. I do not wish to involve the police."

Again the doctor reacted irrationally. "*Tell* the police. No one can touch me now. It is burnt, and Charlie is dead." He grew more calm. "Besides," he said sadly, looking up at George through the straight shank of white hair which had fallen over his forehead, "nothing ever happened, you know. Nothing ever happened."

It had been a strange conversation. There had been no direct questions, no proper answers, but George thought that they had understood each other. He understood, at least, that Paul Derbyshire would talk no more about it. He stood up.

"I would like everyone to be on the island the day after tomorrow. Will you come?"

It was as if the previous exchange between them had never happened.

"Yes," the doctor said. "Give me the details, and I'll come."

Elizabeth was waiting for them in the Land Rover. She was reading a library book. There was an empty sandwich box on the seat beside her. It seemed that she had been there for some time. All three of them sat in the front, squeezed together in relative comfort. She drove down the slipway on to the sand. The sun was very low in the sky. They drove directly towards it. The island was a silhouette suspended between sky and shore. Elizabeth spoke for the first time.

"Not even two murders can spoil it," she said. "It's more important, somehow, than that."

15

George and Molly lit a fire in the common room that evening. They burnt pitch pine, which had been washed up at the north end of the island. It burned beautifully, and smelled of creosote and spice. Elizabeth came to find them there. Molly was knitting and George was reading.

"Why weren't my parents like that? Elizabeth thought with pain and resentment.

"I collected the mail from the post office today," she said casually. "There was a letter for you."

She would have liked to join them, but it was clear that they wanted to be alone. She went back to the flat.

It had been delivered to the post office by hand. The envelope was addressed in a strong upright script, as if painted with a brush. The letter was short and direct:

"Dear sir, I understand that you are interested in my affairs. If you come to my home tomorrow at 11:00 A.M. I might be able to help you."

It was signed A. Todd.

"So," George said, "perhaps I won't need Connibear after all."

"If Albert tells you what is going on."

"Why else would he want to see me?"

"To find out what you know."

"Yes," George said. "There is that. But there must be something going on. Why else would he have written to me? If he's curious about me, that's interesting in itself, don't you think?"

Molly counted the stitches on the knitting needle.

"You *are* sure that it all began with the Todds' business?"

"Yes," George said. "That's the one thing I am sure about."

He went the next day, alone. He left Molly detailed instructions. She tried not to resent them, but watched him off with relief. He had been so restless, so tiresome in the repetition of his orders. John and Elizabeth seemed to have maintained their peace, although Molly thought that Elizabeth had still not given any explanation for her secret trips to the mainland. They spoke very little to each other, as if the peace were fragile and could be shattered by one thoughtless word. She was wearing a loose dress—the first public expression of her pregnancy. John had offered to take George to the mainland in the Land Rover, but George had insisted that he would walk.

Molly walked to the Beacon to watch him go. She stayed there long after he had reached the mainland. It was very calm. The incoming tide crawled in one smooth movement up the shore. These was none of the usual ebb and flow, no breaking waves, no noise.

The lull before the storm, Molly thought, and the cliché dominated her thoughts, so that all day she was tense, waiting for a crisis, and when none occurred, she was left drained, wretched and disappointed.

In one of the houses in Laurel Avenue there was a nursery school. As George got out of the car, the children raced out of the front door to play in the garden. They chased across the grass and threw armfuls of dead leaves at each other. Above the sound of children's voices a church clock chimed eleven times.

The Todds' house stood on a corner and was the biggest in the quiet street. George knocked on the door. It was opened immediately by a motherly, middle-aged woman. She seemed embarrassed, and in the hall she introduced herself as Elsie, Albert's daughter-in-law.

Then she whispered: "You mustn't mind him. Don't be offended. He gets peculiar ideas. It's his age."

She showed him into a small sitting room. George had expected to see a frail and elderly man. He was surprised at once by the size and the power of Albert Todd. He was large and fleshy with rather short legs, so he was stranded on his high chair, like a whale on a beach, but he did not seem ridiculous. He had his eyes shut. That gave an impression not of rest, but of regeneration. He did not acknowledge George's presence in the room, but George was sure that the old man knew he was there. The eyes opened slowly and were fixed, unblinking, on George's face.

"You've been asking questions about me," the old man said. His voice was deep, his accent broad, unchanged since childhood. "Why was that then?"

He spoke slowly, but his eyes were alert and angry.

"Not about you," George said. "About your sons' business."

"It's my business." The reply was loud and furious.

"I'm sorry," George said. "If I had realized I should have come to you first."

"They should all remember that I still own the business. I'm not dead yet."

Then he leaned back on his chair, the anger past.

"Well," he said, speaking slowly again. "You're here now, so ask away."

But George would not go straight to the point. He would not allow himself to be bullied by this formidable old man.

"How did you know that I was asking questions about the business?"

"There's not much about the business that I don't know. At least, there never used to be."

"So you didn't know what was going on between Charlie and your other sons?"

Albert did not answer, but George knew that he had scored a point.

"Did your sons tell you that I'd been asking questions?"

"Laurence said you'd been into the office. I've got other friends who said that someone was being nosy."

"So you know the questions I've been asking. I wanted to know if Charlie had been blackmailing the family. I've been asking if there has been any irregularity or fraud which could have been used against you. I still want to know."

Albert shut yellow, reptilian eyelids. He was thinking. He was obviously coming to a difficult decision. George did not interrupt. He waited until the eyes opened again.

"Are you a friend of young Mardle?" the old man asked sharply.

"Yes," George said. "I suppose that I am."

"Is this in confidence? You won't go bleating to the police?"

"Not unless it's relevant to the murder."

"So that's why you're interested. You don't think that Mardle did it either. I told Savage that the boy wouldn't have killed Charlie. He didn't take any notice. When I heard that you'd been asking questions, I started asking some of my own. They knew that I wouldn't have approved. That's why they didn't tell me. I don't blame Laurence. I don't think he liked it any more than I did."

For the first time Albert was showing signs of his age. The eyes closed again. He was collecting his thoughts. Sunlight slanted through the small window on to his face. His eyes remained shut as he continued to talk.

"There was a planning matter. A certain development in a sensitive position. There would have been objections, bound to have been. They wanted to make sure that it all went through quickly. Ernest knew someone on the council, played golf with the senior planning officer. I don't know any details. I've told you, I wouldn't have approved. But promises were made. We have interests abroad. There were offers of holidays, talk of a share of a villa in Spain. I've stopped it all now. There'd be no point anyway, as

things turned out. But if the press got to hear of it, we'd be ruined. There's no need now for anyone to know.''

"But Charlie knew what was going on, didn't he? That's why he went to the office the Friday before he went north.''

Albert opened his eyes. Bloodshot and triumphant, they stared at George.

"Charlie knew all about it. But he wasn't trying to blackmail us. Quite the opposite. The . . . negotiations I've described. They were all Charlie's idea.''

Molly was walking around the island, following the high-tide line. She walked slowly. Occasionally she stopped and crouched to pull a piece of smooth thick glass from the drying seaweed, before discarding it and continuing her walk. Then she found what George had told her to look for. It had been washed on to the sand and was still quite intact. It was the size and shape of a honey jar and the screw top was still tightly in place. There was no label, no trace of glue on the glass where a label might once have been. She was not sure, at first, what to do with it. Surely all the fingerprints would have been washed off by now. But why then did George think that it was so important? Finally she took out a rather grubby handkerchief, and with that lifted the jar into her small canvas rucksack. The tide was full in now. There was no more that she could do until George came back.

George knew that he would have to see Savage, but he delayed the interview. He drove north along the coast into the steep, wooded valley where Jerry Packham lived and where Charlie Todd had owned a cottage. He could have telephoned. He knew that the trip was an indulgence, a diversion, but he needed time to form his argument before he saw Savage. He could go no further without the police. The valley ran inland, at right angles to the sea. The road twisted down to a cluster of cottages and a small harbour, but Jerry's house was built into the hillside, at the head of the valley. The land fell away beneath the cottage so that despite the trees there was a fine view and a clear light.

Jerry was working. He had a preoccupied air and stained fingers, but he found George a can of beer. He tried not to show how much he minded leaving his easel.

"I'd heard that you were still here," he said. "Have you been able to do much ringing?"

"A bit. But that's not why I'm still on the island."

"You don't think that Nick was the murderer?"

"No."

"How can I help?"

"I wanted to ask you about some rumours. Have you heard any gossip about Paul Derbyshire?"

"I've heard rumours about everyone."

"Please, Jerry. It might be important."

"Pam was always rather cruel about him. She knew him before he was married. She was his receptionist before she had the children."

"What did she say about the doctor?"

"That he made a fool of himself over a couple of the young female patients. Idealized them. Wrote poetry to them."

"Did he take any of them out?"

"Oh, I don't think so. That would have been quite normal. That was the point."

"You've not heard anything recently?"

"Oh no. I think that Marjory keeps him on a very tight rein."

"Had Pamela kept in touch with him, socially?"

"They didn't have much in common, except the island, and the RSPB local members' group, but Pamela used Paul and Marjory to babysit quite often, when the children were small. Sian and Edward are very fond of them. The Todds are a peculiar family and William's parents are dead, so Paul and Marjory have become sort of replacement grandparents."

"I gathered that it was something like that. Did Charlie ever talk about Paul or ever have a go at him, tease him?"

"Not specially."

"Are you usually good at getting up in the morning?"

"What do you mean?"

189

"Could the murderer have taken a chance that you would oversleep? Do you often do it?"

"I'm not at my best in the mornings, but I'm usually reasonably punctual. I think I know why I slept in last weekend. I've had a lousy cold ever since. I may have had a bit of a temperature."

"Can you get over to the island tomorrow?"

"I don't know. I'm very busy. I've this plate to finish by the end of the month."

His eyes were already straying back to his work. George knew that he was losing concentration.

"Do you know why Elizabeth Richards should be visiting William Marshall?"

He said it to shock, to regain Jerry's attention.

"No," Jerry said. "I'm sure that there can be no personal involvement. William's very respectable. Not Elizabeth's type at all."

"Will you come to the island tomorrow? I won't need to trouble you again."

Jerry laughed. "Yes," he said. "I'll come."

There was no excuse now not to go straight to the police station, but George drove slowly up the valley. I should have left all this to the police, he thought, not very seriously. Then there would be nothing to stop me walking through the woods, checking the warblers on the brambles down by the harbour. A bit of gentle birdwatching on a still autumn day is more suited to an elderly gentleman than this.

How can I be right? And if I am right can I prove it? Then he remembered Nicholas, and he thought: If I cannot trust my own logic and my own intelligence, I will never enjoy birdwatching again. If I cannot trust my instinct in this, how will I know, when I see a glaucous gull or a marsh warbler, that it is what I believe it to be? This thing is just as simple. Either Nicholas Mardle killed two people or he did not. Either a bird is a glaucous gull or a herring gull. If ever a time comes when I cannot definitely identify a bird, then I will give it all up. And I know that Nicholas did not kill anyone.

190

He did not know why he was so daunted at the prospect of an interview with Savage. He was, by this time, quite sure who had killed Charlie Todd and Pamela Marshall. Did he expect Savage to shake his confidence? Rather he was afraid of losing his confidence in the policeman. If the superintendent showed himself to be a complete fool, things would be very awkward.

He drove into the town and parked by the police station. Just outside the building he met Connibear. The detective did not attempt to avoid him.

"I'm sorry that it's taken so long to get the information you wanted," he said. "I was going to get in touch today. I've checked with the Inland Revenue and VAT. They've never had any suspicions about Todd Leisure. Ernie employs a clever accountant but it's all quite legal."

"Thank you very much. Sorry to have put you to so much trouble. I seem to have been wrong about that. I managed to see Albert Todd and he was able to clear it up for me."

"No trouble, sir."

"Do you think that Superintendent Savage would be able to see me today?"

Connibear looked fixedly at George, as if he wanted to add extra significance to his words.

"I think he would, sir. I think he might be having . . . second thoughts. Not about being able to get a conviction. No trouble about that. But in his own mind. And then Martindale's resignation shook him."

"Martindale was the young uniformed officer who was there when Pamela Marshall was killed?"

"That's right, sir. But it wasn't his fault. He shouldn't take responsibility for it. He coped well enough. As well as any of us would have done. Mr. Savage was a bit hard on him at the time. He said that Martindale was soft because he believed young Mardle's story, and now I think the superintendent's feeling a bit bad about it. He doesn't say anything, of course, but I think that's how things are. I don't think Martindale will change his mind however things turn out. He says he wants to train to be a teacher. Good

luck to him. The pay's awful, but the hours are better. You've got to be cut out for this job. Look, I've got to go. But you ask to see the superintendent. I'm sure he'll help you.''

He hurried away.

Savage agreed to see Palmer-Jones immediately. He was busy enough. There were files and reports in chaotic disarray on his desk, but he had been staring at each of them in turn all morning without doing any constructive work. He was troubled. It was not, as Connibear had said, that he was worried that a jury would fail to convict Mardle. There was evidence enough for that. Even Mardle's solicitor admitted as much. It was that the boy was beginning to impress him. Nicholas seemed to have matured during his period in the police cells; he had developed a confidence that eventually his innocence would be recognized. He was irritated, occasionally, by Savage's questions but he stuck to his story. Savage's theory depended on the boy's being psychiatrically disturbed, and the superintendent was beginning to believe that fundamentally he was immensely sane. Savage was not afraid of admitting that he was wrong. He had sufficient arrogance to believe that anyone else could have made a similar mistake. The problem was that he was not sure that he was wrong. Mardle was still the most likely murderer. Savage felt too that he had lost touch with the case. He was no longer sufficiently involved, he had no emotional response to the other suspects.

Connibear had told Savage that George Palmer-Jones was still on Gillibry, and that he had asked him to make inquiries about Todd Leisure Enterprises. Savage had been curious. He had hoped that Connibear's inquiries would result in something positive, but when nothing suspicious was discovered, he put that line of investigation from his mind. When the desk sergeant informed him that Palmer-Jones wished to see him, he thought briefly that he had come simply to pursue this line of inquiry, and the thought disappointed him. Connibear was a conscientious and reliable policeman, and if the Todds had been committing some fraud, he would have found it out. Then he remem-

bered Palmer-Jones's power, his reputation. He would have recognized Connibear's ability too. He would have come for more than that.

When George Palmer-Jones saw Savage he was immediately reassured. The man might follow his own theories over-enthusiastically, but he was no fool. Savage stood to greet him.

"I'm glad to see you," he said. "Very glad. I'm sorry that I was too busy to see you earlier in the week. Connibear was ab.e to help?"

"Indirectly," George said. "Albert Todd must have heard that he was asking questions on my behalf. He sent for me and gave me some very useful information himself."

"Did he?" Savage said. "I talked to him, but perhaps I didn't handle him properly. He's quite a character."

He showed George to a seat and waited, giving him his whole attention.

"I think," George said, "that I know now who killed Pam Marshall and Charles Todd. I'm afraid that I can't prove it. I need to talk to Nicholas Mardle. And I need your support."

16

George did not go out with John to collect the remainder of the committee the next day. Molly wished that he had. He would not explain to her what was happening. The weather continued to be still and sultry and she felt tired and irritable. George had not slept. When she had gone to bed at midnight he was still in the common room, sat at the library table writing notes in his tiny, constricted hand. She had given him the jar, and he had seemed pleased. The police would be able to test the inside for chloroform, he had said. When she went to bed she had opened the window, but the room was still airless. She was too hot in her sleeping bag, not warm enough without it. Like the princess with the pea, she felt that she could sense the scratchy, institution blanket that covered the mattress, even through the down of her sleeping bag. She had wanted to get up and go down to him, to say: "Tell me about it. Let me help you." But he knew that she was willing to help him. She did not want him to ask for her help, simply to please her. He must organize the thing as he thought best. There would be a reason for his secrecy, and she must trust it. He had come to bed in the end, and

undressed and climbed into his sleeping bag on the lower bunk. She could sense his tension, physically, as she had sensed the prickly blanket.

"George," she had said, softly, once, just so that he should know that she was awake if he should want her.

But he was engrossed completely, going over and over the details of the case, reassuring himself that he was right. He had convinced Savage. That was easy. He was sure that the facts all pointed in one direction, but he could not leave the thing alone and go to sleep.

"Do you think that he's reliable?" he had whispered. "Can I trust him to do what I want?"

"Yes. He's reliable. You can trust him."

Sleep had settled on her, eventually, like suffocation, but when she woke, very early, she could feel that George was still awake. He had been lying still, afraid to move in case he woke her. When he heard her stirring he got up and went out. He was back to share breakfast with them in the kitchen, and then he went out, with John, leaving Elizabeth and Molly to wash up, but John drove out in the Land Rover, alone.

"Do you know what it's all about?" Elizabeth asked as she piled soapy plates on to the enamel draining board.

"No," Molly said, and she realized suddenly why George had had to keep his discoveries and his plans to himself. She would have found it impossible to lie convincingly.

"If it stays calm I know that George is hoping to do some cannon netting. He's never seen it done before."

"But why has he asked the committee to come to the island? It must be something to do with the murder?"

She was curious. She was even enjoying the drama of it. She did not seem concerned, personally threatened in any way.

At the quay nobody asked John what it was all about. He had been expecting awkward questions, questions which he would be unable to answer. He had performed certain tasks for George, but they seemed meaningless. Perhaps the passengers were frightened to express too much curiosity or interest, in case it was misinterpreted. Even when

they had all climbed into the Land Rover, but John did not begin the slow drive down the slipway and on to the shore, nobody asked the reason for the delay. They talked, among themselves, about the weather, gardening, last night's television. John was looking at his watch and at the lane from the main road. He was beginning to become concerned about the tide. Then he saw the small, red car through the gaps in the hedges. It was driving very fast. John knew what to expect, and prepared to enjoy the surprise of the guests. The car pulled up and Connibear got out of the driver's seat. It must be his own car, John thought. There was a child's seat in the back, and the shelf was untidy with toys. Nicholas Mardle climbed out of the passenger seat and pulled a rucksack after him.

At first they were stunned. They seemed not to take it in, not only because his appearance was so unexpected, but because he seemed to have changed, to be a different boy. In less than a week he seemed to have become thinner, his skin seemed clearer. Perhaps they had remembered only a caricature, investing it with the dark significance of his supposed wickedness, and the reality had not changed at all. But even to John it seemed that it had.

Mark responded first. He jumped out of the Land Rover, ran over to Nick, shook his hand, put his arm around his back. Then they were all out, all asking questions.

Connibear pushed through the small crowd to the boy. Nick disengaged himself, turned to the policeman. They shook hands.

"Thanks for the lift," Nick said.

"Least I could do. No hard feelings?"

"No hard feelings."

"Good luck then."

He grinned, winked and walked back to his car.

John hurried them all back into the Land Rover and drove towards the island.

Elizabeth and Molly had coffee ready for them in the common room. Nick stood by the fire and fended off their questions.

"Yes, I've been released. Savage finally believed my

story. George persuaded him, I think. And then arranged for you all to be here for a sort of welcome-home party.''

George smiled, but he said nothing. When they asked how he knew that Nicholas was to be released, how Savage had been persuaded, he was noncommittal.

''Have they arrested someone else then?'' Jerry asked.

''I don't think so.'' Nick was too intoxicated by his freedom to worry about the implications of it for anyone else. ''Apparently I gave them some information which pointed to the identification of the real killer. They can't act on it yet, but I'm to be the star witness.''

''Do the police still think that the murderer was one of us?'' Jasmine Carson faced the communal fear with characteristic directness.

''I'm sorry. I don't know anything. Savage came to see me today. He said that I was to be released, unconditionally, and asked if I would like to spend the day on the island. He said that George had arranged something special.''

Paul Derbyshire gave a peculiar moan. ''No,'' he said. ''I can't stand it. It's all going to start again. All the prying into our private lives. All the worry and unpleasantness. It's too much.''

''I think,'' Jasmine said, crisply and disapprovingly, ''that Nicholas has suffered more unpleasantness than we have, and that it would be rather churlish not to celebrate his release.''

The doctor seemed not to hear.

''I took the liberty,'' George said, carefully changing the subject, ''as the only committee member on the island, to ask John to prepare his equipment for cannon netting. I must confess that I'm fascinated to see it work, and the conditions today are superb. There have been massive roosts of redshank and oystercatcher all week. I take it that no one has any objection?''

He looked directly at Jasmine Carson. She admitted defeat easily, smiled and shook her head.

Molly had been as surprised as anyone by the appearance of Nicholas Mardle. It was hard now, as he stood by the hearth, the centre of attention, to believe in George's

image of him as a disturbed and miserable adolescent. Could four days in a police cell have changed someone so dramatically? She found it hard to accept. She supposed that she must trust George.

As if in deference to Nicholas's good fortune, they did not mention the murders or the police again. They began to plan the operation of cannon netting. John took charge.

"George and I set the net earlier this morning," he said. "You have to prepare it a long time before high water, so that the birds aren't disturbed. We'll fire a cannon when the birds are roosting, just after high tide. I'll want everyone to keep well out of the way then. It can be dangerous."

"I hope that there will be no harm to the birds." Jasmine had accepted that the operation would take place, but could not refrain from voicing her objections.

"There shouldn't be."

"How exactly does the thing work?"

"The birds have been roosting on that flat, grassy area to the south of the Wendy House. That's ideal for our purposes, because the halfway wall can act as cover. There's a plunger, well behind the wall, which fires a series of projectiles to which the net is attached. The explosion sends the big net over the birds. Then we'll have to be really well organized to ring and process the waders as quickly as we can. I must stress how important it is to stay behind the cannons when we're ready to fire. And do keep away from the equipment now, because it's all set. I'd hate there to be an accident. Especially today. Now, is anyone interested in going round the traps before lunch?"

High water was at three. Molly found that she was continually looking at her watch, counting the hours and the minutes until then. The tide, smooth and clear as baby oil, began to slide round the rocks at the north end of the island, but there were still three hours to go. She was beginning to guess something of what George was doing. What did he hope to achieve with the emphasis on the danger of the equipment? To tempt one of them to suicide? Or to murder? She approached him when they had finished coffee and no one could overhear.

"What do you want me to do?" she asked.

He hesitated. "Nothing," he said. "There's nothing to do now."

There was no more mention of the power of the cannon net, the fear of accident. They had beer at lunchtime, except Elizabeth. It seemed that she had stopped being sick, but that she did not want to drink "for the sake of the baby." She spoke of the baby with reverence and joy. The others got a little bored by her obsession with her condition, but she seemed very happy.

"I know," she said. "Nick can fire the cannon. After all, we're here in his honour."

The afternoon moved slowly to Molly. She pictured it oozing forward like the oily water which now surrounded the island. As the tide came in the waders rose in swarms from the shore and circled in fantastic shapes around Gillibry. As the tide came in so did the cloud, but still there was no wind, not a breath of air.

Perhaps she felt depressed because the others seemed in such a party mood. They carried on drinking after lunch. They sat in the common room and throughout the afternoon they built a pyramid of empty red beer tins. There was a lot of movement. Every so often they wandered out singly, or in groups, to empty the nets or check the wader roosts. Molly could not keep track of all the coming and going. She did not notice that Doctor Derbyshire did not move at all, and that, like her, he seemed unable to enter the spirit of communal gaiety. He was drinking heavily, sitting by the fire, and his face was red. He hardly spoke. Jasmine Carson watched him, Molly noticed, not with disapproval but with concern. She went out to the traps very regularly, more often than anyone else. She would return to the common room and announce concisely the details of the birds she had caught. She was drinking too, but slowly, and she alone had a glass. Mark, John and Jerry were becoming rowdy in a good-natured, rather frantic way. They were planning a ringing trip to the Hebrides. John had been before and grew more and more enthusiastic in his description of the Western Isles. There was a long

story about a visit to a whisky distillery. Nicholas looked on with an amused and adult detachment. George's pile of red cans was as high as any of the others, but Molly knew that he had not drunk enough for the alcohol to have any effect.

Then it was nearly three o'clock and they were all preparing to go out. Elizabeth came from the kitchen to be with them. They drifted, laughing and noisy, into the yard. Molly felt that she could not breathe. She had been drinking too, and the weight of the heavy, black clouds seemed to have settled on her head.

Was anything, after all, going to happen, or would there be an anticlimax, a continuation of the party and the mutual distrust? Then it occurred to her that George might never be able to prove who had committed the murders, and the prospect of his failure was terrifying.

It was a very high tide and the birds were roosting on the island proper because the shore, where they would usually have fed and rested, was covered by water. There were hundreds of birds on the rocks and the grassy slopes to the south of the Wendy House. They were noisy, restless. There were oystercatchers of black and white and orange, heavy grey knot and brown redshank. There was a smell of seaweed, of decay.

They were intent, now, on catching as many birds as possible. John took charge. He sent Nick and George towards the Wendy House. The rest of them were spread along the wall. Molly could see that the plunger, the trigger which set off the net, was positioned right at the easterly edge of the wall, near the edge of the cliff, so that the firer could see round the wall to the birds, without being seen by them. Nick walked through the Wendy-House garden and had reached the firing position. George seemed to have disappeared. Molly felt a mounting tension, even a panic. George's failure to take up his position along the wall convinced her that something had happened. And she was certain that there was something wrong with the cannon. Where was George? He should be here, to prevent a tragedy. What should she do? Should

200

she shout out, prevent the firing from taking place until he arrived? She had promised herself that she would trust him, and he had told her to do nothing, but perhaps there had been an accident, something more sinister than an accident. No one else seemed to have noticed his disappearance. That was not surprising. Each person was crouched now, as John had instructed them, behind the wall, and could only see the individual to the east or the west of him. They were still excited. There was a lot of giggling, stifled. Molly did as she was told, and hid too, leaning against the smooth boulders of the drystone wall. She felt the curves of the boulders against her body as she pressed against it. Elizabeth was about ten yards away on one side of her, Jerry Packham to the other. She did not know how the others had been arranged. She tried to stay calm. I've been imagining it all, she thought. They just want to catch some birds to ring them. Nothing can go wrong. John will have checked all the gear. He will know that it's safe. But she felt the mindless terror and excitement of a child playing hide and seek, as the hunter approaches the hiding place. Then she saw John. He was running, bent double, along the base of the wall. She saw him stop and whisper to Elizabeth. He ran to her, and said:

"We're ready now. As soon as you hear the cannon, get over the wall—there's a stile just beyond Elizabeth if you need it. We'll have to secure the net around the birds."

Then he was gone, and apparently whispering the same message to Jerry. She did not have the opportunity to ask if he had seen George.

Nothing happened. It seemed that she had waited for hours with her cheek against the cold, pink rock of the wall. Still her husband had not come from the Wendy House, and still she was convinced that if the cannon was fired there would be a tragedy. If I stand up, she thought, and shout and wave, all the birds will be disturbed. They will rise, like some noisy multi-coloured magic carpet, and the cannon will not need to be fired. She never knew if she would have had the courage to stand up and expose herself to the others' anger, because the cannon was fired. There

was an explosion which echoed around the estuary, the rush of the net and the beating of wings.

"It's worked!" John shouted triumphantly. "It's worked. Come on everyone. Over the wall."

It had worked. It had not backfired, blown up in Nicholas's face. There were no screams. There was no blood. She felt embarrassment at her foolish anxiety, at the scene she had nearly caused, and an immense relief. She scrambled over the wall. She could see Jasmine Carson and Paul Derbyshire hurrying up from the east. Even they seemed infected by the general excitement. The younger observatory members were already running around the edge of the net, checking that none of the birds had been hurt.

Where is George? she thought. He would enjoy all this. Where is he?

She checked her impulse to join the others, to be a part of the successful operation, and looked back along the width of the island. She began to shout: "George! George!"

Everything happened very quickly then. She saw George running through the Wendy House garden towards the cliff. He was followed by other men, strangers. There was another explosion. A bright red flare lit the sky. It was pretty as a firework. The other observatory members realized that something was happening, that there was some other drama away from the net. John looked up briefly, but he would not let them go. He was responsible for the birds. He yelled at them to stay where they were until all the birds had been bagged. Molly ran along her side of the wall, through the gap at the end of it, to meet George by the cliff.

Nicholas Mardle was in the water. The tide was on the ebb, and a fierce current had already pulled him north, towards the open sea. He was already opposite the observatory garden. He was struggling desperately, but was making no headway against the relentless pull of the water. He had been wearing wellingtons and a bulky anorak, and his heavy clothes seemed to be dragging him under. George was shouting. It seemed to Molly that he was almost crying with frustration.

Then, miraculously, an inflatable boat raced round the north end of the island. It appeared beyond the seawatching hide and circled, sending a cloud of waders from the rocks by the slipway before stopping by the boy. One of the men in the boat pulled Nicholas aboard.

Another man, one of the strangers, had joined Molly and George. "It's all right, sir," he said. "They've got him."

"I should have known," George said, "that the cannon net was too obvious. What a blunderhead I was."

"You were wrong about that perhaps, sir, but right about everything else."

"The boy could have been drowned. You know that he was pushed."

"It's all right now," the man repeated.

Molly interrupted. Her anxiety, her sense of exclusion, had made her furious. "George, what *has* been going on?"

He recognized her anger.

"I'm sorry," he said. "I will explain. As Superintendent Savage says, there's nothing to worry about now."

"I don't understand," she said. Then: "George, you were right? About the murderer?"

"Yes," Savage replied. "Mr. Palmer-Jones was right. I'll just get Connibear, then I'll be ready to make an arrest. Would you rather wait here?"

"No," George said. "I'll come."

They walked through the gap in the wall, to where the others were ringing the waders. They sat in a semi-circle in two ringing teams. John and Jerry were putting the rings on the birds' legs, Paul Derbyshire and Jasmine were weighing and measuring them and Elizabeth and Mark were writing details of the birds and ring numbers in a notebook.

As George, Molly and the policemen approached, they all looked up.

"Superintendent Savage," Elizabeth said. "What are you doing here? Do you want to train to be a ringer?"

"Where's Nick?" asked John. "I saw the flare. Is he all right?"

George nodded, but said nothing.

"Miss Jasmine Carson," Savage said. "I arrest you for the murder of Pamela Marshall and Charles Todd, and for the attempted murder of Nicholas Mardle."

Jasmine Carson stood up stiffly. She straightened her skirt over the swollen joints of her knees.

"I was surprised," she said, "at the strength of the instinct for survival. When I planned to kill Charles, I did not think that I would mind, too much, being caught. So long as I was successful. But when it came to it, I was prepared to fight like an animal to stay free. Well, it's all over now. Somebody had to do it. There was no other way."

She looked at them all, as if to say goodbye, then walked off between the policemen. When she came to the stile to the track, she refused to take Savage's arm, and climbed it alone.

17

*J*ohn *insisted that* they finish ringing all the waders. Nick was brought ashore. He was shocked and cold, but when the tide ebbed away to allow Savage and Connibear to take Jasmine Carson off in the Land Rover, he refused to go with them.

"I'm not going to miss this," he said. "I want to know exactly what happened."

So they sat, that evening, in the common room, with the driftwood fire and the tillies, and George explained it all.

"When did you know that it was Jasmine?" John asked. "I can still hardly believe it."

"I should have known on the night Pamela Marshall died, when I checked all the bedrooms and found Jasmine asleep."

"What do you mean? Could you tell that she was only pretending to be asleep?"

"It's not that, though she may have been acting. No. There were some sleeping pills in her bedroom. I suppose that she took them when her arthritis was painful. I should have known then that she had murdered Charlie Todd. Pamela was a different matter. Nicholas was giving such a

good impression of a homicidal maniac that I was confused. He wasn't the only one of you, of course, who confused the issue. There were Elizabeth's mysterious trips to the mainland, and Doctor Derbyshire's raid of the Wendy House. They shook my faith for a time in my judgement that Jasmine might be the murderer.''

''My dear boy, I'm sure that you never considered, for a moment, that I could have been the murderer.'' Paul Derbyshire was jolly and nervous, and his eyes were watchful. He was wondering what else George would say.

''Not for a moment,'' George answered. ''But you did search the Wendy House, that morning? While John, Nick and Mark went to the seawatching hide.''

''Yes. I didn't know that he was dead then. I thought that he was seawatching. He had something which belonged to me.''

''Had you asked him to give it back to you?''

''Yes. He refused to give it.''

''What was it?''

''A diary.''

Although it was conducted in front of all the others, the conversation was intensely personal. Nobody interrupted.

''Jasmine found a letter, you know, in your waste bin. I saw her find it. That must have pleased her. She would have told me about it eventually, but it suited her purpose much better for me to ask to see it. She expected me to take it to the police, although she was too clever to say so. She was beginning to realize that I found the case against Nicholas unconvincing, and she wanted to give me another suspect. It was, perhaps, foolish to have given her that opportunity.''

The warning had been gently given, but Paul Derbyshire recognized it.

''Oh yes,'' he said. ''Yes. Quite. It won't happen again.''

That was the end of it. Nobody discussed, even among themselves, what the doctor had been hiding.

George turned to Elizabeth. ''Can you tell us why you went to see Ernest Todd and William Marshall?'' he said. ''Or is it still a deadly secret? Molly imagined you as a secret agent of the Todds, sent by them to kill Charlie.''

"Did she? How exciting! How clever of you to find out where I'd been. It's all much more boring than that, I'm afraid. I don't mind explaining now. I've talked to John about it."

She reached out and took John's hand.

"When I was divorced I told Frank that I didn't want any of his money. He was generous and offered me a lump sum as my share of the house. I refused it. I wanted to be independent. I still do, but with a child coming it would be useful to have a little money, a little security. I'd made a big gesture of refusing Frank's money. I felt that John expected me to be very uncompromising, very independent. I didn't want to admit, I suppose, that I had mellowed. I called in to see Ernest, just to ask the name of a good solicitor who might be able to negotiate with Frank on my behalf. He seemed the sort of person who would be able to recommend one. He was very kind, suggested Mr. Marshall and phoned up to make an appointment for me to see him. Then he asked me out to dinner, and got very angry when I refused. I would have told John what it was all about before going to the solicitor, but he found out that I hadn't been to the clinic and started getting pig-headed and autocratic, so I kept it a mystery just out of spite. When I went to the solicitor's I didn't actually see William Marshall. Pam had died by then and he was taking compassionate leave. But I saw someone else who is going to deal directly with Frank's representative, and we'll probably be able to settle it without going to court. I'm sorry if I misled you.

"Now," she said. "Please don't be so provoking. We've disposed of all the red herrings, so do tell us why you should have known, on the night that Pam died, that Jasmine had killed Charlie. And how you finally worked out who had killed him."

"I couldn't understand why the murderer chose that particular time and place to kill him. The crime wasn't committed in anger. There was no evidence of a fight. So, the murderer must have planned to kill Charlie in the seawatching hide. Obviously the killer must have known

that Charlie would be there—that made John an unlikely suspect. But if he knew that Charlie would be there, he would have known that Jerry could be expected too. Although the flaps of the hide give a reasonable view of the island, and there would be some warning of Jerry's approach, it would have been lunacy to choose that particular spot to do it. So, either Jerry was the murderer, or it was someone who could be certain that Jerry wouldn't wake up in time to interrupt.

"Can you remember, on the night before Charlie's death, Jasmine poured out the cocoa? Several of you mentioned that, when you described what had happened after the fire. Usually, her arthritis made her avoid having to do anything of that sort in front of other people. When I went for coffee with her, she made me pour it out. Her hand isn't very steady and it embarrassed her. But on the night of the fire she had to make certain that Jerry would sleep. I believe that you got a strong dose of her sleeping medication. That's why you felt so hungover the next day."

"Did she set fire to the Wendy House, then?"

"Yes. I think that she went to talk to Charlie, having already decided that if he didn't listen to her, she would try to kill him. She wore the duffel coat and boots from the lobby, so that in the poor light if anyone did see her, she would be be fairly anonymous. He refused to be persuaded by her, so she tipped over the lamp as she went past the open window. She hoped that the arson would be thought to be an accident. When Charlie survived the fire, she decided to try again. She would have been able to see from her bedroom window that the fire had been extinguished. It was because of the Wendy House fire that Pam Marshall had to die. She heard Jasmine out on the island on the night of the fire. Jasmine's arthritis gave her a very distinctive walk. Jasmine knew that Pamela wanted to talk to me. I think that Pamela may have given away something of her suspicion. So Jasmine killed her."

"What about the guy rope? Did she take it specially to strangle Charlie?"

"No. she couldn't have done. But she did take it. She

was on the island the week before Charlie died. She saw a Sabine's gull, if you remember. You were staying here too, Nick. You know what a stickler she is for tidiness. I think perhaps you'd left a net out. She tried to put it away, but again, the stiffness in her fingers made her fumble it. She left the guy out. She didn't want to admit that she'd made a botch of it, so she just put the guy in her pocket. Charlie Todd would have been waiting in the hide, that morning. The door would have been open because he was expecting Jerry. The sea and the wind would have been making so much noise that he wouldn't have heard her coming. She was wearing the coat again, and the boots. He would have been surprised to see her, but not frightened. I expect that she sat on the seat behind him. His attention would have been held by the sea. It would have been easy to kill him.''

No one spoke. The edges of the room were in shadow, and in the firelight the faces were expressionless, unfamiliar. George continued:

"It was always probable, of course, that she had killed Pamela too, but there were two points which made me quite certain. The murderer used chloroform to drug Pamela before killing her. Jasmine knew that Pamela already suspected that she was the murderer. If Pamela had woken up to find Jasmine in her room, she would have screamed. Jasmine made certain that she did not wake up. How many of you knew that there was chloroform in the ringing room? Only John. The jar was not marked, so how could you know? But she was a biology teacher. She would have been interested in what the school groups were doing.

"Then there was the fact that the murderer had lit the tilly in Pamela's room. Jerry heard it being pumped. Jasmine wanted to do the thing properly. She would have needed two hands to force in the knife, so she couldn't have held a torch. She knew about anatomy. She knew where she wanted the knife to go. She wanted to see what she was doing.''

"But why?" Mark said. He was distressed, agitated. "Why did she have to kill Charlie?"

"It was because of the island, wasn't it?" Jerry said

209

quietly. "It was all she had. When she retired she lost all her friends, except us. She hasn't got any relatives. She doesn't care about anything else."

"But she knew Charlie," Elizabeth interrupted. "She knew that he was quite likely to change his mind about the island. He was always having weird ideas, but they never usually developed into anything. He wasn't serious about it."

"He was serious about this, though," George said. "It was the lack of motive which disturbed me most. Like you, I thought that Jasmine knew Charlie well enough to realize that he was inconsistent, unreliable. She wouldn't have murdered him because of a sudden whim, which could have been forgotten on the following day. But he was serious about this. And she knew that he was."

"But how could she know? She didn't know any more than the rest of us."

"I'm afraid that she did. I'm sure that she knew more than a week ago that Charlie was planning to sell the island, that he had been thinking about it for a long time, and that he had already begun negotiations.

"Charlie was short of money. He knew that Jerry was losing enthusiasm for illustrating his stories, and that without the pictures the books were unlikely to sell. He could have sold the cottage at Storr, but he was becoming greedy. He wanted more money than that would have fetched. He had become passionate about the canal-boat project, and you know that he enjoyed being a benefactor. But, more importantly, he had a grand dream for the island. He was becoming bored by the observatory. You see, he wasn't going to sell Gillibry, just shares in it. He was planning to develop it.

"That, of course, was why he renewed contact with his brothers. He needed their help to turn his scheme into reality. They recognized the financial possibilities and Ernest began to use his contacts to get some dubious plans agreed by the planning department.

"I was blind. I was convinced that Charlie was blackmailing the Todds. I couldn't think of any other explana-

tion for their reaction to my questions. It was Albert himself who told me that Charlie had instigated the illegal practices which he'd discovered. You can imagine that Jasmine was horrified.

"You see, Charlie's dream was to turn the island into a miniature Disneyland, with a fun fair, bars, and all sorts of attractions. When we were searching the Wendy House we found a ticket for Alton Towers. He had been there while he was in the Midlands. He wanted to turn the island into that sort of amusement park."

"How typical of Charlie," Jerry said with some affection. "It wouldn't have been only the money. He would have loved the idea of it."

"But Jasmine Carson was appalled."

"How did she find out about Charlie's plans?" Mark asked.

"Marie, the Todds' secretary, was one of her ex-pupils. Marie told me that they kept in touch. Savage went to see her last night. She confirmed to him that she saw Jasmine last week. She inadvertently mentioned something of what the Todds were planning, and Jasmine bullied the rest out of her. She was too frightened to tell the Todds about it, and I really don't think she suspected it had anything to do with the murder. So when Charlie dropped his bombshell on Friday evening, Jasmine already knew about his plans. She knew that he wasn't being quite honest. And she had had a chance to brood about it. She is a very logical person, and very ruthless. She didn't have a lot to lose. She is ill, in considerable pain. She weighed up the risk and she took it. And of course she had to act quickly."

"I don't quite understand," Molly said, "what happened this afternoon, and where Nick came into it."

"After Pam's murder," George said, "Savage was convinced that Nick had murdered her and Charlie, because of the way in which the Todds had treated his mother. To be fair, by the time I went to see Savage he had already concluded that he had probably been mistaken. He was prepared to accept my version of events as a working hypothesis, but naturally he didn't want to make another

arrest without adequate proof. So we asked Nick for his help.''

"So when Nick said that he was a vital witness in the police's case, you were hoping that she would try to kill him," Mark said.

"Yes, though I didn't expect her to be so successful. She took the bait, as we had hoped. She believed that Nick did have some information which might convict her. Perhaps she felt that she had nothing to lose when she tried to kill him. Prison will not be so different for her, from her concrete flat on the sea front. Soon she will be so disabled that she would not be able to get to the island to use the observatory. The development would not make any difference to her.''

"But she did stop it all, didn't she?" Elizabeth said. "The fun fairs and the hamburger stalls. She saved my home. I feel somehow that I share her guilt.''

"She helped me," Nick said, "to exorcise mine.''

There was a silence. George wondered if he were talking about the days in prison or the minutes in the water. Through which experience did he feel that he had paid for his desire for vengeance? It was not the time to find out.

"I expect you've guessed that Savage and his officers came over very early this morning and installed themselves in the Wendy House. Connibear came in the inflatable while we were at lunch. I thought that she would see the cannon net as a weapon. She had talked about its danger, the possibility of an accident. Savage was in a position to watch it all day, but she didn't go near it. She knew that Nicholas was to fire it. It would have been easy for her to turn the projectiles so that they faced him, and not the birds. But she didn't. Of course it was too obvious. She was too intelligent. I had started to think that I was wrong, that I had mishandled the whole thing. We would never, then, have been able to convict her. But in the end, as she said, her instinct for survival was too strong. Perhaps she cared too much for the island, and not enough for the people who come here. When everyone was distracted by the cannons, by the spectacle of the net being fired, even

Savage and I, she pushed Nick over the cliff. It was so simple. It could have been another accident. I didn't even see her do it. I was watching Nick. I had seen that she had positioned herself next to him, under the wall, then I lost my concentration briefly, when he fired the cannons. When I looked back he had gone, and she had walked around the wall and was following the doctor to join the rest of you at the net. It was dreadful. For a moment I didn't realize what she had done to him. It was as if she had made him disappear. Then I understood. One of the policemen fired a flare. It was to have been a signal to the men waiting in the inflatable that reinforcements were needed. We were just lucky that they were there. No," he added fairly. "It was not luck. Savage is a good policeman. He had made sure that they were there."

The party which had started that lunchtime continued. They fetched the gramophone from the Wendy House. They were, though, less frenetic, more reflective. There was not a lot of talk, but no one seemed inclined to go to bed.

Molly and George walked out on to the island. It was well after midnight. The gullies around the island were beginning to fill once more. A dog barked on the mainland, and the air was so still that they could hear it quite clearly. The light of the Seldom Seen Buoy flashed. There was a smell of bracken and of salt. Both were imagining a different island, man-made, with metalled causeway, neon lights, a pier of an island, with all trace of natural elements covered by litter and junk, the cries of the seabirds drowned by the shouts of salesmen.

"I can understand," Molly said, "why she did it."

"So can I."

"Did it never occur to you that the case should stay unsolved? That once Nicholas Mardle was released that was enough?"

"No. That never occurred to me."

They walked together back to the observatory, but they avoided the party and went straight to bed.

About the Author

The daughter of a village school teacher, Ann Cleeves
lives near Droitwich, England, where she spends her time
with her two small children and writing. Her introduction
to birdwatching, and her husband, came when she spent a
season on Fair Isle working as an assistant cook at the Bird
Observatory.

Attention Mystery and Suspense Fans

Do you want to complete your collection
of mystery and suspense stories
by some of your favorite authors?
John D. MacDonald, Helen MacInnes,
Dick Francis, Amanda Cross, Ruth
Rendell, Alistar MacLean, Erle Stanley
Gardner, Cornell Woolrich, among many
others, are included in Ballantine/
Fawcett's new Mystery Brochure.

For your FREE Mystery Brochure, fill in the
coupon below and mail it to:

12

D1455479